KONKABOTI

TROILOKYONATH MUKHOPADHYAY (1847–1919) was one of the foremost writers of fiction in nineteenth-century Bengal. He was the prime mover of magic realism in Bengal according to some present-day writers. *Konkaboti* is his debut novel. Troilokyonath was also a trailblazer of indigenous business entrepreneurship in India. His *Visit to Europe* is a treasure trove of information for postcolonial studies.

ARNAB BHATTACHARYA is an author/editor and a translator based in Kolkata. He is a reviewer of books for *The Telegraph*, and is a senior resource fellow in the post-graduate diploma faculty in translation studies at Rabindra Bharati University, Kolkata. Bhattacharya's fields of interest include feminism, nationalism, films, art and architecture. *The Politics and Reception of Rabindranath Tagore's Drama: The Bard on the Stage* (co-edited with Mala Renganathan) (Routledge, 2014), is a recent venture.

KONKABOTI

The Extraordinary Journey of a Village Girl

Troilokyonath Mukhopadhyay

Translated from the Bengali
with a Biographical Note
and a Critical Afterword
by
Arnab Bhattacharya

Orient BlackSwan

KONKABOTI

ORIENT BLACKSWAN PRIVATE LIMITED

Registered Office
3-6-752 Himayatnagar, Hyderabad 500 029, Telangana, India
e-mail: centraloffice@orientblackswan.com

Other Offices
Bengaluru, Bhopal, Chennai, Guwahati, Hyderabad,
Jaipur, Kolkata, Lucknow, Mumbai, New Delhi,
Noida, Patna, Vijayawada

First published 2016
Reprinted 2017

ISBN 978 81 250 6052 9

Typeset by
Le Studio Graphique, Gurgaon 122 001
in Bembo Std 11/13.2

Printed at
Rakmo Press Pvt. Ltd.,
New Delhi

025580
15052017

Published by
Orient Blackswan Private Limited
3-6-752 Himayatnagar,
Hyderabad 500 029, Telangana, India
e-mail: info@orientblackswan.com

To my students

Contents

Translator's Preface ix
A Biographical Note on the Author xi
A Note on the Translation xv
Glossary of Non-English Words/Phrases xix

Konkaboti

Book I

1. An Old Yarn 3
2. Kusumghati 4
3. Tonu Roy 6
4. Khetu 11
5. Nironjon 17
6. Farewell 21
7. Konkaboti 26
8. The Boy and the Girl 30
9. Meni 34
10. Bou-didi 38
11. A Matrimonial Proposal 42
12. Shnareshwor 48

13. Trouble Brewing 52
14. About Godadhor 58
15. Konkaboti's Ailment 65

Book II
1. The Boat 73
2. Underwater 76
3. The Royal Robe 80
4. The Milkwoman 86
5. The Burning Ghat 90
6. The Tiger 96
7. In the Forest 104
8. The In-laws 109
9. The Root 113
10. The Theft 119
11. The Ghost Company 126
12. Frog Sahib 137
13. Putrid Water 145
14. The Master Mosquito 152
15. Khorbur 159
16. The Ogre 165
17. The Wife of the Stars 174
18. The Formidable Sepoy 178
19. The Sati on the Pyre 187
Conclusion 196

Afterword from the Translator: About the Novel 205

Translator's Preface

Even before *Of Ghosts and Other Perils,* my translation of Troilokyonath Mukhopadhyay's stories from the original Bangla, was published by Orient BlackSwan in November 2013, I had decided that I would translate his debut novel *Konkaboti* some day, sooner rather than later. The positive reviews of my first book in journals and dailies, and the enthusiastic responses from readers, speeded up my resolve to follow up my first effort of translation with a translation of *Konkaboti* at the earliest. This novel had not only announced Troilokyonath's arrival in the field of Bengali literature, but my introduction to it also signalled my charmed entry into his vibrantly colourful and humour-filled dominion of fantasy. This translation is an attempt touched with nostalgia at reliving those unforgettable magic moments. This book had a tremendous impact on my adolescence at a time when I was feeling increasingly alienated from the world of adults, and did not have many friends to share my feelings with. I was in desperate need of a personal space that I could inhabit joyfully, and also invite people into. Troilokyonath, with his *Konkaboti,* provided that space, and this work of translation is a grateful acknowledgement of that fact.

As I mentioned in the Preface to *Of Ghosts and Other Perils*, my primary purpose of purveying the enchantment of Troilokyonath's writing is backed up by a secondary purpose of boosting research on him. With that end in view, I have included a biographical note and a critical afterword in this book as well.

Translator's Preface

Hopefully, this book will not be my last effort at translating Troilokyonath, for I believe that at a time of growing worldwide violence and hatred, we need him more than ever before. Troilokyonath's works, like Swift's *Gulliver's Travels*, are much more than children's literature and an anodyne for adult angst.

Kolkata
July 2015

ARNAB BHATTACHARYA

A Biographical Note on the Author

Troilokyonath Mukhopadhyay (1847–1919) is one of the leading authors of fantasy literature in Bengal. His life was eventful and adventurous. Many of his experiences were later translated into fictional escapades that his protagonists undertake. Besides being a literary stalwart, Troilokyonath, or Troilokyo, was socially committed, and he made an earnest effort to mitigate the hardships caused by famine, rather frequent in Bengal in those days, and also to improve the economic condition of his countrymen in general. Troilokyonath's literature needs to be viewed from the perspective of his social activism.

Troilokyo was self-educated, and a pioneer among Indian entrepreneurs. He undertook enterprises in agriculture and industry with a view to strengthening the Indian economy, and wrote reflective articles to kindle his countrymen's interest in research in these domains. He strove to generate people's faith in indigenous products, and to convince them that they could earn revenues by selling them. And, amid all these activities, he wrote stories prolifically. The kind of stories that he wrote was unique and vastly popular in his time, and he was unrivalled in this genre of fiction writing.

Troilokyonath, the second of six children, was the son of Biswambhar Mukhopadhyay, a man of modest means who lived in Rahuta, a village near Shyamnagar (a town about thirty km from Kolkata in the Ganges delta). As a child, Troilokyonath was restless and impish. A real thorn in the flesh of his neighbours, he commanded a large 'army' of lads of his age who stole fruits from trees and roughed people up if they dared to protest. That a streak of the spirit of mischief-making continued in the grown-up Troilokyonath is evident from some episodes and characters in his stories and novels. But for all this delinquency, Troilokyonath always stood first in class. His innovative bent of mind was apparent from his childhood. He invented a language and its alphabet and he etched those letters on blocks of wood and earthen discs, and composed songs, riddles and *shloka*s when he was only about nine; his symbols bear an affinity with Pitman's shorthand.

Troilokyonath's early education started in village schools. Later, he got admitted to Duff's school in Chunchura, Hoogly. In 1862, there was a serious outbreak of malaria in Troilokyonath's village. He was orphaned, and he was attacked by a disease of the spleen. He survived, but his formal education came to a stop. To make matters worse, whatever landed property they had was laid waste by a devastating squall in 1864. In search of a job, he left home in 1865. From then on, it was a long story of hardship, struggles, starvation and sickness for Troilokyonath as he travelled across Bengal, and parts of Orissa too. Troilokyo witnessed the horrors of famine at close quarters. He himself had to starve for days on end and survive only on water. In Troilokyonath's stories and novels we come across characters who undertake, or are forced to undertake, long and arduous journeys beset with numerous perils. These are mostly imaginative re-creations of the journeys that Troilokyo himself undertook in various phases of his life.

He worked as a school teacher in the districts of Birbhum and Pabna (the latter is in Bangladesh now). Later, he was appointed a sub-inspector of police in Cuttack, Orissa, and was subsequently promoted to the post of inspector. He learnt Oriya and even edited a monthly journal, *Utkal Shubhakari*. In Cuttack, Troilokyo met Sir William Hunter, Scottish historian and statistician, and best known for the *Imperial Gazetteer of India*, begun in 1869. With Sir William, Troilokyo developed a deep comradeship and he was given a job in Kolkata in 1870. In 1875, Troilokyo joined as the head clerk at an office of agriculture and industry, of which Sir Edward Buck was the director, that oversaw the central and western parts of India.

There was a rich tradition of artisanship in mid-western India. Silk embroidery and brass work of Kashi, fine needlework, etchings on gold and silver of Lucknow and woodwork of Nagina (now in Bijnor district, UP), among others, were patronised by kings, badshas and nawabs. But artisanship declined during the British rule. Troilokyonath, a precursor of Indian business entrepreneurship, observed that many Britishers liked these objects while the artisans suffered for lack of patrons. Troilokyonath implored Sir Edward to try and ameliorate the artisans' plight. Sir Edward borrowed five thousand rupees from the government, and Troilokyo purchased well-crafted, high-quality articles from the artisans with that money and put those on display in a large hotel near Allahabad station, where Britain-bound sahibs and *mem*s used to put up for a day or two. They took a fancy to those objects and purchased them as gift items, while the hotel owner learnt a lesson in business entrepreneurship. Sir Edward repaid the loan to the government, and took active part in such transactions from then on. It was under Troilokyonath's initiative that shops selling Indian artifacts flourished near all big railway stations in India, and Indian artisans and craftsmen had a new lease of life.

In 1877–78, a famine broke out in the north-western part of India. Troilokyonath stayed in Rajghat near Hardwar for some time. There he bought food for the impoverished populace, spending nearly all his earnings. It was then that Troilokyonath learnt that the cultivation of carrots could be a solution to the aftermath of famines and he wrote to the government about this. The government published his article in its official gazette and its employees were instructed to help the local population by cultivating carrots extensively and expeditiously. After a couple of years, another famine struck Raebareli and Sultanpur, but the cultivation of carrots saved lives then.

In 1882, Troilokyonath got a job in the revenue department of the Government of India. He published a book containing information on what products were manufactured in India, where they could be obtained, and at what price. The book opened the eyes of foreigners to the wide range of the variegated Indian market. People from the West purchased Indian artifacts worth lakhs of rupees, which paved the way for foreign exchange earnings. His diverse domains of interest and activity are manifest in the articles that he wrote for the periodical *Jonmobhumi* on steel manufacture, cattle rearing, gold mining and many other topics.

In 1883, a fair of Indian goods was organised in England. Troilokyonath went there to spread the network of Indian commerce, and he was welcomed by the British nobility and royalty. Troilokyo went to Scotland, too, as well as countries in the Continent, recording his experiences in his *Visit to Europe*.

In 1886, Troilokyonath joined service at the Indian Museum when he wrote *Art Manufacture of India* at the behest of the Indian government. The book was immensely beneficial to Indian artisans and craftsmen. He retired from service in 1896 because of failing health.

His ailment persisted even after his retirement. In order to recuperate, he started living by the seaside at Puri in Orissa. On 3 November 1919, he breathed his last.

A Note on the Translation

Jacques Derrida, in the section '... That Dangerous Supplement' in his *Of Grammatology,* shows that Jean Jacques Rousseau, in both his *Emile* and *Confessions,* expressed 'a perpetually reanimated mistrust with regard to the so-called full speech'. Derrida writes that in order to reconstruct it through *écriture* or writing, Rousseau in those two books simultaneously 'valorizes and disqualifies' writing. Writing thus becomes a 'dangerous supplement' to speech, which very often conceals or counterfeits 'the presence' of the speaker, a necessary evil in the act of communication itself. If Rousseau's idea is transposed to the notion of translation, we should not object to accepting translation as another form of necessary evil. By common agreement, it is the only possible means of trans-linguistic and trans-cultural communication, and also a portentous (maybe also pretentious) tool of possible mis-communication. It is entrusted with a solemn task, but ironically, only by default, and hence remains discredited from the beginning. Translation as an activity thus can at best aspire for a left-handed compliment, and at worst be prepared for a disparaging dismissal.

My take on this issue is somewhat different. For me, translation is not a 'dangerous' but a creative supplement. It is not a simple tool for transferring a message or information from one culture to another, but a process of creative intervention that, as Walter Benjamin brilliantly argues in 'Task of a Translator', not only brings two disparate cultures closer, but also seeks to transform both. Alongside this, I believe that translation is an exercise in the art of persuasion, like histrionics. Actors playing a role have to persuade the spectator as part of their professional obligation that they *are* actually the persons whom they represent on the stage or the screen. They exhaust themselves in the role they play, and yet, some indelible parts of their real life self (like their way of speaking, their gait) get transmitted into the character they are playing. The spectator recognises these twin aspects of acting, and yet remains convinced that the actors *are* the persona they are playing for the time being. Translators, similarly, persuade the reader to believe that their translation *is* the original, and yet leave a signature style of their translation on the body of the translated text. The readers will be convinced that the text *is* original, while recognising at the back of their mind that this actually is a specific act of translation. That is why translation is not a mechanical proxy, but a creative supplement.

I have attempted to make my translation a creative supplement to Troilokyonath's text. A translator has to fuse, and simultaneously diffuse, cultures. As Susan Bassnett points out in 'Culture and Translation', a translator is like a traveller who must create a 'third language' to make an 'otherness' acceptable to the target reader. While translating *Konkaboti*, I have tried to diffuse nineteenth-century Bengali culture into that of the twenty-first century English-speaking readership, by interspersing the target language with British informal words/phrases and idioms. This is what Lawrence Venuti calls 'domestic inscription'. And in this sense I have consciously sought to make my translation not only a trans-cultural, but also a trans-temporal, dialogue of languages, which highlights what Venuti calls 'diachrony-in-synchrony'. But 'to diffuse' does not mean 'to defuse', and so I have tried not to defuse the identity markers of the source culture. As in my previous translational enterprise *Of Ghosts and Other Perils*, here too I have used borrowings and calques [or, loan translations, that is, words or phrases borrowed from another language by literal translation], liberally, while using transpositions and equivalences only sparingly. Here too a glossary of non-English words/phrases has been incorporated to prevent the possibility of unintelligibility. And alongside this, notes are to be found at the end of most chapters.

A point about an orthographic variation needs to be highlighted. I have used 'o' to indicate the shorter 'a' in this work, unlike in *Of Ghosts and Other Perils*. Thus, 'mahashay' of my earlier work has become 'mohashoy' in this one, and '*shraddha*' has become '*shraddho*' to approximate the standard Bengali pronunciations more closely. However, in the spellings of such words as 'dharma' and 'Brahman' which have found their ways into the English vocabulary, and in those of some well-known names like 'Vidyasagar' and 'Lakshmi', the use of 'o' for short 'a' has been avoided.

ARNAB BHATTACHARYA

Glossary of Non-English Words / Phrases

aaha: Expression or interjection of happiness.

aha: Expression or interjection of regret, akin to 'alas'.

alta: Red pigment smeared on the sides of women's feet, especially by married ones.

anna: Coin, one-sixteenth part of a rupee, now obsolete.

apsoras: Damsels of heaven, according to Hindu mythology.

babaji: Common nineteenth-century form of address for one's son-in-law.

bachha: Literally, 'child' (different from 'bachcha', child, with no other connotation), an address of endearment, especially by elderly Bengali women for a young person in the past, sometimes used sarcastically to address a grown-up person to preface an insult.

basorghor (also, basor): Room in which a newly-wed couple are supposed to spend a wakeful night. This ritual, known as 'basor *jaga*' or 'staying awake in the basor', harks back to *Monosamongol Kabyo* of the fourteenth century in which Lakhinder, the bridegroom, was bitten in his basor by a snake sent by Goddess Monosa, desperate to extract devotion from the merchant Chand, the groom's father and a devotee of Lord Shiva.

bata: Bengali name for a variety of small silvery-white fresh-water fish.

batasa: Light, convex sweet-drop made of sugar or molasses.

Bhadro: Fifth month of the Bengali year, which corresponds to mid-August to mid-September.

bhetki: Species of fresh-water fish.

Bilat: Indian reference to a European country, especially England.

Bilati: Resident of or related to Bilat (above).

boidyo: Physician, particularly rural.

Boishakh: First month of the Bengali year, corresponding to mid-April to mid-May.

bongsojo: A Brahman lineage originally of *kulin* descent, but lowered in social hierarchy because of matrimonial alliance with a family of an 'inferior' caste.

borokh: Ice; now written and pronounced in Bengali as '*borof*'.

boron: Ritual in Bengali Hindu weddings, in which the bride is welcomed ceremoniously.

bou-didi: Standard Bengali address for the wife of one's elder brother; 'bou' means 'wife' and 'didi' means 'elder sister'.

Brahmani: Wife of a Brahman.

brohmottor: Piece of rent-free land given away to a Brahman as a gift, also called 'brohmotro'.

broto: Ritualistic practice performed mainly by Hindu women, of which fasting is often an essential part, to appease the gods.

byanjon: Cooked dish, used commonly with reference to vegetables.

chhi: Interjection, often repeated, to express one's feelings for something shameful.

chhotak: Earlier measure of weight equal to 1/16 *ser*, or a little over fifty-eight grams.

chochhori: Dish of spiced vegetables cooked in oil, sometimes with fish bones, popular among Bengali middle-class and lower middle-class people.

chondal: A 'low-caste' man in the Hindu hierarchy once considered 'untouchable', whose profession was to cremate corpses.

chorka: Spinning wheel, especially one manually operated in the past.

chotuspathi: Private educational institution of rural Bengal usually owned by a Sanskrit scholar, its other name being '*tol*'.

chowkidar: Sentry who maintained nocturnal vigil, mostly in rural areas.

dada: Elder brother, often used as a suffix (sometimes shortened to 'da') to male names as a sign of respect or affection.

dadamohashoy: Grandfather.

dadathakur: Reverential form of address for an elderly male particularly in nineteenth- and early twentieth-century Bengal.

didi: Elder sister, also used as a respectful form of address in regard to any woman older than the speaker.

ekadoshi: Day (eleventh of the lunar fortnight) for ritual fasting by Bengali Hindu widows.

gamchha: Thin towel, also used to bundle up small objects.

ghat: Riverbank, often used for cremation ('burning ghat').

gonda: Sum of money in an obsolete currency.

gurumohashoy: Teacher of a *pathshala*.

haan: Word to signify 'yes'.

hai, hai: Expression or interjection of lament or regret.

Hé: Prefatory form of address before the utterance of the name of a godhead.

hnari: Urn-shaped clay pot, used mainly to boil rice.

hobishyo: Boiled sunned rice and ghee, eaten by near relatives of a deceased person as part of ritualistic mourning by Bengali Hindus.

ish: Interjection of regret, at something missed, opportunity lost, etc.

jhumjhumi: Rattle for infants, a popular toy.

jobon: Non-Hindu, originally referred to Ionian Greeks, but later referred to Muslims as well; infidel.

joggo: Fire lit ritualistically on an auspicious occasion, like making sacrifices, invoking gods and chasing away evil spirits. *Puranic* tales are replete with references to such joggos, which were also occasions for social gathering.

jok: Mythical spirit believed to be guarding hidden treasure. The popular superstition was that if children were killed in some underground treasure trove, their spirits would turn into 'joks' to watch over that treasure. This belief prompted a criminal practice of infanticide.

joté buri: Mythical haggard, unkempt woman believed to scare children.

jyathaima: Standard Bengali form of address for the wife of one's paternal uncle ('*jyatha*') older than one's father.

kaka: Bengali form of address for or a reference to one's father's younger brother. The English equivalent 'uncle' is too generalised a term for this, and hence avoided in the translation.

kando: A chapter is so called in the Ramayana.

kansi: Flat plate with raised edges made of bell-metal and used as a musical instrument, especially during idol worship, producing a clangorous sound when beaten by a stick.

katla: Variety of flat fresh-water fish, similar to the *rohu* but with a larger head.

khansama: Valet of a sahib, or of a Westernised gentleman.

khero: Thick coarse cloth dyed in red, used especially for wrapping books.

khoi: Very light food prepared by frying paddy in sand heated on an oven.

khuri ma: Form of address of endearment and respect for an elderly lady in olden Bengal. Literally, 'khuri' means 'the wife of an uncle (father's brother)', 'ma' meaning 'mother'.

kobiraj: Village physician who prescribes herbal medicine.

koi ga: An especially rural form of address, which roughly translates as 'O what is this?' Literally, it means 'Where are you?'

kola bou: Plantain dressed as a bride, believed to be Lord Ganesh's wife.

Koli: An age or era of sins, which the present is sometimes believed to be, at the end of which apocalypse or total destruction is to set in according to the Hindu scriptures. Also, the fourth or last era of creation according to that belief, the first three being *Sotyo*, *Treta* and *Dwapor*. Koli is the age in which dharma is supposed to be in a state of decline, reaching almost the nadir. This is when Lord Vishnu is expected to appear in his tenth avatar, namely *Kolki*, to bring the apocalypse about, and recreate the universe.

kora: Coin of the smallest value, now obsolete.

krosh: Now obsolete measure of distance equal to 8,000 cubits/ a little more than two miles/ three kilometres.

kulin: An elite Brahman who enjoyed high social prestige, and was entitled to many marriages in the past.

kulki: Kind of ice-cream, now spelt and pronounced in Bengali as '*kulfi*'.

kulo: Flat and light vessel made of bamboo for winnowing grains, etc., also used for fanning.

kulodharma: Rituals or customs pertaining to a particular clan among some 'upper-caste' Bengali Hindus.

kush: Kind of grass, regarded as holy, often used in Hindu rituals.

logno: Specific time mentioned in the Bengali Hindu almanac as the auspicious hour of marriage. If the time is over, the bride is said to be '*lognobhroshto*', meaning 'one who has missed her logno'. Such a bride once carried a social stigma and had to remain a spinster all her life.

luchi: Indigenous pancake fried in boiling ghee or oil, ideally spherical; a popular food item for Bengalis.

ma thakurani: Respectful form of address for an elderly woman (or a woman of 'higher' caste) in nineteenth-century Bengal.

magi: A common, particularly nineteenth-century, slang term for a woman.

malsa: Small earthen basin.

masi: Sister of one's mother, but often used as a respectful form of address for an elderly woman. 'Aunt' is too generalised an equivalent for this term, hence avoided.

mem (short for memsahib): Feminine gender of 'sahib'.

minshe: Pejorative reference to a man; the word derives from '*manush*', meaning 'human'.

mohashoy: Bengali equivalent of 'Mr' or 'sir' when addressing, or speaking of, elderly or respectable males.

muri: Common food for Bengali middle- and lower-middle-class people, made by parching rice on hot sand.

namaboli: Scarf or wrap with names of Hindu deities printed on it.

noa: Iron ('loha,' corrupted as 'noa') wristlet worn by women as a mark of their marriage.

nomoskar: Typical Indian/Bengali gesture of paying obeisance, especially by joining palms.

noté: An edible creeper.

obhiman: Feeling of wounded sentiments, which originates from love and affection, with no exact equivalent in English.

ogo: Form of address, often in a pleading tone.

ombol: Kind of sour broth taken as a delicacy.

pathshala: Educational institution of rural Bengal.

pindo: Offering of food to the dead.

pnuti: Small fresh-water fish.

Poush: Ninth month of the Bengali year, which corresponds to mid-December to mid-January.

prohor: Indigenous measure of time equal to three hours.

projapatya: Strenuous Hindu expiatory ritual for not performing a promised act.

pronam: Typical Bengali gesture of obeisance offered either by prostrating on the ground, and making one's head touch the respected one's feet, or by touching their feet with the hands while bending down.

puranic: Of or having to do with Hindu mythological texts ('*puranas*').

rampakhi: Facetious reference to the cock or hen, for reasons obscure.

rudraksho: Kind of dried fruit used as a bead in a rosary used by devout Hindus.

sati: Chaste and faithful wife (apart from the sense of the former practice of a Hindu wife burning herself with the body of her dead husband).

ser ('seer'): Obsolete Indian measure of weight equivalent to 1/40th of a *mon* (maund), somewhat less than a kilogram.

shaala: Literally brother-in-law, also a commonly used slang term of abuse.

shal: Tree of hard wood like teak, used in making furniture.

shastric: Relating to *shastras*, Hindu scriptural texts, including the *Samhitas*.

shloka: Couplet of classical Indian text in Sanskrit verse.

Shrabon: Third month of the Bengali year, corresponding to mid-July to mid-August, and hence a month that experiences heavy showers.

shraddho: Hindu ritual performed after somebody's death, wishing for the deliverance of his/her soul; the word derives from '*shroddha'*, meaning respect; observed monthly among certain sections of the people.

Shudra: Fourth, and the 'lowliest', caste in the Hindu hierarchy.

shuk bird: Bird whose female counterpart is '*shari*'; Bengali fairy tales are sometimes presented through dialogues between these two birds.

sirni: Sweet made of milk, *atta* (a wheat product), sugar, and banana, offered to deities.

sondesh: Popular dry sweetmeat of Bengal.

songsar: Word with an expansive spectrum of signification, ranging from 'the family' to 'the world' one lives in.

Sotyo, Treta, Dwapor: See 'koli' above.

srijukto: Bengali form of address or reference to a male as a mark of honour.

tamasha: Literally 'fun', often that derived from someone else's discomfiture; a trick.

thakur: Especially nineteenth-century Bengali form of address of respect for Brahmans by 'lower-caste' people; literally, god or idol.

thala: Circular metal plate with raised edge, used to eat from.

thangares: Groups of brigands who waylaid passers-by in open, desolate fields and killed them to take possession of whatever they carried. They were a source of terror for people who had to travel long distances for commercial or other purposes. Also known as thuggees, they are mentioned in Barani's *History of Firuz Shah* which dates from around 1356. Lord William Bentinck exterminated this menace with the assistance of his administrative chief, William Henry Sleeman, in 1830.

tiki: Tuft of hair on a tonsured or a closely-cropped head as a Hindu practice among some males.

tip: Dotted mark with sandal paste, vermilion, tinsel or saffron, etc., put on the forehead especially of women as a personal decoration or as a mark of sanctity.

tithi: Astrological term meaning 'a lunar day'; religious rituals are performed on these days, as prescribed in the Hindu scriptures.

tola: Small part, a measure of weight of 180 grains, or approximately twelve grams.

torpon: Hindu ritual of offering food and paying obeisance to one's ancestors.

trisondhya: Ritualistic worship that a devoted Brahman is expected to perform thrice a day. The word is a combination of '*tri*', meaning three, and '*sondhya*', meaning conjunctional period of the day, i.e., dawn, noon, or evening.

tthan didi: Common Bengali term in the past for one's granny.

tusser: Brownish silk textile obtained from a moth.

zamindar: Landlord in the past, wielding monetary and social power.

Konkaboti

Book I

1

An Old Yarn

Everybody knows Konkaboti. Bengalis have heard of her in their childhood.

Konkaboti's brother brought a mango. Having lodged it safely at home, he alerted everyone with these words: 'Take care that no one eats this mango; if somebody does, I'll marry the wrongdoer.'

Konkaboti had no knowledge of this. She was but a child! Without understanding anything, she ate the mango.

Her brother said, 'Now I'll marry Konkaboti.'

His parents tried to reason with him, 'How can a brother marry a sister?'

But he did not heed their words. He said, 'Why has Konkaboti eaten my mango? I will and I must marry Konkaboti.'

Konkaboti was hugely embarrassed, she was frightened. Rendered helpless, she built a boat. She boarded that boat and floated away in her backyard pond. Her brother's plan to marry her was thus thwarted.

This is how the saga goes. But this is incredible. Would someone want to marry his sister for a mango? That is impossible. Now I will narrate what *is* possible.

2

Kusumghati

There is a village called Kusumghati among the forests, away from the city. Large and quite heavily populated, the village is skirted by a field. In olden days, it was trampled by many feet. At opportune moments, rogues from neighbouring villages would often kill pedestrians and plunder their belongings. The miscreants would bury their victims in the ponds dotting that field. Even to this day, skulls are exhumed from the beds of those ponds.

There was yet another way of concealing bodies. Those ruffians would kill a passer-by, carry his lifeless body to another village, and leave it there. Before leaving, they would squeak, 'ku.'

Hearing that sound, the *chowkidar* would immediately know that a corpse had been laid at some fringe area of his village. He would then think apprehensively, 'If a corpse is found at my boundary, I will be hauled up for murder.'

Having reasoned thus, he too would carry that corpse with the assistance of his friends to some other village, and leave it there, squealing 'ku.'

In this manner, a corpse would travel a distance of about ten to twelve *kroshes*. Matters regarding where the victim hailed from and who murdered him were not looked into at the back of beyond.

So this land was forested, and on top of that it abounded with unnatural deaths! At such a place, ghosts can never be scarce. The village folk believe that a wide variety of ghosts live among the

1

An Old Yarn

Everybody knows Konkaboti. Bengalis have heard of her in their childhood.

Konkaboti's brother brought a mango. Having lodged it safely at home, he alerted everyone with these words: 'Take care that no one eats this mango; if somebody does, I'll marry the wrongdoer.'

Konkaboti had no knowledge of this. She was but a child! Without understanding anything, she ate the mango.

Her brother said, 'Now I'll marry Konkaboti.'

His parents tried to reason with him, 'How can a brother marry a sister?'

But he did not heed their words. He said, 'Why has Konkaboti eaten my mango? I will and I must marry Konkaboti.'

Konkaboti was hugely embarrassed, she was frightened. Rendered helpless, she built a boat. She boarded that boat and floated away in her backyard pond. Her brother's plan to marry her was thus thwarted.

This is how the saga goes. But this is incredible. Would someone want to marry his sister for a mango? That is impossible. Now I will narrate what *is* possible.

2

Kusumghati

There is a village called Kusumghati among the forests, away from the city. Large and quite heavily populated, the village is skirted by a field. In olden days, it was trampled by many feet. At opportune moments, rogues from neighbouring villages would often kill pedestrians and plunder their belongings. The miscreants would bury their victims in the ponds dotting that field. Even to this day, skulls are exhumed from the beds of those ponds.

There was yet another way of concealing bodies. Those ruffians would kill a passer-by, carry his lifeless body to another village, and leave it there. Before leaving, they would squeak, 'ku.'

Hearing that sound, the *chowkidar* would immediately know that a corpse had been laid at some fringe area of his village. He would then think apprehensively, 'If a corpse is found at my boundary, I will be hauled up for murder.'

Having reasoned thus, he too would carry that corpse with the assistance of his friends to some other village, and leave it there, squealing 'ku.'

In this manner, a corpse would travel a distance of about ten to twelve *krosh*es. Matters regarding where the victim hailed from and who murdered him were not looked into at the back of beyond.

So this land was forested, and on top of that it abounded with unnatural deaths! At such a place, ghosts can never be scarce. The village folk believe that a wide variety of ghosts live among the banyan, *peepal* and *bel* trees. Once evening sets in, they sit and talk about phantoms, and these tales make children's flesh creep.

Witches too are not at all rare in the village. Grandmas caution the children, 'Witches lie about as hay on the road, do not ever tread on those, or else witches will gobble you up.'

The village folk, thus, are beset with perils on land. In water, too, dangers lurk aplenty. A stream flows by that village. Coursing down from a mountaintop, the brook gurgles its way towards the sea. True, there are no sharks or crocodiles about, but the rill throws up some other perils. The *joté buri* is there carrying shackles, and besides, the riverbed is replete with live stones. Given half a chance, these fears of the unknown sit heavy on the human heart.

Hill ranges are visible at some distance from Kusumghati. The hills are cloaked in woods in which tigers and bears prowl. Tigers carry off cattle all the time. In a while a tiger learns to devour man, and once it does that, it eats nothing else but man. The beleaguered villagers then have to kill that tiger.

But some tigers are so cunning that nobody can kill them. Word goes that these are not real tigers, but humans. There is a variety of roots spread all over the woods which a man can wear on his head to instantly transform himself into a tiger. If someone picks a quarrel with someone else, the former makes a headdress with that root and turns into a tiger in order to kill his adversary. Having performed the deed, he takes that root off, and becomes human again. If someone perchance fails to remove the root after the mission is accomplished, that person then remains a tiger for good. Tigers of this ilk spell real trouble for human beings.

These beliefs dwelt in the minds of the rural folk of Kusumghati. But their fears are being dispelled nowadays. Some of these folk often come to Kolkata with *tusser* cocoons and lac. Some take up accommodation in Kolkata lodges. Some have studied English, and do not believe in ghosts or witches. If somebody raises the topic of ghosts, they quip, 'Ghosts do not exist. And even if they do, what harm can they do us?' Watching these fellows, today's children too have mustered some courage.

3

Tonu Roy

Srijukto Ramtonu Roy *mohashoy* lived at Kusumghati. Nobody called him 'Ramtonu Roy'; rather, he was known as 'Tonu Roy'. He was an aged Brahman who ritualistically carried out priestly duties. He performed *trisondhya*, *shraddho* and *torpon* for his forbears, paid obeisance to deities and gurus, and participated in sectarian movements. He nursed a grudge against modern men for their indifference towards religious activities.

He said, 'Today's young men are all atheists, nobody should take water offered by them.'[1]

He himself abided by religious norms and performed rituals unfalteringly. He had profound respect especially for the norms pertaining to *kulin*s and *bongsojo*s.

He was a Brahman of the bongsojo lineage. He said, 'Since God has made me a bongsojo Brahman, I must adhere to my bongsojo dharma, failing which I will insult God Himself, commit a sin, and head for hell. Now, if you ask what this bongsojo dharma is, my answer is that it consists in the injunction that a man, having offered his daughter to a prospective bridegroom, will accept a mere pittance from the latter (unlike the prevalent practice of extracting higher amounts from older grooms). The person who, despite being a bongsojo, does not go by this ruling, has his dharma laid waste to; that person is cast very low in the social hierarchy—so goes the *shastric* mandate.'

Since he did everything by the book, Tonu Roy was widely revered. Women, while performing *broto*s, considered him as the first

Brahman.[2] Everybody said, 'A devout Brahman like Roy mohashoy is extremely rare in this world.' He had the pride of place especially in the Shudra community.

Tonu Roy was a bongsojo of a high order. People wisecracked, 'His is a family of bachelors for generations. It is doubtful if their fathers and grandfathers married at all.'

The fact was that his own marriage ceremony had had a rather rough ride. Promising to pay five hundred rupees, he had decided on his marriage with a girl. He had collected that amount by selling *brohmottor* lands. With that money he went to marry the girl. The bride's father had counted and jingled the coins.[3] The *logno* of the marriage had drawn near, but the bride's father made no efforts to formally offer his daughter to the bridegroom. Nobody could figure out why he dragged his feet.

Then he had spilled the beans, 'Little could I guess that the bridegroom is this old. That is why I agreed to make the deal for five hundred rupees, but now I have changed my mind; unless I get another hundred, I will not offer my daughter.'

These words of the bride's father had set the cat among the pigeons. The logno got transgressed in that bedlam, and it was almost daybreak. By then, some people had liaised with both the contending parties and offered the solution that Roy mohashoy would have to pay another fifty rupees to be able to marry the girl. Tonu Roy had borrowed fifty rupees against a bond, handed that money over to the girl's father, and concluded the nuptial.

Tonu Roy had rehearsed a few songs, intending to sing those in the *basorghor.* But everything had ended in a fiasco, for the basor itself did not take place as it was already dawn. This grief remained in Tonu Roy's mind for ever.

Tonu Roy had three daughters and a son. He preserved his *kulodharma* and offered the daughters to eligible grooms. The sons-in-law did justice to Tonu Roy's social prestige. One paid five hundred rupees, and the other one thousand rupees in cash. So they must have been quite eligible grooms.

In order to command more prestige than usual, Tonu Roy had allowed his daughters to grow up before marrying them off. He used to say, 'If I marry them off at a tender age, and if subsequently they are widowed, who is going to shoulder the burden of that sin? One should marry off only grown-up daughters. The kulin and bongsojo Brahmans cannot be faulted for that. This is the shastric commandment.'

When the Act regarding the bridal flower-bed was passed,[4] Tonu Roy said, 'I have been abiding by this law since my early days, why then this new legislation?' He opposed the law tooth and nail, organised meetings, collected subscriptions, and eventually, appropriated the money.

Tonu Roy's sons-in-law were not exactly greenhorns. A young bridegroom was his anathema. Such a groom usually wants to settle the negotiations with only a hundred or two hundred rupees! As such, he picked on slightly elderly grooms to marry off his daughters to. One of them was aged seventy, and the other seventy-five.

When the local women cast aspersions on the grooms' ages, Tonu Roy explained, '*Ogo*, O women, you don't understand. Brides are cosseted and coddled only when the grooms are a wee bit long in the tooth.'

The grooms' ages had ripened a tad too much, for within a year after their marriages, both the daughters were widowed.

Tonu Roy was a man of gumption. He might have been overpowered with grief over his sons-in-law's deaths, but he quickly recovered, consoling himself with these words, 'It is all destiny! Who can overrule it? There are people who marry their five-year-old daughters off to twelve-year-old boys. Why are their daughters widowed, pray? Whatever is destined to happen, will. Nobody can escape the divine decree.'

Tonu Roy's son was a chip off the old block. Now, he was no longer a tot, but past twenty-five. He had not received an education, but, like his father, was well-versed in shastric knowledge. He was quite happy that his father was making money by marrying daughters off, for he was his father's only successor. Who were those widows, after all? But he always eulogised the widows of his family.

He said, 'Our widows are the embodiments of goddess Saraswati.[5] They are always committed to dharma, always devoted to philanthropy. They are always preoccupied with the thought of feeding father and me well. They prepare five-course dinners for us, even having fasted for three days themselves. These two sisters of mine are like Ahalya, Draupadi, Kunti, Tara or Mandodhori.[6] They are the ones whose names you would like to remember in the early morning.'[7]

He sometimes lamented that sati had been abolished, for in case it hadn't been, his sisters would have sailed to heaven in a trice. They would not have had to be fed by his father then.

O, why should the sahibs have latched the door of heaven like this?

Tonu Roy's wife was of a different nature, though. As her daughters tied the knot one after the other, she broke into sobs, watching the 'graceful' bridegrooms. Tonu Roy took her to task and said, 'Try to remember how your father acted!' Occasionally, he bore down on her with jeers and sneers. The issue of their daughters' marriages was an eternal apple of spousal discord. Looking at the faces of her widowed daughters, the mother's tears knew no bounds. The mother too sort of performed *ekadoshi* with the daughters; on that day, she ate nothing, though she sipped a drop of water or two, fearing that her full fasting might augur ill for her husband.[8]

Every day, having worshipped each godhead, she tapped her head at their feet, and prayed to them, '*Hé* Ma Kali! *Hé* Ma Durga![9] Hé dear gods and goddesses! See to it that the groom for my Konkaboti be the one after my heart.'

Konkaboti was Tonu Roy's youngest daughter. She was a mere infant then.

Notes

1. 'Today's young men ... offered by them': Taking water from someone to drink was a mark of social acceptance in days of yore.

2. '... consider him as the first Brahman': This is a gesture of paying obeisance to 'higher-caste' people, especially Brahmans.
3. 'The bride's father counted and jingled the coins': This suggests that the bride's father wanted to check if the coins were real or fake.
4. '... the Act regarding the bridal flower-bed ...': A reference to the Age of Consent Act of 1891, which raised the age of consent for sexual intercourse for girls from ten to twelve years. The Act was passed on 19 March, and was hotly debated, with some members of the legislative assembly blaming the Act for interfering with orthodox Hindu customs.
5. Goddess Saraswati: The goddess of learning for Hindus.
6. 'Ahalya, Draupadi, Kunti, Tara or Mandadhari': Illustrious women in Indian mythology. Ahalya is a devotee of Lord Rama in the Ramayana, Draupadi is the wife of the five Pandavas in the Mahabharata, Kunti is the wife of Pandu in the same epic, Tara is the wife of Lord Brihospoti, and Mandodhori is Ravan's wife in the Ramayana.
7. 'They are the ones whose names ... in the early morning': This is a gesture of paying respect to someone, especially one who is no more.
8. 'Though she sipped ... her full fasting might augur ill for her husband': Full fasting by a wife on the day of ekadoshi is believed to bode ill for her husband, since this is a ritual reserved for observance exclusively by Hindu widows.
9. '*Hé* Ma Kali! Hé Ma Durga': Kali and Durga are female godheads particularly revered by Bengali Hindus.

4

Khetu

In Tonu Roy's neighbourhood lived a grief-stricken Brahmani. People called her 'Khetu's mother'. She was now woebegone, but she had seen better days. The late Shibchondro Mukhopadhyay, her husband, had been educated; he had been in service in Kolkata and earned a decent sum.

But money burned a hole in his pocket. People's misery appalled him, and he bent over backwards to help. He used to feed many people, and paid for the education of a large number of boys. Such a man and his money are soon parted.

His wife bore him a son at an advanced age. The son was named 'Khetro', and that was why people called her 'Khetu's mother'.

When the son was born, Shibchondro thought, 'Now I will have to scrimp on my expenses. I must ensure that my wife and son do not have to scrounge for food when I am no more.'

The thought occurred to him all right, but it stopped short of being implemented. The world is laden with sorrow, and the person who looks upon this sorrow as his own has to live and die a pauper.

When Khetu was only four, his father passed away. He left his wife and his child truly in deep waters. Khetu's father had once done a good turn to many. Some of them had now become rich. But when his family was in trouble, none cared to redress their plight. Nobody deigned to ask, 'Khetu's ma, do you have provision for *hobishyo*?'

In such a time of distress, they had only one man to look up to. And that man was Ramhori Mukhopadhyay.

Ramhori was their kin, but a distant one. Khetu's father had once got him a petty job. There was none to look after his family in his country home, and that was why Ramhori had to live with his family in Kolkata. He had to make do with what little he got as salary.

How was such a man expected to save money? Still he managed to collect some amount and give it to the widow; he wandered from door to door for help. Those who had once been fed by Khetu's father today grumbled and groused, and hurled snide remarks at Ramhori before doling out a rupee or two. With this pittance, the shraddho was performed for Khetu's father. And Ramhori sent Khetu and his mother back to their country home with the little money he had managed to save.

Once Khetu's mother returned home, Ramhori used to bear her expense of buying rice. He could not afford more. Khetu's mother used to snip sacred threads[1] to make ends meet. There were no friends nearby. Only Nironjon *Kobirotno* looked after them,[2] and it was always he who stood by them in troubled times.

In this manner, Khetu's mother spent her hard days. Her boy was growing up to be quiet and gentle, yet brave and strong. His grace and virtues, his affection and sympathy made his mother forget her grief. When the boy turned seven, Ramhori came once to their village.

He told Khetu's mother, 'Khetu has attained the age of learning, now he should no longer be kept here. I want to take him with me to Kolkata, but what is your opinion?'

Khetu's mother said, 'O, good gracious! How can that be? How shall I live apart from Khetu? I cannot survive even for a moment when Khetu is out of my sight. No, *bachha*! I cannot send Khetu away to any place as long as I am alive.'

Ramhori said, 'If Khetu lives here, his education will surely suffer. You know what the condition of Mathur Chakraborty was. He used to live off worshipping Lord Shiva during the Gajon festival.[3] People used to look down on him as "the Brahman of the Gajon".[4] His son, Shnareshwor, used to cook in your house for some time. Shibkaka took pity on him as he was a small child,[5] and admitted him to a school. Now, he has become an advocate, and is rolling in money.'

Khetu's mother shot back, 'Shut up, please. If the education at Kolkata begets a Shnareshwor, my Khetu need not be educated.'

Ramhori said, 'It is true that Shnareshwor tipples, and accepts taboo food from his Muslim coachman, and alongside all these, chants the hymns of Hori as well. But that does not imply that everybody would be like him. A male child *does* need education, doesn't he? A male craves for education as much as he longs to live.'

Khetu's mother answered, 'Yes, that is true. A male child desires education more strongly than he prays for life. Those parents who do not impart education to their sons are their arch enemies. But please try to understand that I have a mother's heart, that I am a lone, helpless widow! I have none in this world; I live in this *songsar* with this slip of a boy. I always worry about him. If he delays a bit in coming back from play, what shall I say of the premonitions that trouble my mind? I have misgivings that either Khetu has drowned, or been burnt, or fallen from some tree, or been beaten up by local boys. When Khetu sleeps at night, I get up from time to time and put my hand under his nose to see if he is breathing. Now, try to understand how a mother's heart pines and languishes when she has to part with the apple of her eye. That is why I sob, and say in protest, "no".'

Khetu's mother continued, 'Ramhori, my Khetu is a child of fine qualities. After only two years at the *pathshala* he has mastered the palm leaf, and been graduated to the banana leaf.[6] *Gurumohashoy* says that Khetu is a cut above the rest of his pupils. Listen, Ramhori, my Khetu is a well-behaved boy. He does whatever I ask him to. And he never does anything that I forbid him to. One day the Das's daughter came running and told me, "*Ogo*, hello, local boys are roughing Khetu up." I rushed off at the double. Reaching the spot, I rescued him and picked him up in my lap. Khetu wiped his tears and said, "Ma, I did not cry in front of them lest they should think that I am scared. None is really a match for me by himself, so six of them laid into me in a body; still I *did* hit back at them, and whenever I meet any one of those six all alone I will beat the daylights out of him." I said, "No bachha, you shouldn't do that. If you fight with everybody, whom will you play with?" Khetu heeded my words. After that, often Khetu met each of those six boys all alone, and if he so wished he could have thrashed each to a pulp, but since I forbade him he desisted.

'Another day I told him, "Khetu, don't throw stones at Tonu Roy's mango tree. Tonu Roy is bad-tempered, he will call you names." Khetu said, "Ma, the mangoes of that tree are so sweet! One of those mangoes ripened red, and I held a stone in my hand, so I thought what if it fell down." I said, "Baccha, the mangoes of that tree may be sweet, but the tree is not ours. If you throw stones at other people's trees, they will get angry. When the mangoes fall off by themselves, you may pick those up and eat them, for that no one will tell you a thing."

'Once, Khetu came and told me, "Ma, mangosteens ['*gaab*'] have ripened in fishermen's trees. Local boys climbed a tree and were eating the fruit, they called me and said, "Khetu, come, O brother! We cannot get to the fruits that are so high!" But then, ma, I didn't climb that tree. I didn't because the mangosteen tree is not ours. Why should I climb it then? I stood underneath it. Boys dropped a mangosteen or two. Ma, how can I describe to you how sweet those mangosteens were! I have brought one for you, just taste it, O ma! If we had a mangosteen tree, it would have been so very nice!" I told him, "Khetu, elderly people don't eat mangosteens, better you have it. And plucking mangosteens of others' trees is not an offence; the fishermen won't chide you for that. But remember, don't climb up to the edge, and don't step on a thin branch for that may snap and you may have a heavy fall. Lick up the seeds of the mangosteens, and then throw them away, don't try to eat those too for they may stick in your gullet." How can I tell you how over the moon my child felt once he got the permission to eat mangosteens?

'Another time, a man came to this village to sell *sondesh*. Local boys stood around him. The parents bought sondesh for their boys, as many as each of them could afford. My Khetu stood there with a glum face. I ran up to Khetu quickly, and picked him up in my lap. My heart broke, and I cried. I came back home with my son, still wiping my tears. But Khetu kept mum, he didn't utter a single word. I could not tell what he was thinking in his tender mind. After a while, he touched my face and asked, "Ma, why are you crying?" I said, "Son, once there used to be sondesh galore in my home, even the servants could barely manage to exhaust the stuff after having their fill. But today I have not been able to buy you one paisa worth of sondesh, so how shall I get over this sorrow? O son, what an unfortunate mother has brought you forth!" Now, listen to what that seven-year-old said, "Ma, those sondesh are not good at all. Haven't you seen that those are all rancid? And mother, you know, eating sondesh makes me sick. You must remember that once I went to attend an invitation at the Choudhuris', ate sondesh there and took so very ill the next day. One should not eat sondesh, rather, one should eat *muri*. Ma, in case you have muri at home, give me some, please."'

Khetu's mother could not speak enough of her son! What shall I say of the accounts of her son that she gave to Ramhori?

At last, Ramhori said, '*Khuri ma,* don't be afraid. I will take care of Khetu more than I do of my own children. I have once been greatly served by Shibkaka. It is thanks to his efforts that I now feed my family. I can hardly allow his son to remain illiterate. I will always write to you about how Khetu is doing, and how he is studying. When Khetu learns to write, he will write letters to you himself. I will send Khetu back home during the pujas and the summer vacation. He will stay with you for two or three months in a year. Today is Friday. Next Wednesday is auspicious. I will take Khetu along to Kolkata on that day.'

Notes

1. 'Khetu's mother used to snip sacred threads': It was a common occupation for poor women in nineteenth-century Bengal.

2. 'Nironjon Kobirotno': 'Kobirotno', meaning 'a gem among poets', was a title for Sanskrit scholars in nineteenth-century Bengal.
3. 'Gajon festival': A festival of Lord Shiva celebrated mainly by Bengali Hindus, especially in rural Bengal. Fairs are organised widely as part of this festival.
4. 'The Brahman of the Gajon': A Brahman who worships Lord Shiva in the Gajon festival does not usually belong to an elite class of Brahmans, and hence is socially slighted.
5. 'Shibkaka': 'Kaka' is a paternal uncle younger than the father, and is suffixed to names as a form of respectfully addressing older males.
6. '... he has mastered the palm leaf, and ... the banana leaf': In rural pathshalas of Bengal, pupils were first taught to write on palm leaves which are small, and once they acquired some skills in writing, they were made to write on banana leaves, which are larger.

5

Nironjon

Tonu Roy and Nironjon Kabirotno were not on good terms. They were neighbours.

Nironjon said, 'Roy mohashoy, don't marry off your daughter in exchange for money, as that is a cardinal sin.'

And so Tonu Roy hated Nironjon's guts. On the days Tonu Roy gave his daughters' hands in marriage, Nironjon left the village for another. He said, 'Seeing or hearing of somebody selling his daughters is a sin.'

Nironjon was a great scholar. He had studied many shastras. But learning never ends, so he always pored over books. He didn't like to parade his learning. So his fame had not spread far and wide. Days ago, many students came to him to study. He used to teach them day and night, and derived immense pleasure from it. He gave them food to eat and clothes to wear, and looked after them as his own sons. When he visited other people's houses, he would never get into an altercation over the farewell gifts[1], since he was well off. He had inherited a lot of brohmottor land.

He had a dispute with Jonardon Choudhuri, the *zamindar*, over these lands. Once, at the second *prohor* of the day, the zamindar sent for him, with a bailiff carrying the order.

The bailiff came and told Nironjon, '*Thakur*, Choudhuri mohashoy has sent for you, come.'

Nironjon said, 'My lunch is ready, I am set to eat now. I'll go to zamindar mohashoy after I have eaten. You may go.'

The bailiff said, 'That cannot be, you must come with me right at this moment.'

Nironjon said, 'The second prohor of the day is past now, the seat has been arranged, and the meal is ready; I'll go after having my meal. If I don't take my meal, my wife will not take hers, and my pupils too will starve."

The bailiff said, 'No, that cannot be, you will have to come this instant.'

Nironjon said, 'I see, I have to go this very instant, indeed? Okay, then let's go.'

When Nironjon reached the zamindar's house, Jonardon Choudhuri said, 'The land that you have in Bamunmari plain has measured up to fifty-five bighas instead of fifty. Since you have perfectly legitimate documents, I do not intend to take away the whole of the land. I claim only the extra portion.'

Nironjon answered, 'O yes, mohashoy, I have legal documents. Please check if these are the papers that you meant.'

Jonardon Choudhuri took the papers, and said, 'Yes, these *are* the papers. I saw these earlier; I don't need to check them again.'

Saying this, he returned the papers to Nironjon. Nironjon threw the papers down into the *malsa* that contained fire for smoking tobacco. The papers caught fire and burnt to ashes in the blink of an eye.

The zamindar said, 'Dear O dear, what are you up to?'

Nironjon said, 'Why only five bighas, from today onwards, my entire brohmottor land is yours. The One who created life will feed this Nironjon.'

Jonardon Choudhuri got cold feet; he now feared that a Brahman's curse might take its toll.

He said, 'My legal papers are lost forever, but I don't regret that loss. You enjoy the land; I'll bear no grudge against you.'

Nironjon answered, 'No, mohashoy! The One who created life will feed the living. It is better to meditate on that Friend of the poor, and spend one's days in total surrender to Him. If thoughts of wealth and property hamper the conduct of dharma, and distract the mind, wealth and property are best got rid of. It is because I had some land that I had to bear with your bailiff's insolence at this hour, isn't that so? So that land is no longer of any use to me. To a man who has overcome desire, the king and the subject, the rich and the poor are all equal. You are a propertied man, so you are unlikely to understand what I say. Even if you do, you are inextricably fettered by this songsar. You will have to chase the mirage. You cannot get away from this blanched, parched desert land. Now, bless me so that I don't ever have to ask for favours from anybody for anything.'

With these words, Nironjon turned his back on the zamindar.

From that day on, Nironjon was plunged into hard times. He spent days on the rack. His students left him one after another, and went to Gobordhon Shiromoni's *chotushpathi*.[2]

Gobordhon Shiromoni was Jonardon Choudhuri's court scholar. He fed a number of students, but he was hard-pressed for time to teach them. He had to attend Choudhuri mohashoy's court, and besides, had to attend invitations of other teachers, and move from pillar to post. So the students were given over to self-teaching.

But this did not dampen their spirit. They neither grumbled nor grudged. The reason for this was that Gobordhon was extremely honey-tongued; he cajoled people with pleasant words. In particular, if he came across a moneyed man, he showered sweet talk like the *Shrabon* torrents, and the listeners, like thirsty *chatok* birds, slurped it up.[3]

One day, Tonu Roy was discussing the shastras at Jonardon Choudhury's. Nironjon, Gobordhon and some others were around.

Tonu Roy said, 'One should accept some honoraria on offering one's daughter in marriage. This is the shastric mandate.'

Nironjon asked, 'Which shastra decrees so? Scriptural texts absolutely prohibit extracting such payments.'

Gobordhon whispered to Tonu Roy, 'Tell him that the Mahabharata commands so.'

Tonu Roy failed to hear his words. He racked his brain, and blurted out, 'It is prescribed in *Karna, the Great Donor*.'[4]

Nironjon sniggered. And this ruffled Tonu Roy's feathers.

Nironjon said, 'Roy mohashoy, accepting money by marrying daughters off is a great sin. Commit sins if you like, but do not apportion blame on the shastras, do not tarnish the holy texts, please. You do not know the shastras, you have not studied them.'

These words made Tonu Roy's hackles rise. He could not restrain his anger any longer. He vented his ire on Nironjon. 'You say that I have not studied the shastras? Well, well, well, why at all should I read the shastras written by others? If I so wish I can make a raft of shastras. Why should one who can make the shastras on one's own peruse those written by other people?'

Nironjon now had to throw in the towel. He had to admit that one who can make the shastras on his own is in no need of reading those by others.

Notes

1. '... he would never ... with people over the farewell gifts': Brahmans in earlier days would get substantial farewell gifts, and those were among their major sources of income. Hence, they were never shy about expressing their discontent if the gifts did not match their expectations.
2. 'Gobordhon Shiromoni': 'Shiromoni' is a title of honour for Sanskrit scholars.
3. 'Chatok birds': Birds that are believed to slake their thirst only with rain water.
4. 'Karna, the Great Donor': Karna is a character in the Mahabharata, and is famous for his proverbial generosity.

6
Farewell

The day Khetu's mother had the conversation with Ramhori, she told Khetu at night, running her affectionate hands over his body, 'Khetu, my son, I want to tell you something.'

Khetu said, 'What is it, ma?'

His mother answered, 'Bachha, you will have to travel to Kolkata with your Ramhoridada.'

Khetu asked, 'Where is that place, ma?'

His mother said, 'Don't you remember? It is the place where vehicles and carriages ply.'

Khetu said, 'O, is it that place? You will go with me, won't you?'

His mother answered, 'No, child, I won't, I will stay where I am.'

Khetu said, 'In that case, I too won't go.'

The mother said, 'But you will have to go, son. I am a woman; I should not go to such a place. You will go with Ramhoridada, what is there to be afraid of?'

Khetu said, 'Afraid! I am afraid of nothing, ma. But, ma, I will miss you sorely there, that is why I say I won't go.'

The mother said, 'Khetu, do you think I am sending you out of my own sweet will? Son, there is no way out. Send you I must, and that is why I am sending you off. You are grown up now; it is about time that you studied at a school. If you don't study, you will become a dunce, and nobody loves or respects a fool, you know. If you go to school and study in right earnest, you will be loved by everybody and, Khetu, this poor ma of yours will see happy days. Look, I can no longer nick thin threads, I have turned bleary-eyed; maybe, in a short while, I won't be able to shear thick threads either. Tell me, how will I manage a decent income then? If you become educated and earn money, I won't have to snip threads. I will then live in style, worship idols, and pray to godheads, "My Khetu is an excellent boy, do please grant him a long life."'

Khetu said, 'If I go, won't you cry?'

The mother replied, 'No, son, I won't.'

Khetu said, 'But ma, you are already shedding tears!'

His mother answered, 'I am feeling weepy at this moment, but I won't cry henceforth. And Khetu, it's not that you will have to live there all the year round, for you will come back home on vacations. I will look forward to your return, I will go to the bank of the Dutta's pond well in advance when I get the news that you are coming, and from there I will take you in my arms and bring you home. If you study well, you will learn to write letters to me. You will write tons of letters, which I'll carefully preserve and not let anybody open or read. When you come back home, you will open those letters yourself and read them out to me.'

Khetu asked, 'Ma, will I find rosaries there?'

The mother said, 'Rosaries? What do you mean?'

Khetu said, 'Ma, don't you remember you told me once that you cannot sleep at night, and that you would like to count beads if you had a rosary.'[1]

The mother said, 'O yes, son! Rosaries are available aplenty there.'

Khetu said, 'I will buy you a good rosary.'

The mother answered, 'Okay, that makes sense! Bring a rosary for me.'

After such a conversation between mother and son, Khetu fell asleep.

The next morning, Khetu woke up and said, 'Ma, for the next few days, I won't go to the pathshala, nor to play, but stay by your side the whole day.'

His mother replied, 'Okay, that's fair enough, but make it a point to visit Nironjonkaka and offer him *nomoskar.*'

Khetu said, 'I will do that, ma. And yes, another thing. For the next few days, I will eat from your plate after you have taken your food. Do you know why I forbid you to leave food in the plate? Whatever tastes delicious to you, you leave that for me, denying yourself. So I say, ma, don't leave food for me at noon for I am not hungry then. I do feel the sting of hunger, and when I do, I pick up berries and fruits scattered plentifully under other peoples' trees, and eat my fill. But when, ma, you are hungry, you don't eat that stuff. So I ask you not to leave food in the plate lest your hunger is not sated.'

The Brahmani took Khetu up in her lap, ran her hand over his head, and said, 'Son, these are not tears of sorrow! Why should the woman who has borne such a gem of a son ever be sad? Your honeyed words make me apprehensive—will you, born of such an ill-fated woman, have a long life?'

That day, after lunch, Khetu's mother took up sewing Khetu's tattered clothes.

Khetu said, 'Ma, let me hold the two parts of the torn cloth together, and you start stitching from the other side, for that will expedite things. And yes, ma, when the string runs out, I will thread the needle, for you cannot spot the eye of the needle with your weak vision, and that slows you down.'

With this kind of talk between mother and son, the sewing went on. Mother then washed the sewn clothes. This was how the preparation for Khetu's journey to Kolkata proceeded.

In the evening, Khetu went to Nironjon's place. He did *pronam* to Nironjon and his wife, and took the dust off their feet.[2] He told them about his plan of travelling to Kolkata. Nironjon had heard about this from Ramhori.

Blessing Khetu and giving him some advice, Nironjon said, 'Khetu, always speak the truth, never lie. Tell your Ramhoridada of your joys and sorrows, don't keep anything back from him. You will have to study with a number of boys, some of whom are naughty and some gentle. So there will be quarrels among the boys. Never beat anybody up mistakenly. And never beat the weak. Do not join in with five others to beat up one. Rather, take the side of the weak if somebody attacks him. In case you have to take a few blows yourself while defending the weak, even that is preferable. When you turn in every night, contemplate what good and bad deeds you have done during the day. If you have done anything wrong, resolve not to repeat it.'

Khetu then took leave of Nironjonkaka.

On Tuesday night, mother and son didn't sleep a wink. Both chatted away, their words flowed on and on.

His mother admonished him time and again, 'Khetu, now go to sleep. Or else you will fall ill.'

Khetu protested, 'No, ma, I cannot sleep tonight. Ma, I will not be able to talk to you tomorrow night. I will have gone so far away. Whenever I come to think about that, I feel like crying.'

The mother said, 'The puja vacation is round the corner. The next few months will pass quickly. You will again come back home then.'

Ramhori turned up in the morning. Khetu's mother put a drop of curd[3] on Khetu's forehead, and tied a marmelo leaf ['*bilwopotro*'] at the end of his wrap.[4] Then she placed Khetu's hand in Ramhori's. Tears threatened to burst forth, but she fought those back with a struggle.

In the end, she managed to utter only these words to Ramhori, 'Here I give a miserable woman's treasure over to you.'

Ramhori said, 'Khetu, do nomoskar to your mother.'

Khetu did nomoskar and Ramhori too did the same. The two then took their leave.

As long as those two could be seen, Khetu's mother looked unblinkingly in the direction of the path they took. Khetu too turned round from time to time to have a glimpse of his mother. When they were no longer visible, Khetu's mother slumped down on the dusty road. Prostrated, she soaked the dust with the tears coursing down her eyes unceasingly.

Notes

1. '... count beads if you had a rosary': A common religious practice, particularly of nineteenth-century elderly Bengali women.
2. '... and took dust off their feet': A gesture of respect, still in vogue, though to a lesser extent.
3. 'Khetu's mother put a drop of curd': This act by a mother is believed by Hindu Bengalis to be propitious for the children.
4. '... tied a marmelo leaf at the end of his wrap': Marmelo leaves are believed to be sacred, and propitious for one's journey.

7

Konkaboti

While Khetu's mother wept profusely on the road, Tonu Roy's wife came to the spot.

She took her by the hand and helped her up, and said, '*Didi*, don't cry like that. Shedding tears is not good; it bodes ill for the son.'

Khetu's mother said, 'I know that, but what can I do? I cannot restrain my tears, they roll down on their own. Today my world has turned empty! How shall I go back home? Today my Khetu will not come back from the pathshala caked in mud and dust, and famished. Today I have no work left! By now, Khetu must have travelled far enough. *Aha,* bachha must be feeling broken-hearted and forlorn!'

Tonu Roy's wife said, 'Didi, let us go inside. There we will talk about Khetu. Truly, what a brilliant and virtuous boy he is! Such a boy is rare in these parts. If you are lucky, Khetu will live long. Or else, everything will go up in smoke.'

Having said this, Tonu Roy's wife gently led Khetu's mother to her room. There they chatted for long about Khetu.

Khetu had left after having his lunch; Tonu Roy's wife scrubbed the utensils and cleaned the room. She sliced vegetables and made a paste of spices for the meal that Khetu's mother would cook for herself later in the day.

Khetu's mother said, 'Leave it, sister, stop this, please. O, to think of cooking and eating today! Today, I won't have my meal.'

Tonu Roy's wife protested, 'No, didi! One should not fast like this, for that will augur ill for Khetu.'

'That will augur ill for Khetu'—these words promptly silenced Khetu's mother. How could she do something that would bode ill for her son?

Tonu Roy's wife continued, 'I have arranged everything. Do your cooking later in the day. I will come back in the afternoon after finishing my household chores.'

Tonu Roy's wife kept her word and came again. This time, she brought along her baby daughter.

Khetu's mother said, '*Aaha*, what a beautiful daughter you have, sister! Her face is as winsome as her hair and complexion.'

Tonu Roy's wife said, 'Yes, everybody says that this daughter of mine is a glory of my womb. But didi, why are such daughters born in this accursed womb? When a daughter is born, the man at my home is on cloud nine, but I feel like killing her in the birth chamber itself by thrusting salt into her mouth. When, in the days of ekadoshi during summer, my daughters' faces parch, and they thirst and pine for a drop of water, O didi, tell me how a mother is supposed to feel at heart. What a dastardly decree! If I could ever come across the person who made such a ruling, I would strike him squarely with a broom. Had that blackguard left a provision for drinking a little bit of water, I would consider sparing him.'[1]

Khetu's mother said, 'Sister, a person in this birth suffers the consequences of the deeds in the previous birth, and will reap the fruits of the deeds in this birth in the next.'

Tonu Roy's wife answered, 'That is true, indeed! But a mother's heart does not find solace in these words, does it?'

She continued, 'Sometimes I feel, if Vidyasagar's opinion is endorsed, I will offer an oblation of *sirni* to godheads.'[2]

Khetu's mother answered, 'Sister, that's enough, please! *Chhi, chhi*! What a shame! Please, don't utter those words. If the sahibs, heeding Vidyasagar's words, command that no women will be allowed to remain widowed in this land, and that each and every widow will have to remarry, then—chhi, chhi, shame, what a distasteful idea! Where shall I go in this old age! I shall have to end my life either by hanging myself or by drowning.'

Tonu Roy's wife replied with a smile, 'Didi, you had long been in Kolkata, but know so little! Vidyasagar mohashoy has not advocated for the remarriage of all widows including the old and the senile. He has pleaded only for the remarriage of the young and child widows. And that too is optional, meaning only those who want to get their widowed daughters remarried may do so, and those who don't, may not.'

Khetu's mother said, 'That may be true, sister, but I don't know all that.'

Tonu Roy's wife had two widowed daughters; she was distressed by their sorrow. That was why she was always keen on listening to discussions about widow remarriage. What Khetu's mother, even after having lived in Kolkata, did not know, she did.

Tonu Roy was a pundit. The moment Vidyasagar mohashoy's view was aired, Tonu Roy grabbed it with both hands.

He said, 'If the shastras rule in favour of the remarriage of widows, why should you people not obey it? Overruling the shastric verdict is a grave offence. And why only twice? Marrying widows off even ten times is not a sin, rather, it is a virtue. But this ill-fated country is replete with superstitions, it is simply beyond redemption.'

People were initially taken aback by these words uttered by a devout person like Tonu Roy. Then everybody came to think—'Aha, an afflicted father's soul speaks out here! He has two widowed daughters at home, these words spring from the depth of his anguished heart!'

Only Nironjon said, 'Yes, if widow remarriage comes into vogue, Tonu Roy will make a killing.'

For such talk, people vented their spleen on Nironjon. They said, 'Nironjon has an exceptionally spiteful mind. Or else, why would he have come to such rack and ruin? One who once had two hundred bighas of brohmottor land is now in extreme want and struggles to keep the wolf from the door.'

Khetu's mother and Tonu Roy's wife were talking on various topics.

Khetu's mother asked, 'This daughter of yours is about a year old, isn't she?'

Tonu Roy's wife answered, 'Yes, she will step into her second year very soon.'

'What have you named her?'

'Her name is Konkaboti.'

Khetu's mother said, 'Konkaboti! That's a fine name! The name is as sweet as the girl herself.'

Thus Khetu's mother and Tonu Roy's wife gradually became friends. During her leisure time, Tonu Roy's wife visited Khetu's mother, visits which the latter reciprocated. Occasionally, Tonu Roy's wife left Konkaboti in the care of Khetu's mother.

The girl was not yet a toddler. She moved about on all fours, at times she played while sitting down, at other times she stood up, holding on to some support. Khetu's mother did her chores, and spoke a word or two to her. The girl giggled, and a cherubic smile spread across her countenance. She was a quiet girl, and never cried at all.

Notes

1. '... that blackguard': The literal translation of the Bengali term in the original ('*mukhpora*') is 'burnt-faced', a common, particularly nineteenth-century, invective used chiefly by rural women.
2. 'Vidyasagar's opinion': Pandit Ishwarchandra Bandyopadhyay (1820–91), who was conferred the title 'Vidyasagar' for his scholarship (vidya=learning, sagar=sea, hence 'sea of learning'), was a social reformer too, and campaigned vigorously for the remarriage of child widows.

8

The Boy and the Girl

Arriving at Kolkata, Khetu started studying hard. Calm, gentle and sensible, Khetu won everyone's heart with his qualities.

Ramhori had an infant son called Norohori, and after three years, he sired a daughter who was named Sita.

Ramhori and his wife loved Khetu more than their own son. Khetu's sharp intelligence made everyone at his school gape in wonder. Khetu was quick on the uptake, and he had a formidable memory. He was easily the best in his class, and none ever managed to surpass him. It was difficult to outsmart Khetu with questions from the books he studied. He was thus promoted from one class to another.

Ramhori used to give Khetu one paisa to buy snacks. Khetu had his refreshments on some days, on some other days, he didn't. Ramhori somehow came to know about this.

He asked him, 'Khetu, why don't you eat? What do you do with the money?'

Khetu was caught somewhat on the wrong foot; after a pause, he replied, 'Dadamohashoy! The days I am very hungry, I take some food, but on the days I feel that I can do without it, I eat nothing. Whatever I have managed to save in this manner is with me. The day I took leave of ma, I told her, "Ma, I will get you a rosary." I am saving to that end.'

On hearing this, Ramhori put his hand on Khetu's head, and stroked his hair. Khetu realised that Ramhori was not at all angry; rather, he was being affectionate.

After a pause, Ramhori said, 'Khetu, tell me when you intend to buy the rosary, I'll get a good one for you.'

Later, with the puja vacation approaching, Khetu asked Ramhori, 'Dadamohashoy, will you now buy me the rosary that you promised?'

Ramhori said, 'Bring the coins you have saved so far. Let me see how much those add up to.'

Khetu brought his savings to his dada. Ramhori counted the coins and found that the sum came to more than one rupee. Ramhori bought a nice rosary made of *rudraksho* beads for eight *anna*s, and returned the rest of the money to Khetu.

Khetu said, 'Dadamohashoy, what shall I do with these coins? It's better you take them.'

Ramhori answered, 'No, Khetu! These are not mine, but yours, take these to your mother, she will certainly be delighted.'

The day of homecoming drew near. Khetu, and his mother at home, were walking on air! Merchants selling tusser and lac were then returning to their homes. Ramhori sent Khetu along with them, and let Khetu's mother know in advance the expected time of his arrival.

Khetu's mother went, no, not to the bank of the Dutta's pond, but much beyond that point to welcome him. Khetu spotted his mother from afar, and went running to embrace her. Khetu's mother clasped her son to her bosom, and savoured heavenly bliss.

Khetu said, '*Oi ja,* O my goodness, ma, I forgot to do pronam.'

His mother answered, 'Never mind, let that be, I have no use for your pronam! I bless you that you live long and that your pen and inkpot turn golden.'[1]

Khetu said, 'Ma, I thought you would be by the pond of the Dutta's. I had not imagined that you would come this far.'

His mother said, 'Bachha, I would go all the way to Kolkata if I could. But Khetu, you have grown so thin!'

Khetu answered, 'No, ma, I haven't. Weariness of the journey has made me look so. Now ma, let me walk home, you cannot carry me all this distance.'

His mother said, 'No, that cannot be, I'll carry you all the way in my arms.'

While travelling in his mother's arms, Khetu surreptitiously tied the coins at the end of his mother's sari. When, on reaching home, his mother put him down, she felt the end of her sari was rather heavy.

His mother said, 'What's this, Khetu! You have tied coins at the end of my sari, I presume!'

Khetu broke into a laugh, and said, 'Wait, ma, I will show you another trick.'

Saying this, Khetu slipped the rosary round his mother's neck, and said, 'Ma, you remember my promise, don't you?'

His mother gently tapped his cheek, and said, 'Very naughty boy!' Khetu laughed out at this, and his mother too joined in his happiness.

The next day, Khetu noticed that a little girl had come to their house from somewhere.

Khetu asked, 'Ma, whose child is she?'

His mother said, 'Don't you know her? She is the youngest daughter of your Tonukaka. Tonu Roy's wife visits me regularly these days. I snip sacred threads, and chat with her. Sometimes she leaves her daughter in my care. The girl plays by herself, she never creates any trouble; she loves being with me.'

Tonu Roy was by no means related to Khetu. Khetu called him 'kaka' for he was his neighbour.

Khetu told Konkaboti, 'Come here.'

Konkaboti moved towards him. Khetu said, 'Look, ma, see how she toddles!'

Khetu's mother said, 'Her legs are not yet strong.'

Khetu offered her a leaf, and said, 'Take this.'

Konkaboti reached out for the leaf, and smiled.

Khetu said, 'Look, ma, see how she smiles!'

His mother replied, '*Haan,* yes, bachha, this girl smiles a lot, she never cries, she's very well-behaved.'

Khetu said, 'Had I known that she would be here, I would have bought a doll for her.'

His mother said, 'Bring it when you come back home next time.'

Note

1. '... that your pen and inkpot turn golden': A blessing in earlier times to wish learning and wisdom for somebody, particularly a young student.

9

Meni

When the puja vacation was over, Khetu went back to Kolkata; there, he once again knuckled down to study. He came back home twice a year during his holidays. He brought this thing or that for his mother, and dolls or toys for Konkaboti. Konkaboti stayed with Khetu's mother much of the time, and she in turn doted on Konka.

When Khetu was merely twelve, he started tutoring a rich man's son. That man used to pay Khetu five rupees.

Khetu gave his first few months' fees to Ramhori, and said, 'Dadamohashoy, from this month on, do not pay for the rice for my mother, please; instead, give this amount to her. I have heard that you have run into debt, so I have taken pains to earn this money.'

Ramhori said, 'Khetu, you have done well. Effort, zeal and vigour are a human's most prized virtues. I will send this money to your mother. I will write to her that you have earned this. I will tell everybody around that our Khetu, a twelve-year-old, is taking care of his mother.'

When Khetu came back home the next time, he brought a *namaboli* for his mother and a scarlet sari for Konkaboti. Konkaboti was in seventh heaven. She ran off to show that to her mother.

Khetu said, 'Ma, we can educate Konkaboti, can't we?'

Mother said, 'Yes, but son, Tonu Roy is a strange sort of man. If we offer such a suggestion, who knows what he will say?'

Khetu said, 'But what's wrong with Konkaboti studying? In Kolkata, so many girls go to school.'

Mother said, 'Okay, I'll raise this point with Konka's mother, and seek her opinion.'

That afternoon, when Tonu Roy's wife came to visit her, Khetu's mother, in the course of their conversation, told her, 'Khetu was saying, "When I come back home next time, I'll bring a book for Konkaboti and teach her gradually how to read." I told him, "No bachha, better not attempt such a thing! Your Tonukaka may not take kindly to it."'

Tonu Roy's wife answered, 'Why should he take exception to that? This is the order of the day. Today's girls wear blouses,[1] read and write. But we live in a village, so we are strangers to these things.'

Later that day, Konkaboti's mother told her husband, 'Khetu has come home; he has brought a beautiful scarlet sari for Konka.'

Tonu Roy said, 'Khetu is a good boy, is attentive to his lessons. He will, I believe, earn his bread, but the thing to watch out for is if he turns out to be as wasteful as his father.'

His wife said, 'Khetu was telling his mother, "When I come home next time, I will bring a book for Konkaboti, and teach her bit by bit how to read."'

Tonu Roy said, 'Of what use is reading and writing to a girl? Learning is pointless for a woman.'

Tonu Roy had blurted out these words off the top of his head. But when he thought over it, he came to realise that learning has many benefits.

Today's grooms prefer marrying educated brides. These brides are well-regarded, and are priced high too.

But the point to consider was whether this act was against the shastric law. If the shastras took a dim view of it, Tonu Roy could never approve of his daughter's education. Tonu Roy thought hard, turning the shastras over in his mind.

He concluded that although the shastras had prohibited women's education, the ruling was valid for the *Sotyo*, *Treta* and *Dwapor* eras, and not for *Koli*. What had been common in the past was prohibited in the present, an example being human sacrifice—if somebody performed it now, he would promptly be sent to the gallows. Another instance was sea voyage; now a sea-voyager was an outcast, whereas in earlier ages such voyages had been permissible.

That was why, when his mother had been alive and had desired to sail across the sea, Tonu Roy had stubbornly set his face against it.

He had explained, 'Ma, seafaring should not be done. It is absolutely prohibited. The sea and the shastras are sworn enemies. It is a sin to catch sight of the sea, and to touch sea water. Why then, ma, should you spend money to acquire sins? Why, ma, should you sacrifice your caste and clan?'

Tonu Roy reasoned that what had been permissible earlier was now proscribed. So, conversely, what was forbidden in the past should now be acceptable. Learning had been debarred for women in earlier days, so now it could not be a sinful act.

Tonu Roy thus fudged the shastras, and reconstructed them. When he felt that the shastras had been moulded to his liking, he said to his wife, 'Well, if Khetu wants to educate my daughter a little bit, I do not object.'

Tonu Roy's wife conveyed these words to Khetu's mother. And she in turn relayed them to Khetu.

When Khetu came home this time, he brought the first part of *Borno Porichoy*[2] for Konkaboti. Konkaboti was initially ecstatic at the idea of learning how to read and write.

But after some days, she understood that learning was not quite a pleasant job. To her eyes, all letters were much of a muchness. And while reading, she confused this letter with that.

Khetu lost his temper. He said, 'Konkaboti, learning lessons is not your cup of tea. You will stay ignorant all your life.'

Konkaboti was cut up with *obhiman*. She broke into tears and said, 'What can I do, I just cannot remember these things.'

Khetu's mother said, 'It is not right to scold a little girl. She has to be taught with sweet words. Come, child, come to me. You have had enough of this business of studying.'

Khetu said, 'Ma, Konkaboti whiles away her time with Meni the whole day. Can she learn her lessons that way?'

Meni was Konkaboti's pet cat. She was her pampered protégée.

Konkaboti said, '*Jyathaima*, I teach Meni the alphabet; but the rub is that Meni is as much a birdbrain as I am. Am I right, Meni? Meni cannot read, just as I cannot. Meni is a tot, just like me. She will learn how to read when she will grow up, just as I will. Meni, will you not?'

Khetu burst into laughter, and said, 'Konkaboti, you must be as nutty as a fruitcake.'

However, Konkaboti managed to get over her primer.

Khetu said, 'I'll leave for Kolkata pretty soon. I put you through the primer, but the lessons have not been learnt all that well. Memorise this book thoroughly in the next few months. Next time, I will bring the second part of the primer.'

When Khetu came back home again, Konkaboti got through the second part. Khetu did not have to teach Konkaboti this time, she learnt by herself. Khetu bought Konkaboti a book on arithmetic. She learnt her sums from that book. Khetu helped her only once in a while.

Konkaboti was fond of reading. Khetu sent her various books and dailies from Kolkata. Konkaboti read even the advertisements in newspapers.

Notes

1. 'Today's girls wear blouses ...': Wearing blouses or any such garment for the upper part of the body was not customary for women, especially in rural Bengal, in the nineteenth century. Such a practice was looked upon as an influence of Western education, and elicited mixed responses from different echelons of society.
2. *'Borno Porichoy'*: Literally, an introduction to the letters of the alphabet, this is the name of a Bengali primer for young learners written by Ishwarchandra Vidyasagar, which was immensely popular in the nineteenth century and even beyond.

10

Bou-didi

Khetu passed the first exam in English at thirteen, and he got a scholarship. With the money, he employed a maid for his mother. His mother was ageing, and he wanted to ensure that she did not suffer hardship. He helped Ramhori's household too by bringing this thing or that, and buying them clothes.

At fifteen, Khetu got through another exam. His scholarship increased. At seventeen, he passed yet another. His scholarship was enhanced even more.

Khetu began to earn money, and with that money he put an end to his mother's hard times. She now got everything she needed, soon after she asked for it. She was left in no want whatsoever.

One day, Khetu's mother failed to collect flowers with which to worship Lord Shiva. Khetu heard of this, and laid out a beautiful flower garden near his house. He brought a wide variety of saplings from Kolkata, and planted them in the garden. The garden beamed the year round with varicoloured flowers.

Ramhori's daughter Sita had now grown up. Since his mother lived alone, Khetu sent Sita to stay with his mother, after obtaining Ramhori's permission. With Sita by her side, Khetu's mother's life brimmed with joy.

Konkaboti too loved Sita. They went together to sit in the garden in the afternoon. Konkaboti now did not venture out in front of Khetu. She felt shy in his presence.

But she loved to talk and hear about Khetu. She was too embarrassed to talk about Khetu to somebody else, or to hear words about him from somebody, and she had all these conversations only with Sita. In the afternoon, they both went to a grove. Konkaboti stitched flowers into garlands with which to adorn Sita. She made her wear garlands round her neck, on her head, round her arms, and wherever those fitted. Then she sat and listened to what Sita had to say about Khetu.

Khetu did not forget his Nironjonkaka. Whenever Khetu came back home, he brought something or the other for him. Nironjon and his wife blessed him with all their heart.

As the days passed, Khetu brought for Konkaboti some articles besides books and journals. From Kolkata, he had bought for her a chemise and other garments that were fashionable those days.

Although Khetu contributed to Ramhori's household, Ramhori could not easily be persuaded to accept that favour. Once Khetu bought a couple of sets of clothes for Ramhori. When Ramhori came to know about this, he gave Khetu a scolding. Khetu was seized with a profound obhiman. He did not protest to Ramhori, but gave vent to his feelings to Ramhori's wife. Khetu called her *bou-didi.*

Noticing that Khetu was deeply hurt, his bou-didi said, 'You were lost for words when your dada snubbed you, and so have come to me to settle the score, I suppose?'

Khetu answered, 'Bou-didi, it was the two of you who brought me up. You should look upon me as you do your son Norohori. If you don't do that, I should be allowed to think that I am not one of you. And in that case, what is the point in quarrelling with you? Dadamohashoy has deemed me an outsider, and now, if you too think in the same vein, then the discussion ends there.'

Bou-didi said, 'Suppose we do that, what then, Khetu?'

Khetu replied, 'What then? Nothing much. Then I'll not take pains to earn money, or to talk to you, or even to stay here in your house. I'll then be inclined to think that these people simply gave alms to my beggarly mother, and this body of mine, this flesh and these bones are all nourished on their alms. Then I'll never mingle with gentlemen, never venture into a gentlemen's community, and never speak with my head held high in gentlemen's company. I am but the son of a distressed beggar woman; how is a person who has been fed on charity and alms supposed to sport a dignified face?'

Bou-didi said, 'Chhi, Khetu, shame! One should not utter such words. You are related to me as a brother-in-law, but I love you more than my own son. You are truly an eligible son, whatever you decide to do will get done. What is this obhiman for?'

Khetu said, 'Bou-didi! To keep ma and your family happy is the cherished desire of my soul! Now I am capable, but if you do not let me fulfil that desire, I'll be sorely grieved.'

Bou-didi said, 'Hail to your mother who conceived you! Now Khetu, let me bless you that you soon tie the knot with a beautiful bride!'

That day, Ramhori's wife told Ramhori persuasively, 'Look, our plight has aggrieved Khetu sorely. He has begun earning. He says, "As these people have brought me up like their own son, I too, like a son, will take care of them." So if Khetu does his bit in meeting our family expenses, don't stop him. When you do that, Khetu takes it to heart.'

Hearing his wife's words, Ramhori sent for Khetu.

When Khetu came, Ramhori told him, 'You feel bad, dear boy? This earth is a terrible place to live in. When you are my age, you will know how people around the globe hanker for money. For that reason, Khetu, I forbade you to spend money for my family. Our plight is everlasting. Our wants will never be removed. But why should I make you share this misery? For a long time now, I have not been in the habit of having breakfast or snacks. When I come down with fever, I cure myself through fasting. You are just a boy, why should I allow you to be stricken with such penury? With this thought in mind, I had asked you not to spend money on our family. But I did not think then of the father who sired you. Khetu, what shall I say of him? He was like a real angel on this earth. I bless you, brother, so that you too may grow to that angelic stature.'

Tears started falling from Ramhori's eyes. His wife too wiped her eyes. Tears welled up in Khetu's eyes too.

Khetu passed three exams, and fathers of daughters started visiting Ramhori's residence. Each craved to marry his daughter off to Khetu. One said, 'I'll give this much gold and money,' another said, 'I'll give this and that.' People thus started auctioning their daughters off.

Ramhori explained to everyone that until Khetu's studies were over, and until he started to earn a decent sum, he would not arrange his marriage.

But fathers saddled with daughters had no ears for such level-headed words. They pleaded with Ramhori to change his mind. At last, Ramhori thought to himself, 'Damn it, let me give my word to one among them, so that these people will pester me no longer.'

Reasoning thus, he went on to see many prospective brides. In the end, he selected the daughter of Jonmejoy Bandyopadhyay. Jonmejoy was a well-heeled and well-bred person. But Ramhori could not give him his full consent. How could he decide on such a matter without consulting Khetu's mother?

11

A Matrimonial Proposal

As time went by, Konkaboti's beauty bloomed all the more. Her loveliness illumined every corner, and dazzled every eye that fell on her. Her complexion was bright and fair, as if it glowed from within. It was so lucent and lustrous that you could almost see the water she drank, as it were. Her body was neither plump nor thin. She was like a doll! What a ravishing beauty she was! Her face was as if sculpted by God Himself. Her nose was pointed, her eyes were large, and eyelashes long, thick and jet black. When she looked downward, her upper eyelashes resting on the lower created a strange comeliness. And these eyes were arched by the kind of delectable, fine, dense brows that befitted them. Konkaboti's cheeks were not quite full, but they dimpled when she laughed. And that smiling, dimpled face could mollify even an enemy's heart. Her lips were thin. They did not need to be tinged with betel leaf juice, but stayed crimson on their own. When she spoke, two or three milk-white teeth loomed from behind those red lips, and sparkled bright. Konkaboti had a good head of hair which was ebony black; when undone, her curly tresses cascaded down her back. The parting of her hair in the front was like a faint white line drawn with a brush. In effect, Konkaboti was a paragon of beauty; passers-by feasted their eyes on her, but even repeated glances could not quite slake their thirst for seeing her. When Konkaboti played about with her companions of the same age, lightning truly seemed to flash.

A Matrimonial Proposal

Konkaboti was growing up. Now she did not run about with her friends the same way. But the other day, she came home running for some reason or the other. That made her face glow red, and that tinge spread over her cheeks, and her face radiated an ethereal beauty. The earth seemed too small to contain such heavenly grace.

Her mother noticed this, and told Tonu Roy, 'Just look at your daughter! Don't cast away such a golden idol. Konkaboti is goddess Lakshmi herself. Have you ever seen a girl with such auspicious signs in all your life? If the Mother goddess has come to this hapless cottage of her own will, don't dishonour her. Just as our daughter is a graven image of goddess Lakshmi, find out such an image of Lord Narayan to marry her off to. This time pay heed to what I say.'

Tonu Roy cast a glance at Konkaboti, and was startled. The sight took his breath away. He thought, 'What is this feeling? Is it what people call filial affection?'

Tonu Roy did not respond to his wife's words.

Another day, Tonu Roy's wife told her husband, 'See, Konkaboti has now attained a marriageable age. You must listen to what I say. Please, fulfil at least one desire of my heart in this life.'

Tonu Roy asked, 'And what is that?'

His wife said, 'My desire is that I will spend some happy time with my daughter and son-in-law. You married off two daughters earlier, but that did nothing to fulfil my desire; on the contrary, those marriages have been crushing my heart day and night. However, let us not cry over spilt milk, now get a good groom for Konka. My elder daughters say, "We are undone by our destiny, let that be, now we will be happy if we get to see our youngest sister spend happy days."'

But neither wife, nor son, nor daughter was dearer to Tonu Roy than money. Even so, anything said about Konkaboti made his heart flutter. Was it tenderness or fear that stirred his soul? He could not pluck up enough courage to give away Konkaboti, who was to him an incarnation of a goddess. But, on the other hand, he had an unquenchable avarice. All these years he had nurtured the hope of making a whopping sum of money by selling his exquisitely beautiful daughter. How could he now extirpate that long-cherished ambition? Tonu Roy was now in two minds. Never had he been on the horns of such a dilemma.

Thinking for a while, Tonu Roy said, 'Okay, I agree not to demand money in giving my daughter over in marriage, but in any case, I cannot agree to spend money from my pocket to marry her off. The scenario of marriage negotiations is such nowadays that you cannot hope to get an eligible groom unless you spend a lot of money. What about that?'

His wife answered, 'Okay, in case I get an eligible groom for Konkaboti for free, will you agree to that marriage?'

Tonu Roy asked, 'Where will you get such a groom? Who is he?'

His wife said, 'Old age brings the curse of poor vision and witlessness. Can't you see that person who is always right in front of your eyes?'

Tonu Roy said, 'O, please tell me who he is.'

His wife replied, 'Why, Khetu?'

Tonu Roy said, 'Is that worth considering? He does not have property, nor connections. How can I offer my Konkaboti to such a penniless orphan? Okay, I won't demand any payment, but I shall have to make sure that my daughter lives in comfort, and gets to wear some ornaments; what do you say of that?'

His wife retorted, 'Do you mean to say that Khetu will never make it? Don't you yourself say, "Khetu is a good boy, he will earn some money one day"? This very Khetu will embellish Konka with ornaments, if it is in our stars. But no matter if Konka wears jewels or not, her groom must be a good boy, which is my wish. Where can you find such a gem of a boy like Khetu, tell me? Khetu is as priceless a groom as my Konkaboti is a gorgeous bride. God has made them as two flowers on the same twig.'

Tonu Roy said, 'Well, time will tell if such assumptions are well-founded. We needn't rush.'

Some more days passed. A missive came to Khetu's mother from Kolkata. She got the letter read out to her by Tonu Roy. Ramhori had written the letter. It read:

'Many people are approaching me for Khetu's marriage. They are pleading with me persistently. My wish is that Khetu will first complete his studies, and then marry. But these fathers encumbered with nubile daughters are loath to heed that. They say, "Let us settle the matter, marriage may take place later on." I have seen many prospective brides. Among them, I have selected Jonmejoybabu's daughter. That girl is graceful, gentle and demure. She is of a good lineage, and there is no taint on it. She has her parents, brothers and sisters. The girl's father is an affluent man. He will adorn his daughter with sumptuous ornaments and lavish the son-in-law with huge wealth while conducting the wedding. If you let me know your opinion, I will give the girl's family my final word.'

Tonu Roy was taken aback. He was disinclined to give away his daughter to Khetu on account of his financial background, and here were many people looking up to the same Khetu with an eye to making him their son-in-law, offering so much pelf!

Khetu's mother wrote back to Ramhori, 'I am but a woman, why ask me at all? What you decide to do will be done. I nursed one desire in my heart, but now I see that stands little chance of fulfilment, so there is no point in discussing that.'

On receiving the letter, Ramhori brought it to Khetu's knowledge, seeking his opinion.

Khetu said, 'Dadamohashoy, I have understood what the desire of my mother's heart is. As long as there is a chance of fulfilling that desire, don't give your word to anybody, please.'

Ramhori said, 'Rightly said. Yes, I too agree that I should not commit to anybody about this marriage right at this moment.'

The moment she heard that Khetu's marriage was being settled with another girl, Konkaboti's mother was prostrated with grief. She would not cease crying in her husband's presence day and night.

Tonu Roy, on his part, was a little worried too. He thought, 'I am growing old. I am burdened with two widowed daughters and an illiterate son. They need a guardian. The manner in which Khetu is acquiring education and his gentle demeanour suggest that he will make a mark later in life. It does not matter if he fails to pay me a handsome sum right now; later on, I'll extract sums from him in monthly instalments.'

Thinking thus, Tonu Roy told his wife, 'I will not object if you can settle Konka's marriage with Khetu, but I will not pay a paisa.'

Having got the permission, Tonu Roy's wife went running to Khetu's mother, and having taken the dust off her feet to put on her own head, she narrated everything there was to tell.

Khetu's mother said, 'I have all along wished that Konkaboti will be my daughter-in-law. But, sister, if only you had told me a couple of days earlier! I have asked Ramhori to settle the marriage elsewhere. In case Ramhori has already given his word, we will be in no position to go back on that. And I fear as much!'

Tonu Roy's wife said, 'Didi, when you have consented to this marriage, Khetu and Konka will tie the knot. Please get a letter written to Ramhori. I will arrange for its being sent to him.'

The next day the two mothers sent a messenger to Kolkata, carrying a letter from Khetu's mother.

In the letter, she wrote, 'I wish that Khetu and Konkaboti tie the knot. Tonu Roy and his wife have approached me for that match. In case you have not given your word to somebody else, please settle the match by writing to Tonu Roy.'

This letter gladdened Ramhori, Ramhori's wife and Khetu.

Ramhori handed the letter over to Khetu, 'This is your mother's decree. This cannot be overruled.'

Khetu said, 'What my mother desires will be fulfilled. But we are in no hurry. Tonukaka marries off his daughters when they are sufficiently grown up. He will not grudge keeping Konkaboti in his custody for two or three years more. By that time I will pass the remaining exams, and should also be able to earn a decent sum. Please write to Tonukaka to this effect.'

Ramhori did what Khetu advised him to. Tonu Roy agreed to the proposal. He was not at all sorry for the delay in his daughter's marriage, rather, he was elated.

He thought to himself, 'I have agreed to this proposal for the present in order to calm down my blubbering wife. Let me see whether I can manage to get a bridegroom better than Khetu. If I find one—well, I'll decide on that in due course.'

Khetu's mother told everything to Nironjon. Nironjon thought, 'With age, Tonu Roy is now getting dharma-minded.'

Konkaboti had looked crestfallen the last few days. Today, people saw her with a radiant face. And on that day, she laid her heart bare to her Meni. What shall I say about what she shared with Meni and what she didn't? Meni was no longer a kitten now, she was a full-grown cat. So what wonder that Konkaboti would make her privy to her innermost thoughts?

12

Shnareshwor

A few days before the pujas, Khetu came upon Shnareshwor on his way to Kolkata.

Shnareshwor said, 'Khetu, when are you going home? I have booked a vehicle, and you are welcome to accompany me.'

Khetu said, 'My school holidays are yet to begin. I have not decided about when I will leave.'

Shnareshwor said, 'Khetu, what's that in your hand?'

Khetu replied, 'This is a miniature throne. Ma models the image of Lord Shiva with clay every day, and worships that. I have bought a stone idol for her. And this throne is for that idol.'

Shnareshwor asked, 'Where is that idol? Let me have a look.'

Khetu brought it out of his pocket, and handed it over to Shnareshwor.

Shnareshwor said, 'What, did you put that idol in your pocket?[1] I must admire your devotion!'

Khetu answered, 'This idol is yet to be worshipped. So what's wrong with putting it in the pocket?'

Shnareshwor said, 'O, I see.'

With these words, Shnareshwor handed the idol back to Khetu.

Talking about this thing and that, Shnareshwor said, 'Look, this is the mansion of the Christian priest. You know this man, I suppose! Come on, let us pay him a visit.'

Shnareshwor and Khetu went in to meet the priest.

After a brief conversation, Shnareshwor told the cleric, 'Do you know, mohashoy, Khetu has bought a stone idol for his mother to worship, and he has kept it in his pocket.'

The clergyman said, 'My goodness! Shocking! Shame, shame, Khetu, I never imagined that you could commit such a despicable act. We have built so many schools for your community, but all our efforts have come to naught! This community of Bengalis is a band of liars, frauds, perjurers, scallywags, rogues, scoundrels, the basest of the base, slaves, sons of slaves, grandsons of slaves.'

Khetu said, 'Ah, what mellifluous words of dharma I have heard today! My entire body has been soothed. I feel like converting to Christianity right away. If you have water in your house, get that quickly, why procrastinate? Come on, sprinkle it on my head, and baptise me. The way you people are showering pleasantries on the Bengalis has drenched their minds with the ambrosial syrup of your Christian religion! So, what's there to ponder over? The Bengalis are falling over themselves for conversion! Again, when people will come to hear of your fraternal feelings for the black Christians in America, and get to know of your immense sympathy and compassion for the unarmed African blacks, none of this country will remain unconverted. This poor country will then swarm with Christians throughout its length and breadth! Salaam to you, for the time being!'

Khetu left that place with these words. Shnareshwor too followed him with a smile.

Khetu asked Shnareshwor on their way back, 'I have heard that every evening you sing devotional hymns of Hori.[2] Why then did you scoff at me like that in front of that clergyman?'

Shnareswor said, 'It was not you that I took a dig at. Anyway, it is already evening, and it is time for singing hymns. Come and have a look at my devotional activities. Even witnessing such acts is pious, you know!'

Shnareshwor's residence was in the vicinity. Both Khetu and Shnareshwor went in. Khetu found that the singing of hymns had already started in Shnareshwor's house. But Shnareshwor did not go and join the singers; instead, he went straight upstairs to his drawing room. Asking Khetu to wait there for a while, he went inside the house.

After a while, Shnareshwor came back, and said, 'Come, Khetu, let us go to another room.'

Entering that room, Khetu found two of Shnareshwor's friends sitting there. And an arrangement for dinner was in progress.

All this while, singing of hymns continued unabated downstairs. Shnareshwor was a lynchpin of Hindu dharma and the Hindu community.

A little while later, dinner was served. And the persons in charge of that were two Muslims.

Khetu said, 'Well, then, you enjoy yourselves, and permit me to leave.'

Shnareshwor said, 'O no, stay a little longer, please. See all these things, for even looking on may bring piety. What we are having now is a broth of meat. This is called soup. Khetu, will you have a helping?'

Khetu said, 'I never tasted such stuff, and I don't relish the prospect of having this either. Please go on eating.'

Then again, after some time, Shanreshwor said, 'Khetu, what we are having now is *bhetki* fish. You have nothing against eating fish, I suppose! Have a bite, will you?'

Khetu said, 'Mohashoy, don't request me. You have your fill, I am sitting over here.'

Shnareshwor said, 'In that case, take a sip of this, please. This is an excellent bottle of brandy. The clergyman's words must have weighed heavily on your heart; this will remove your affliction.'

Khetu said, 'Mohashoy, I plead with you with joined palms not to request me. And please let me go home.'

A friend of Shnareshwor's said, 'Well, then, have a bit of ham and chicken. This ham, you know, is the meat of *Bilati* pig. It came here straight from Bilat. You are forbidden to eat village pigs, but not Bilati pigs. And this chicken too is a great cock that we call

'*Rampakhi.*' It has been purchased at Hogg market, so you may rest assured that this is not just any old chicken.'

Then another friend of Shnareshwor's said, 'Now, here we have this super special cutlet. Come on, Khetubabu, this time we will not take no for an answer.'

What stuff the *khansama* brought that time we will do well to leave undisclosed. The hymns were being sung with great gusto downstairs. Let us hear that and comfort our souls.

After a while, the three friends put their heads together to discuss something. One of Shnareshwor's friends then stood up and held Khetu tight, and the other tried to force brandy down his throat. Shnareshwor sat smirking.

Khetu, who was a strong lad, now went berserk. With two vigorous shoves he floored both. Then he upturned the table. He threw down and smashed the glass utensils and tumblers, and whatever he could lay his hands on. Having thus caused mayhem, Khetu left the scene.

Notes

1. 'What, did you put that idol in your pocket?': Putting an idol in the pocket is deemed a sacrilege by a devout Hindu.
2. '... devotional hymns of Hori': Hori is another name for Lord Vishnu, and singing hymns of Hori is a routine ritual for devout Vaishnavs (followers of Vishnu).

13

Trouble Brewing

Three years passed uneventfully. Khetu was now twenty. He had passed all the school exams. And he passed some other exams too. Now he had reason to hope that he was in line for a plum job.

Ramhori and his wife thought that now the time had come to get Khetu married. They wrote to Khetu's mother to settle the date for it.

In her reply, Khetu's mother talked about this thing and that, and then wrote, 'I am yet to broach the subject of marriage to Tonu Roy. He is extremely busy these days; it is pretty difficult to arrange a meeting with him. Jonardon Choudhuri, meanwhile, has lost his wife. Her shraddho will be conducted with much fanfare, and Tonu Roy has become the organiser-in-chief. Jonardon's wife is indeed lucky, she passed away leaving behind sons and grandsons from both sons and daughters brimming with life, her head resting on the lap of her octogenarian husband. What more acknowledgement of her virtue can a woman aspire for? I went to look when her cortège was heading towards the cremation ghat. The parting of her hair was smeared copiously with vermilion, and she had a scarlet-border sari on. Ah, how graceful she did look on her last journey! Anyway, I will broach the subject of marriage to Tonu Roy when he has some free time.'

Some days later, Khetu's mother wrote another letter to Ramhori. It read like this:

'A terrible, terrible news has reached me! Tonu Roy has gone back on his word. There is no decent bone in his body; he is pitiably devoid of any sense of dharma. I have heard that he is making secret plans to marry Konkaboti off to Jonardon Choudhuri. What a horrific idea! And what about that fellow—*Jonardon Choudhuri*? Has he taken complete leave of his senses? He has his sons, and sons of sons and daughters swarming round him! He is so very old! His knees tremble while walking! He knows full well that his days are numbered! Why at this age should he at all entertain the mischievous idea of remarriage? Is this what one is supposed to do if one has money to burn, and property enough and to spare? Yes, I admit he is a man of stature, a zamindar, a feudal lord. But does that mean that he is at liberty to exhibit monstrous indiscretion? Doesn't that decrepit fellow know that his death is imminent? The condition he is in right now makes it evident that soon he will be going the way of all flesh. He can barely take a step without a stick. What dreadful news! And that Tonu Roy—is he absolutely stone-hearted? How can he bring himself to offer that tender, cherubic child Konkaboti to this moribund octogenarian? O, will this be the fate of Konkaboti? Whenever her face flashes in my mind's eye, my heart is rent in sorrow. I have come to hear that Konka's mother is weeping herself sick day and night. I sent for her, but she did not come. She sent the messenger back with the words, "Never again will I show this face to didi. Nor will I show this shame-tarnished face to anybody else." O, woe is me! Since the time I came to hear of this marriage, I have been in agony. Alas, for the girl's mother it must be heart-rending!'

On receiving the letter, Ramhori showed it to Khetu.

Khetu said, 'Dadamohashoy, I must go to my country home immediately.'

Ramhori cautioned, 'Jonardon Choudhuri is a wealthy man, and you are but a helpless boy, what do you think you can do to thwart his plan?'

Khetu concurred, 'It's true that I can do little about this. Even so, I cannot stay idle. I must at least strive to bail Konkaboti out of danger. I may not succeed, but so what?'

Khetu went home. He gathered all relevant pieces of information from his mother and neighbours. He came to know that Jonardon had been initially reluctant to give his consent to this marriage. But, Gobordhon Shiromoni, his court scholar, had got him round after a great deal of persuasion.

It did not matter that Jonardon Choudhuri was old. He had a graceful appearance, had good taste and had a heart brimful of desire. A five-faceted rudraksho rosary, which is difficult to come by, adorned his neck. Since he had a chronic cough and cold, a plaited cap always covered his hoary head. Decked in this attire when he consulted Gobordhon Shiromoni on the proposal of marriage, his elegance put even Indra, Chandra and Vayu to shame.[1]

Khetu came to know that Jonardon Choudhuri had now gone crazy about his impending remarriage and was not prepared to wait any longer. The twenty-fourth day of *Boishakh* was slated for the marriage. Jonardon was counting down the days. His sons and daughters were all opposed to this marriage, but they lacked the courage to utter a word. Only Jonardon's eldest daughter once emboldened herself to raise a voice against the idea. Since then, Jonardon had had no truck with that daughter.

Initially, Tonu Roy too had hesitated to give his daughter over to Jonardon. But when Jonardon said, 'I will give to the new bride East India Company's papers worth ten thousand rupees, a settlement, gold enough to swathe her body, and also two thousand rupees in cash to the bride's father,' Tonu Roy could resist the temptation no longer.

Even so, Tonu Roy shilly-shallied, looking at his daughter's face. But his son, once he came to hear of the money that Jonardon promised, eagerly fell for the bait. With tough words, he made his father consent to the proposal. Now both father and son were in a frenzy of pleasurable anticipation.

Tonu Roy did not have the guts to spill the beans to his wife. His son said, 'Well, you needn't tell her, I will go and tell ma.'

So he approached his mother to break the news. He told her, 'Ma, Konkaboti will get married to Jonardon Choudhuri. Father has set everything up.'

His mother was thunder-struck. She responded, 'What did you say? O, what is it that I have heard! O my goodness, Jonardon Choudhuri is a doddering old man! He has one foot in the grave! Dear O dear, how can you say that he will be the groom for my Konka?'

Her son replied, 'Did anyone say he is not old? That he is a youth in full bloom? Or he is a toddler? Or licks cotton dipped in milk?[2] Or that he plays with a *jhumjhumi*? O ma, come on, talk sense, please. He has promised to give Konka ten thousand rupees, gold enough to drape her body, real estate, and to father, two thousand rupees in cash. What more do you want, pray? Once that old man expires, Konka's money and ornaments will all be ours. That he is on his last legs is all the more reason for our jubilation! Had he been a strong fellow, we could not have possibly hoped for his early death, could we? Ma, you don't understand practical matters at all.'

There was no more to be said. The mother slumped to the ground. Tears came gushing down from her eyes. She thought, 'O mother earth, split yourself open, please, and let me enter your depths.'[3] Her two elder daughters too wept their hearts out, but to no avail. Konkaboti was dumbfounded. How can a girl whose soul blazed have tears in her eyes?

Khetu came to know all this from his mother and neighbours. He went to Tonu Roy first. He tried to dissuade him from this negotiation. He said, 'Mohashoy, don't fix Konka's marriage with such an octogenarian, please. If you don't like me, choose another eligible bridegroom. In case you cannot find her perfect match, I will help you to do so.'

At this, both Tonu Roy and his son were hopping mad. They drove Khetu out, with fierce tongue-lashing.

Khetu then went to Jonardon Choudhuri, taking Nironjon along with him. With joined palms, and great humility, they forbade Jonardon to marry. Initially Jonardon laughed their advice out of court. And then, when Khetu called him old a couple of times, he went ballistic, trembling all over. He had a chronic cold; anger induced such a terrible spasm of cough in him that everybody feared he might choke to death.

He coughed out his command, 'Throw this brat out of my house by the scruff of his neck!'

Ordered thus, Jonardon's attendants literally went for the jugular.

Khetu, quick on the draw, lifted Jonardon's stick and calmly proclaimed to the advancing henchmen, 'Do not attempt to touch me, for if you do, your heads will roll instantly.'

Khetu's inflamed look frightened the life out of everybody around. Nobody dared come up to lay hands on him.

Nironjon intervened to calm both sides down, and escorted Khetu out.

Khetu departed. But Jonardon's wrath did not abate, nor did his cough. His body shook vigorously in fury, and his cough developed into more frequent and convulsive spasms.

He sputtered through his coughs, 'What effrontery! He dared call me old!'

Gobordhon Shiromoni protested, 'O no, why should you be old? The person who calls you old is himself so.'

Shnareshwor was present there. He said, 'That young man must have been drunk. Didn't you see that his eyes were blood-red?'

Nironjon said, 'Don't say that! Some people, we know, do drink, let them. Everybody knows who takes drinks, and eats chicken.[4] Don't try to slander a man.'

Shnareshwor said, 'Let everybody take note that this gentleman has declared that I drink, and eat chicken too. I will bring a defamation suit against him. I will have him rot behind bars.'

Gobordhon Shiromoni said, 'I don't know whether Kshetrochondro consumes liquor or not. But this much I know that he drinks water from *jobons*. He eats what you people call '*borokh*'—the thing that the sahibs manufacture in their factories. And Godadhor Ghosh has seen him do that.'

Jonardon Choudhuri asked, 'What? What did you say?'

Shnareshwor said, '*Sorbonash*! Calamity! He eats 'borokh'? The thing that the sahibs produce with the blood of cows? Now we see that our dharma is heading for perdition. *Hai, hai,* the end of the Hindu dharma is nigh.'

Nironjon said, 'Shnareshworbabu, please try to remember how you were once helped by Khetu's father. Do not do Khetu a bad turn.'

Jonardon Choudhuri said, 'Put aside all this piffle now. Send for Godadhor Ghosh.'

One of his attendants rushed to fetch Godadhor Ghosh.

Notes

1. '... Indra, Chandra and Vayu': Hindu godheads.
2. '... he licks cotton dipped in milk': A reference to the rural practice of feeding new-born babies.
3. 'O mother earth, split yourself open, please, ... your depths': A reference to Sita, wife of Rama in the Ramayana, who, unable to put up with the distrust of her husband, sought refuge in the earth, her mother, and entered the nether world.
4. 'Everybody knows who ... eats chicken': Drinking alcohol and eating chicken were taboo for Hindus in the nineteenth century.

14

About Godadhor

Godadhor Ghosh was brought before Jonardon Choudhuri. He offered nomoskar to Jonardon with joined palms, and squatted some distance away on the floor.[1]

Choudhuri mohashoy said, 'Godadhor, what is that abominable thing that I have heard? That the son of Shibchondro, that Kheta, ate taboo food?[2] Did you see him do that? Or did you hear of it? Did you talk to him? Come out with everything, I command you.'

Godadhor said, 'Mohashoy, I am stupid and illiterate. I know very little, understand even less. I will narrate exactly what happened.

'Last year, I went to Kolkata. There I was looking for a place to stay. So I went to Ramhori's. I sat in his outer house in the evening when I heard a *minshe* walking along the road with a *hnari* on his head hollering a trade cry. Attracted by that noise, Ramhori's son barged out of the inner house, and pleaded with Khetu, "*Kaka*, O kaka, that man is carrying *kulki*, please get me that." Khetu bought him two paise worth of that stuff. Then he asked me, "Godadhor, will you have kulki?" I said, "No, *dadathakur*, I don't eat kulki." Ramhoribabu's son asked Khetu, "Kaka, won't you have one?" Khetu said, 'O no, I am thirsty, but this stuff doesn't quench thirst, rather I would eat raw borokh." Saying this, Khetu stepped out of the house. A little while later, he came back with a glistening, glass-like white slab of stone tied in his *gamchha*. Then he broke that stone into fragments, put those into water and started sipping it. I asked, "Dadathakur, what is that stuff?" Khetu said, "This is called borokh. When the throat gets parched in sweltering summer noons, you can drop this stuff into water to make it cold." I asked, "Dadathakur, do all pieces of glass make water cold?" Khetu said, "O no, this is not glass, this is borokh. It is made by freezing water. This is just another variety of water. This is but the water that you get to see in your rivers and streams. The only difference is that this specimen here is frozen, as simple as that. The hailstones that fall from the sky are the same as this. The sahibs manufacture borokh in factories. Come on, stretch your hand, and feel it." Saying this, he placed a bit of that stuff on my palm. Instantly, my palm felt like being ripped apart as if with a saw. I could not hold it, and let it drop. Then Khetu said, "Godadhor, why don't you put a bit of it into your mouth? There is no offence in doing that." I said, "No, dadathakur, you have studied English, you're rid of taboos on food, and so there's no offence in that. But I have not studied English. We cannot eat things that the sahibs produce in machines. If we do, we will violate the strictures of our dharma, and will be cast out."'

Now, Godadhor addressed Choudhuri mohashoy, and said, 'My lord, I have narrated the entire incident exactly as it unfolded. After this, Khetu asked me so many questions about so many things of the olden times, but I need not report all that stuff here now.'

Jonardon Choudhuri said, 'Oh no, don't keep anything back. Report the entire conversation you had with that chap. I need to know everything.'

Godadhor addressed Gobordhon Shiromoni, and said, 'Shiromoni mohashoy, then I will have to narrate the story of that silk-selling Brahman.'

Shiromoni mohashoy protested, 'O, that is but an old wives' tale. You needn't tell them that.'

But Jonardon Choudhuri was insistent. 'No, I wish to hear about the entire conversation you had with Kheta. Yes, I do.'

Godadhor said, 'Okay, then let me narrate it. After that borokh episode, Khetu asked me, "Godadhor, I have heard that in our fields people were killed by brigands in the days of yore, and have also heard that you were one such leader of brigands. Is this true?" I answered, "Dadathakur, what's the use of raking over the ashes of what I did in my adolescent years? Those days are no more. The Company has clamped down on those activities.[3]" Khetu said, "That is true, but I long to hear about those *thangares*. I have heard that you killed people with your own hands, so I want a first-hand account from you. You are among those very few old men still alive. When you people are no longer around, this portion of the past will be well and truly buried. And besides, what's there to be embarrassed about? Everyone in this village knows that you commanded a gang of freebooters." I said, "O no, dadathakur, when there are people like you around us, how can we be the ringleaders of some activity? You are Brahmans, you are our deities! You are the born leaders of all activities." Then Khetu asked, "Who then was the leader of your gang?" I told him, "The leader of our gang was Komol Bhattacharya mohashoy. Since we worked together, we called him by his first name, Komol, in a spirit of camaraderie. He is no more." Khetu asked, "Godadhor, have you ever killed Brahmans?" I said, "Yes, in the midst of the sprawling fields we killed whichever pedestrian we came by. No offence in that. Getting to know one's identity before killing a person is absurd. And getting to know what a chap has in his possession before taking his life is not a viable option either. We had to kill the passer-by straightaway. Then, after having slain the fellow, if we noticed the sacred thread wound round his neck, we would come to know that he was a Brahman by caste. If he did not have that thread, we would know that he was a *Shudra*. We would get out of our victims whatever we were fated to get on a given day. It happened so many times that we got not a paisa from our victim looking through the various parts and folds of his clothes. Those people were indeed scamps, rogues, ill-begotten. When you are out on the street, you should have a paisa or two. Does it make sense to travel penniless? Is not this a felony, dadathakur? It takes a lot of effort to kill a man, does it not? Those scoundrels travelled without a paisa on them, if only to scupper all our efforts." Khetu asked me once again, "Godadhor, do you mean that man doesn't give up the ghost all that easily?" I said, "Everybody doesn't have the same life force. Some lost their lives in fear even before they actually got beaten up, and some did not give in even after being battered fifty times by three or four of us. Once we ran into serious trouble while killing a Brahman." Khetu wanted to know what had happened.'

Now, Godadhor cast a glance at Gobordhon Shiromoni, and said, 'Shiromoni mohashoy, now I am coming to that part!'

Shiromoni said, 'Choudhuri mohashoy, you needn't listen to those unholy words. Come, let us decide what we can do about this Khetrochondro. There is little doubt that having drunk water from the sahibs, he has acquired sahibhood.'

Jonardon Choudhuri said, 'O no, I must know about the entire conversation Godadhor had with Kheta. The brat must have had some crooked design up his sleeve, or else why should he have asked Godadhor so many questions? Come on, Godadhor, tell me what happened next.'

Godadhor picked up the thread of his yarn once again, and continued, 'Khetu asked me, "Why did you have trouble in killing that Brahman?" I said, "Dadathakur, once three Brahmans came to our village to sell silk clothes. They failed to find a suitable place to stay and were on the lookout for one. I bumped into them. I was then seeking the dust off a Brahman's feet,[4] carrying a leaf in my hand. It is part of my daily routine that I never drink water until I take the dust off a Brahman's feet. Knowing they were Brahmans, I took the dust off their feet, and offered them my house for their accommodation. They accepted my offer. They stayed for three days in our village, sold many clothes, and earned a tidy sum of money. I shared that news with Komol. We hatched a plan to finish those three off. But we did not let our other members know of it, lest they claimed their share of the spoils. I told Komol, "You go and hide somewhere in the field. I will take them along with me to that field in the small hours. Then the two of us would carry out our business." Very early at dawn, I went with them to show them the way. And by divine grace, the day was so exceptionally foggy that even a man standing right in front of us was not visible. As we approached the pre-fixed spot, Komol came out and hit one Brahman on the head with his stick. I too struck a blow on the other's head with a stick. Both fell poleaxed. When we were busy applying the coup de grâce, the third fellow took flight. Komol chased him, and I too having done my job followed them. That Brahman entered the village, and bolted into Shiromoni mohashoy's cottage, begging for shelter, praying, "Save this poor soul, for God's sake, they are going to spill a Brahman's blood." With great affection Shiromoni mohashoy helped him up, and said, "Life is transient like water on a lotus leaf.[5] Why then are you so desperate to save it?" With these words, Shiromoni mohashoy carried the Brahman out of his cottage, dumped him down, and shut his cottage door. Now, Komol chased that Brahman once again in the direction of the field. When that Brahman found that he could not escape, that Komol was almost breathing down his neck, he suddenly turned round and clasped Komol tight. A scuffle ensued, which was short-lived. Komol had the strength of an elephant, how could the Brahman put up a fight? Komol knocked him down, and tried to slay him. But the Brahman had such immense life force that he neither died nor fainted. He only screamed, "Hé Modhusudon, save my life! O save me, Lord Modhusudon.[6] Is there anybody around? A Brahman's blood is being spilt! Save me, O save me." I had lagged behind. Because of the fog, I had no clue in which direction the Brahman had fled or Komol had chased him. Now, I ran in the direction of the Brahman's scream. I found that he lay on his back on the ground, Komol was sitting on his chest, he had pinned the Brahman's hands down, his left knee was planted firmly on the ground, his big toe was thrust into the Brahman's belly, and he was trying to pierce his navel with all his might. The Brahman, lying supine, was yowling his life out. Komol muttered, "This Brahman is a downright rascal. He refuses to die. Godadhor, do something about it, or else this guy will bring a crowd here with his screams." I had then no stick in my hand. A stone lay about. I took it up and smashed his head in. And then, the Brahman breathed his last. Anyway, although we really had a trying time to knock that fellow off, we profited handsomely. We got quite a substantial amount of cash, and a good many pieces of silk clothes. But somehow another gang leader, Nosiram, got wind of it. He demanded a portion of the booty. We said, "You played no part in this business, why then do you want a share?" Komol and Nosiram got into a fierce squabble over this, and were on the verge of coming to blows. Komol tore off his sacred thread, and cursed Nosiram.[7] Komol Bhattacharya was a Brahman, you know. He was almost like the incarnation of godhead Ogni! And he had many clients and disciples. So, no wonder his curse would take its toll! Within five to six years Nosiram died, vomiting blood. Anyway, from the bundle of silk clothes that we plundered, I gave one to Shiromoni mohashoy. When he went about in that silk shirt with the silk scarf on one of his shoulders and with the holy mark on his forehead, everyone said, 'Aaha, look, as if Kondorpo himself is out on a stroll."[8] In that full bloom of youth, Shiromoni mohashoy had the looks to bowl an onlooker over! Am I not right, mohashoy?'"

Shiromoni mohashoy said, 'Godadhor! You shouldn't make such statements. I don't have the foggiest notion of what you have said. You must have taken leave of your senses from prolonged illness. I vow to offer basil leaves to Lord Narayan for your sake.[9] Then your sin will be expiated.'

Nironjon had been listening to this narration all this while, emitting long and heavy sighs intermittently, and saying, 'O Lord Modhusudon! O Lord Deenobondhu!'[10]

Jonardon Choudhuri kept mum for a moment or two, and then asked again, 'Godadhor, what happened thereafter?'

Godadhor answered, 'Nothing happened after that. Khetu fell silent for a long time, and then asked me, rather absently, "Will you have a bit of borokh, Godadhor?" I said, "No, dadathakur, I won't have that stuff, for if I do I will lose my dharma and my caste."'

Jonardon Choudhuri said, 'Then you confirm that Khetu ate borokh?'

Godadhor answered, 'Yes my lord, I saw him do that with my own eyes. You are a Brahman, I swear touching your feet that this is the truth.'

Notes

1. '... squatted quite a distance away on the floor': An indication of the caste hierarchy in Hindu society, which decrees that 'low-caste' men do not have the privilege to come too near a 'high-caste' person, or take a seat at the same level as the latter.
2. 'Kheta': A belittling reference to Khetu.
3. 'The Company has clamped down on those activities ...': A reference to Sir William Henry Sleeman who, on behalf of the East India Company, put an end to the menace of the thangares or thugees in 1830.
4. '... looking for the dust off a Brahman's feet ...': Taking the dust off a Brahman's feet was deemed a propitious act by 'lower-caste' men in nineteenth-century Bengal.
5. '... like water on a lotus leaf ...': A common metaphor used in ancient Indian poetry and scriptural texts to indicate the transience of life.
6. 'Modhusudon': A name of Lord Vishnu, who is invoked when somebody is in danger.
7. '... tore off his sacred thread, and cursed Nosiram ...': This is a common gesture by Brahmans while issuing a curse, especially in the past.
8. '... Kondorpo himself': Kondorpo is the Hindu godhead of love, and is believed to be exceedingly handsome.
9. '... offer basil leaves to Lord Narayan ...': Basil leaves are believed by Bengali Hindus to be Lord Narayan's favourite.
10. 'Deenobondhu': A name of Lord Vishnu, literally, 'friend of the poor'.

15

Konkaboti's Ailment

Having heard what Godadhor had to say about Khetu, Jonardon Choudhuri sent for the elderly gentlemen of the village, including Tonu Roy.

When everybody arrived, Jonardon said, 'Today, I heard something that is plainly calamitous. Now, our caste, clan, dharma—everything seems to be in grave danger. If we come to lose all this, we stand simply no chance to offer water to our ancestors.[1] Koli, the age of the apocalypse, is knocking on the door, I believe!'

Flabbergasted, they all asked, 'What's the matter, mohashoy? You look terribly distressed!'

Jonardon answered, 'We have come to know that Kheta, the son of our late Shibchondro, who has been living in Kolkata to study English, eats borokh. This borokh is something that the sahibs manufacture in factories, it is nothing but water made by the sahibs. Shiromoni mohashoy has given his mandate that by consuming that stuff, one attains sahibhood. Someone who keeps in touch with one who acquired sahibhood is in danger of turning into a sahib himself. So now it seems that by keeping in close touch with Kheta, we are on our way to becoming sahibs ourselves!'

Hearing this, the whole tribe of village folk was shell-shocked. Sorbonash! Khetu eats borokh! Well, well, well, now everyone is done for! The very existence of people's dharma and caste is in jeopardy!

Of them all, Shnareshwor was the one most taken aback. True, he did not wail aloud, but his dharma-minded soul was really and truly mortified. What shall I say about the number of times he moaned 'Alas, O woe is me!'?

Anyway, it was unanimously decided that Khetu would be excommunicated.

Nironjon was the only one who stood against this verdict. He said, 'As long as I am alive, none can ostracise Khetu. We two then will be ostracised together.'

Nironjon continued, 'Choudhuri mohashoy! What I have heard since early morning today has convinced me that Koli really is round the corner. I have heard about the slaying of men and Brahmans! Choudhuri mohashoy, you are a sagacious fellow, you are wise and learned, the blessed son of Mother Lakshmi; God has always been benevolent to you. This conspiracy does not become you. There is no glory in casting a man out from a community, our job is to rescue the downfallen. Lord Vishnu is called "the rescuer of the fallen" because that is what he does. All virtuous people of this world represent the divine grace of "the rescuer of the fallen". How can people like Shnareshwor, who are besotted with alcohol and taboo food, those like Tonu Roy, who earn revenue by selling their daughters, people like Gobordhon, who are guilty of such heinous offences as murder of men and Brahmans, people who are but slimy, grimy worms of hell like those fellows—how can they know the spirit of dharma?'

Nironjon departed with these words.

When Nironjon had left, Gobordhon Shiromoni said, 'He has lashed out at Shnareshwor babaji. Shnareshwor babaji is a hero of this village. None I suppose will be able to live in this village having insulted Shnareshwor babaji.'

Jonardon Choudhuri intended to demonstrate that Khetu had been ostracised. And to fulfil that desire, he invited people of seven villages, including his own, to his house on the occasion of his wife's monthly shraddho. Everyone came to know the condition Khetu was in, every corner buzzed with the news that Khetro, the son of the late Shibchondro and dweller of village Kusumghati, had turned a Christian by consuming 'borokh'.

That very night Shnareshwor brought four bottles of mohua liquor, and got chicken cooked from Tarikh Sheikh's house on the sly. He and four of his friends got together to party, and guzzled that stuff. However, for a moment their gala spirit was under threat of being disrupted. While eating, Shnareswor had a sneaking suspicion that Tarikh Sheikh might have mixed 'borokh' in the chicken soup. He took his hand off, declaring, 'I cannot eat this stuff. Do you want me to forsake my dharma and caste by eating 'borokh'?' Then everyone around took great pains to convince him that borokh was never mixed in the soup. Convinced, Shnareshwor once again turned his attention to the scrumptious food. When the binge got over, they went near Nironjon's house, and started hurling stones and cattle bones at it. Every night from then on, Nironjon's dwelling was pelted with such missiles. When things went beyond the point of endurance, Nironjon and his wife, with tearful eyes, left their ancestral home for another village.

Khetu said, 'Kakamohashoy, you go first. And I too will be following you very soon.'

Khetu's mother had a female domestic help. She gave up her job. She said, '*Ma thakurani*, how can I serve you any longer? The other people of the village will refuse to take water from my hand if I work here. So I have no option but to leave.'

Khetu's mother was tormented in various other ways. When she went to the riverbank, the women there gave her a wide berth lest she accidentally touched them.

The wife of Komol Bhattacharya, the one-time gang leader of whom Godadhor spoke, one day blurted out to Khetu's mother, 'Bachha, if one knows how to be careful, one need not have to put up with invectives. If one knows how to sit, none needs to ask one to get up and move. Your son has eaten "borokh", and so you are now outcast. But does that warrant you to ruin our castes as well? I see you do rather uncannily prefer this riverbank to all others. The other day, the moment I stood up with the water-filled earthen pitcher to hold it on my flank, water from your body got sprinkled on mine. I had no option but to discard that three-paise-worth pitcher and take another cleansing bath. Bachha, what have we people done to you that you are always up to such mischief?'

Khetu's mother did not reply. She came back home weeping.

Khetu said, 'Mother, do not cry. We will not be staying in this village much longer. We will go away.'

His mother said, 'Bachha, I am not hurt by the words those wretched people say. But, I feel deep anguish when I look at your face. You don't eat and sleep properly. You are always restless. Your face has turned pale, and your body has grown thin. Khetu, please, for my sake, stay calm, son.'

Khetu said, 'It is now a matter of seven days, ma. Today is the seventeenth of this month. Konkaboti will get married on the twenty-fourth. That day, all my hopes will be snuffed out. That will be the day of our taking leave for good from this land.'

His mother said, 'I have learnt from the Das's daughter that Konkaboti has changed beyond recognition. She, I am told, has lost her grace, her complexion, and her smile. Alas, for all her sorrow, she is trying to allay her mother's pain. She, oblivious of her own affliction, is consoling her mother day and night. Her mother is weeping constantly, and Konkaboti is trying to soothe her.

'Konkaboti told her mother, "Don't cry, ma. If father makes some money by selling these few bones of mine, why should we grudge him that, ma? Such bones lie scattered plentifully in cremation grounds, but no one pays for them. If my bones are so high-priced, and if father and brother come up trumps with the money that these bones can bring, why should we rue that, ma? But ma, I feel so weak and there is no joy left. I fear that I may meet my Maker within the next few days. In case I die before he gets hold of the money he is craving for, father will be very cross with me. By then I will be burnt to ashes, but whenever father will remember me, he will berate me no end."'

Khetu's mother went on, 'Khetu, I don't tell you all that I come to know about Konkaboti for I fear that it will make you restless. I have heard that she has wasted away completely, and that her days are numbered.'

Khetu said, 'Ma, I told Tonu Roy, "Roy mohashoy, you needn't marry Konkaboti off to me if you do not like to, but get her married to an eligible groom." But ma, Tonu Roy turned a deaf ear to my words. He abused me and dismissed me from his presence. Well, ma, I don't think we are all that hard done by, after all! If we find it difficult to live here, we can easily leave this village for another. But Konkaboti! That poor girl will have to stay in this hell with a sorrow-laden soul forever and ever. That is, O ma, what pains me the most. The feeling that I am so worthless that I failed to do anything to remove her sorrow is what, O ma, gnaws at my heart. In any case, ma, if you get to hear anything more about Konkaboti, let me know of it, please. Do not keep me in the dark about it. O, why did we send Sita back to Kolkata? Had she been here, I would have got the correct information daily.'

The next day, Khetu's mother told him, 'Today I have heard that Konkaboti is laid up with a high fever. It's no wonder that the child will fall ill, weighed down by so many worries! I don't know if she is going to survive this. Jonardon Choudhuri has sent in a *kobiraj* with the command that he must, by any means, bring Konkaboti round within four days.'

Khetu said, 'You are right, ma. I too have a premonition that Konkaboti's life may not be saved. O ma, if Konkaboti's cat comes here, feed her amply on fish and milk. Ma, if we leave this village, her cat will not come here, will she? Maybe, moving over to a rich man's home she will forget about us.'

Khetu's mother did not reply. She kept wiping her tears with the end of her sari.

The next day, Khetu's mother got the news that Konkaboti's fever had not abated at all, and that she had lost consciousness.

Konkaboti's ailment kept worsening day by day. Seven days passed, and the day of the wedding arrived.

That day Konkaboti's entire body had a terrible burning sensation, and her throat was parched. She was totally bedridden. Her malady had completely overpowered her. She was unconscious most of the time. Even when awake, she could not recognise anybody. She was on the brink of death.

Note

1. '... we stand simply no chance to offer water to our ancestors': Offering water to one's ancestors is believed by devout Hindus to be a sacred ritual.

Book II

1

The Boat

Her throat was parched. And her body smarted from a terrible pain.

Konkaboti said to herself, 'Let me go to the river bank, there let me sit and drink water to my heart's content, and sprinkle water on my body, for only that may bring relief and solace.'

Konkaboti sat by the riverbank, sprinkling water all over her body. Then, all of a sudden, someone called out, 'Who is it? Konkaboti, is that you?'

Konkaboti looked around, but could see nobody. No one was about. Konkaboti had no clue as to who the speaker was. Only a *katla* fish was floating up and down in the river water. That was about all she could see.

Once again, someone asked, 'Who is that? Konkaboti?'

The girl now answered, 'O yes, I am Konkaboti.'

The same voice asked again, 'Is your body racked with a burning sensation? Is your throat parched?''

Konkaboti answered, 'Yes, you are right. My body feels as if it is on fire and my throat is dry.'

The voice said, 'Why then don't you do one thing? Why don't you swim to the midstream? There are chambers under the surface of the river water. If you enter one of those, your thirst will be quenched, and your blistering pain will be allayed.'

Konkaboti answered, 'The midstream is quite some distance off. How will I swim that far?'

The voice said, 'Why worry? See, there is a fishermen's canoe afloat. Why don't you go and get on that boat?'

Konkaboti got onto the fisherfolk's craft.

Meanwhile, in Konkaboti's house, everyone was looking for her. 'Where has Konkaboti gone? Where could she have gone?'—these words were on everyone's lips. A great hue and cry broke out. Someone called out and said, 'Ogo, hello, your Konkaboti has gone in the direction of the riverbank.'

Everyone in her household thought that Konkaboti had left home to avoid her marriage with Jonardon Choudhuri. So to call her back, one of her elder sisters rushed towards the riverbank. Having reached there, she found that Konkaboti was sailing away to midstream in a dinghy.

The elder sister said,

> Konka, dear Konka, come back to the shore,
> Am I to believe you love me no more?
> We are three sisters, two of them widows,
> Ma loves you the most, everyone knows.

From the boat, Konkaboti rejoined,

> Under the water, in an abyss,
> There is an abode full of peace.
> There go I, sister, farewell to thee,
> Sail, O my boat, there directly.

While the sisters were so conversing, Konkaboti's boat sailed farther into the deeper part of the river.

Then Konkaboti's brother came to the bank, and pleaded with her,

> Come back, Konka, don't bring on us shame,
> Father is livid, and swearing at your name.
> The world is complex, you're a child 'tis plain,
> Return, don't make your father groan in pain.

Konkaboti answered,

> What you say, brother, I can't follow,
> What pain I am in, how can you know?

Go back, brother, and on wealth gloat,
Go on, keep sailing, O my boat.

While these words were being exchanged, Konkaboti's boat sailed deeper into the river water.

Then came Konkaboti's mother, and told her,

Konka, my darling, come back, dear,
My heart bleeds, O come near,
Rice at home has gone cold, *byanjon* gone stale,
You're starving, daughter, and have turned pale.

Konkaboti replied,

Thirst is so acute that I can't bear,
My body is as if on fire.
To douse that fire, ma, I am afloat.
Sail, keep sailing, O my boat.

Konkaboti's boat sailed farther away as she spoke these words.

Then her father came, and said,

Konkaboti, come back home, and get married,
Get wonderstruck with the array I have made.
Wear jewels aplenty, and satin dress,
Money will cascade, quite limitless.

Konkaboti answered,

For money and ornaments I have no desire,
My body, father, is now on terrible fire.
Acute pain drives me to the brink,
Now, O my boat, dip and sink.

The moment Konkaboti uttered these words, her boat plopped under the river water.

2

Underwater

As the boat sank, Konkaboti too was drowned. She was sinking down, down, and further down. She sank leagues and leagues down under the water. There, all the fishes gathered round her. A great din and bustle broke out in the fish community. It was abuzz with the news that Konkaboti was coming. *Rohu* said, 'Konkaboti is coming!' *Pnuti* said, 'Konkaboti is coming!' All the fishes echoed, 'Konkaboti is coming!' The aquatic animals waited for her with bated breath, gazing at the way along which she would come. At last, Konkaboti *did* come among them. Everyone welcomed her cordially, and greeted her with, 'Come, Konkaboti, come.'

The infant fishes said, 'We will play with Konkaboti.'

The old dame Katlani snubbed them, 'This is not the time for Konkaboti to play with you. I have called her down here from the riverbank, having noticed that she was suffering from a severe burning sensation. Aha, bachha had to travel such a long distance! See, her face looks so drawn and withered from fatigue. Come, child, come to me. Rest awhile and then we will decide what we can do for you.'

Konkaboti went slowly towards Katlani the old dame and sat by her side.

Konkaboti rested, and meanwhile the aquatic creatures met in a great assembly. Mango-fish was conferred the post of president because of the beard that he sported. The members of the assembly discussed and debated what they could do with Konkaboti.

After a flurry of lectures, the canny *Bata* proposed, 'Comrades, we can make Konkaboti our queen, can't we?'

All of them happily agreed to the proposal. Konkaboti's name came to be hailed with great fanfare. It was proclaimed with drumbeats in all streets and highways, lanes and bylanes underwater that Konkaboti would be the queen of the fish community.

The joy of the fishes knew no bounds. They talked among themselves, 'Brothers, if Konkaboti becomes our queen, our hard days will come to an end. If somebody catches any of us with a hook and a fishing line, Konkaboti will snap the string. If fishermen cast their nets in the river water, Konkaboti will cut the nets with her knife. If she becomes our queen, we will have nothing to worry about. Let us go and implore her, "Konkaboti, please be our queen."'

After such a round of consultation, the members of the fish community approached her, and said, 'Konkaboti, we have decided to make you our queen. Please, accept the offer, for our sake. O Konkaboti, please do.'

Konkaboti said, 'I cannot be your queen now. I am not well physically, and not happy in spirit either. So now I am not in a position to be your queen.'

Hearing these words, Katlani the old dame asked the fishes, 'You have organised a meeting and delivered lectures all right, but have you cast your "votes" in her favour? That is the legal procedure, you know!'

The fishes answered, 'Oh, we did not cast votes in her favour! We forgot that part of the legal formality.'

Katlani said, 'Then how do you expect Konkaboti to agree to your proposal?'

The fishes cried out in unison, 'O yes, now we understand! We must vote for Konkaboti, otherwise she will not agree to be our queen. Come on, comrades, let us all vote for Konkaboti.'

Having said this, all the members of the fish community started voting for Konkaboti. Finally, they took the tumbler carrying their vote slips to Konkaboti. They then removed the piece of cloth that covered the mouth of the tumbler, and told her, 'Come, Konkaboti, take a look, you have got such a shipload of votes. Now you can hardly turn down our entreaty to be our queen.'

Konkaboti answered, 'O no, friends, this is not a matter of votes. I cannot consent to your proposal to be your queen now. The troubles that I am going through only I know!'

Then Katlani said to the fishes, 'Have you prepared royal robes for her? Unless you give her royal robes to wear, why should she agree to be your queen?'

Hearing this, the fishes chorused, 'O yes, now we understand. Konkaboti will not consent to our proposal unless she is given royal robes to wear. She will have to be provided with colourful garments, and mem-like outfits. Only then will she agree.'

Konkaboti said, 'O my friends, once again you are making a mistake. Colourful garments are not at issue here. I have lost all desire to preen myself. I now have only one wish—which is to cry long and cry alone.'

Then Katlani said, 'O you fishes, have you decided who the king will be? Unless you find her a king, how will Konkaboti be a queen? No wonder, without the right match, she wishes to weep alone.'

Konkaboti answered, 'O no, friends, that is not the reason for my sorrow. I don't need any king. I am Konkaboti, the disconsolate girl. It is only to assuage my anguish that I have come to your place underwater.'

Katlani said, smiling gently, 'O you don't need a king, is that so? But in case we decide to make Khetu the king, what then?'

Konkaboti was startled, and looked at Katlani's face. She thought, 'How amazing! How did this news travel from above the water to the midstream so far down below?'

Katlani correctly guessed the working of her mind, and said, 'You people think that fishes don't know a thing, that they are there only to be caught and eaten, don't you? But you are wrong, Konkaboti, take my word for it. We too keep abreast of certain worldly matters. When we roam about near the riverbanks, we overhear a word or two that are routinely exchanged among the women who gather there. Now, Konka, please listen to my advice, and get up. Come on, change into royal robes, and be the queen. Cry no more, O my dear lady.'

The words of Katlani the old dame calmed Konkaboti's distressed soul quite a bit.

She said, 'Okay, if I agree to be your queen, what am I supposed to do?'

The fishes answered, 'What you are supposed to do? You need to do a very simple thing right now. You will have to go to the tailor who will take your measurements for the royal robes.'

Then they all told the crab, 'Crab mohashoy! You can travel both on land and in water. You are a clever fellow. When you bat your eyes, they sparkle with intelligence. You please take Konkaboti along to the tailor's. Ask the tailor to take the correct measurements and make a gorgeous robe for her. Take enough money and gold coins on the turtle's back. Give the tailor as much money as he wants, and make Konkaboti a winsome vesture.'

Crab mohashoy answered, 'I will certainly go. Who does not want that Konkaboti gets to wear beautiful clothes? If we do not keep our queen in the finest of fabrics and the choicest of ornaments, it is we who will be disgraced. You load the turtle's back with money and gold coins, and meanwhile, let me put on decent clothes and brush my hair back with a neat parting in the middle.'

The turtle's back was loaded with money and gold coins. And the crab turned out in his glad rags and brushed slick hair, all raring to go.

3

The Royal Robe

What could Konkaboti do except accompany the crab and the turtle? The crab led the march, while Konkaboti was in the middle, followed by the turtle. This was how the three advanced.

Initially they travelled long in water, then they travelled long on land. They crossed hills and mountains, woods and forests until they ultimately came to an old tailor.

That old tailor was sewing clothes with glasses on his nose and scissors in hand. He looked at the distant hills and noticed some fellows approaching him. He wondered who they were, but when they came near, he could recognise them.

The old tailor said, 'Who is that, my crab brother, I suppose?"

Crab mohashoy answered, 'Yes, brother, you are right. How are you?'

The tailor said, 'Brother, there is but little difference between our being and *not* being well at this age. I am waiting for the last round, while you are dandies, so our worlds are as different as chalk and cheese. Now tell me the mission on which you have come here.'

The crab replied, 'We have made Konkaboti here our queen. She needs splendid apparel to wear, so we have come to you.'

The tailor said, 'O, I see. Yes, brother, I have a large store of splendid garments. I have a good stock of *khero* garments from Patna. This is blood-red khero with wash-proof dye and wear-proof material that I have hem-stitched entirely. Now, if your Konkaboti is silky-cottony, make her wear it, she will look bewitching in it, I bet. The price will not be an issue here. Now, press her body to make sure if she is silky-cottony or not.'

Crab mohashoy pressed Konkaboti's body with his claws. Then he looked at the tailor's face, and said with a touch of disappointment, 'Not really, I don't think she is as soft as silk-cotton.'

Crab mohashoy then blew hard at Konkaboti, and turning to the tailor, said dejectedly once again, 'O no, she has not been blown away, I see!'

The tailor said, 'O what a pity! Okay, check if she is coconut coir; in case she is, that will do.'

Konkaboti said, 'What do you mean to do with me? Do you want to make a pillow of me? You have made me your queen just a little while ago, why then do you propose to make a pillow of me?'

The tailor said, '*Ish*! This girl seems to be much too full of herself! If you don't want to be a pillow, what do you want to become then? A cushion for the back?'

These cruel words from the tailor cut Konkaboti to the quick. She broke into sobs.

Crab mohashoy said, 'You are but a child, Konkaboti. Why do you intervene in our conversation? We will do whatever we deem fit for you. Keep mum, and keep watching. Be quiet! Crying is shameful, you know.'

Consoling her with these words, Crab mohashoy wiped Konkaboti's tears with his long claws. And Konkaboti's face got scratched because of this act of fondness.

As she stopped crying, Crab mohashoy once again pressed Konkaboti's body long and well enough, and told the tailor sullenly, 'O no, she doesn't seem to be coconut coir either!'

The old tailor now said, 'Then I am helpless. I don't have a garment that will suit her. I can neither cut nor stitch her clothes. Konkaboti, if you were silky-cottony or, at any rate, coconut coir, I would make you a gorgeous outfit, for sure. But unfortunately, you are not blessed that way.'

Crab mohashoy asked, 'So what option are we left with? Where will I then get a suitable robe?'

The old tailor then said, 'You do one thing, go to Khalifa sahib. He is an excellent artisan, the best in the world. He has a large stock, and even if a blunt-nosed creature gets to wear his clothes, his nose will look sharp.'

These words touched Crab mohashoy on the raw. He shot back, peeved, 'Are you jeering at me? Maybe your nose is pointed, and mine blunt, but does that warrant mockery?'

The old tailor answered, 'O no, is that ever possible that I will cock a snook at you? And why should I, anyway? Your nose is not at all ugly, but is invisible, and that is a pity.'

Such dulcet words from the old tailor mitigated Crab mohashoy's ire. Flattered, he said, 'Now, that indeed is a valid point. My nose is truly beautiful, but its only flaw is that it is invisible. Sometimes, I myself am hard put to search it out. If perchance it were visible, then everybody would certainly have said, "Aaha, what a charming nose! O, it looks exactly like a flute!" And those who compose rhymes would certainly have written, "A nose more attractive than a sesame flower!" or "A nose more exquisite than the beak of a *shuk* bird." Whatever you people say, my nose is really wonderful!'

Konkaboti thought to herself, 'I wonder what is happening here! I am in the company of some crackpots, I suppose. This crab is raving mad. He should best be accommodated in a lunatic asylum.' But then, she did not speak her mind.

Everybody moved on from there. Crab mohashoy led the way, with Konkaboti in the middle, followed by the turtle. They proceeded in this formation. They had to travel a long way before they reached Khalifa sahib's place. Khalifa was then in the inner part of his house.

Crab mohashoy called out from outside, 'Khalifa sahib! Khalifa sahib!'

Khalifa answered from within, 'Who is there? Who calls me?'

Crab mohashoy said who he was. 'Will you come out, please? We have important business with you.'

Khalifa came out and gave the crab a hearty reception.

Khalifa said warmly, 'Welcome, Crabbabu.[1] And O, here I see Turtlebabu as well. Come, please be seated on that stool. And you, Crabbabu, you please take that chair. But where shall I make this girl sit? This girl is so graceful! Crabbabu, is she your daughter?'

The crab answered, 'No, she is not. I am a bachelor. But it is for this girl that we have come to you. We have made this girl our queen. We have come to you with a plea for making a gorgeous outfit for her to wear.'

Khalifa remarked, 'I can make a royal robe jolly well. I have silk, wool, satin, and even brocades from Benaras.[2] But it takes a lot of effort to make a royal robe. You have got to attach diamonds, pearls, sequins and laces and other precious material to such robes. That calls for a large sum of money. Are you prepared to pay that sum?'

The crab answered with an assuring smile, 'Do you think we are short of funds? When ships get wrecked, where do you suppose their treasure goes? All that is rightfully ours. Now, let us know how much you charge for your fee.'

Khalifa said, 'If you give me two bundles of currency notes, I can proceed.'

The crab took two bundles of gold coins from the turtle's back and threw those down in front of Khalifa. He had made many royal robes, many outfits for fops and bridegrooms, but none had offered him two bundles of gold coins.

The moment Konkaboti saw those gold coins, she pleaded with the crab with all humility, 'Ogo, I appeal to you, please give me those coins! O, please do! My father adores money, and he will celebrate if he gets this. I agree to be your queen with these shabby clothes of mine, I don't need richer garments. I fall at your feet, give me those coins, I'll give those to my father.'

The crab chided Konkaboti, saying, 'I am surprised to find that you are such a disobedient girl. Haven't I told you once that you, being a mere child, should not interrupt when the elders talk? Just hold your tongue, and watch how we go about it.'

What could Konkaboti do? She fell silent. Khalifa got the gold coins, and was on cloud nine. He said, 'Let me go inside the house, and bring out the finest of fabrics. I will make your queen the royal robe in no time at all.'

Khalifa went in with the two bundles of gold coins. Elated to the bone, and grinning from ear to ear, he showed those coins to his wife.

His wife was gobsmacked. 'Wonder of wonders! How fortune has suddenly smiled on us!' she thought. Then she spoke, 'Now, with these coins you must make me a diamond-studded amulet, okay?'

Khalifa then took Konkaboti inside his house. He told his wife, 'She is a queen. Her name is Konkaboti. I will have to make her a royal robe. Take her measurements with care!'

Khalifa's wife took the girl's measurements. Khalifa put many people on the job and made the robe with extreme swiftness. His wife made Konkaboti wear that robe with great care. Adorned in that attire, Konkaboti cut a real dash, and her grace dazzled everybody.

The wife said, 'O what an enchanting beauty!'

Khalifa murmured, 'Her loveliness is bewitching!'

Everyone around said, 'Such beauty is matchless!'

The royal robe having been prepared, the crab and the turtle wended their way homewards with Konkaboti. They crossed many rivers and many lands to reach their place under the river water. There, everybody was overwhelmed with Konkaboti's captivating charm and her grand apparel. They all hailed her wholeheartedly. Everyone said, 'We are really lucky to have a queen like Konkaboti!'

Now a great worry descended on them. The aquatic animals started to wonder where they would accommodate their queen. And this queen was no ordinary queen, this was Queen Konkaboti! The palace must be embellished, ornamented and marvellous enough to befit the enthralling and radiant grace of the Queen herself. Thinking hard and long on it, they unanimously decided that for Queen Konkaboti, the *Motimohol* would be the most appropriate accommodation. The word '*moti*' means 'pearl', so 'motimohol' is a place where a pearl resides.

Now the fishes, like Rohu and the others, told Konkaboti with joined palms, 'Queen Konkaboti, Your Highness, please oblige us by consenting to live in the Motimohol, which is a dwelling befitting your glory and majesty.'

Greeting Konkaboti with such reverential words, the fishes showed her an oyster. Since an oyster contains a pearl, it is called motimohol. Konkaboti stepped into that oyster. And from within that oyster, Konkaboti started discharging her queenly duties.

Notes

1. 'Crabbabu': Babu is a suffix to a male name used as a mark of respect.
2. 'I have silk, ... and even brocades from Benaras': In the nineteenth century, and even in the twentieth, Benaras was famous for the fabrics mentioned. There is a special brand of silk sari called 'Benarosi', which is a traditional bridal outfit for Bengalis even now.

4
The Milkwoman

Some days passed. It so happened that a milkwoman stepped into that river. While she was taking a bath, that woman's feet brushed against the oyster shell which housed Konkaboti. The woman took a dip, and picked that oyster up. She found the oyster really beautiful. She took it home, and tucked it in the slats that thatched her hut.

Bolting her hut door from the outside, the milkwoman went out every day to distribute milk to her customers. At that time, Konkaboti stepped out of the oyster. The first day, as soon as she put her foot on the ground, her royal robe vanished, and her previous outfit took its place. Konkaboti was stupefied to notice this change. Every day, emerging from the oyster, she did all the household chores for the milkwoman. She tidied her room, scrubbed her utensils, cooked rice and byanjon, and then, she herself ate, and readied the meal for the milkwoman.

When the milkwoman came back home, she was astounded. She thought to herself, 'Who is it that does all my work? The door remains locked just as I leave it while going out. Nobody has entered the house from outside. Then who is the person that does all this?'

The milkwoman was baffled, and remained clueless. The same thing was repeated every day.

Then at last, the milkwoman thought, 'I must find who the person is. I must know who does all my work.'

Having made up her mind, that day the milkwoman came home early. Quietly and gingerly she opened the door, and lo, she found an exceedingly beautiful girl scrubbing her utensils!

Noticing the milkwoman, Konkaboti hastened to get back into the oyster, but before she could retreat, the milkwoman got hold of her. And having caught her, the milkwoman was startled to find that the girl was none other than Konkaboti.

Mystified, the milkwoman asked her, 'Konkaboti, is it you? How come you are here? I heard that you were drowned in the river!'

Konkaboti answered, 'Yes, *masi*, I am Konkaboti indeed! And yes, I was really drowned. I took refuge in that oyster under the water. Now, you have brought that oyster home, and lodged it in the laths thatching your hut. That was how, masi, I entered your house.'

The milkwoman figured everything out. Now things fell into place for her.

Konkaboti told her, 'Masi, don't tell my people at home now that I am here. If I go back empty-handed, father may haul me over the coals. I saw a pile of wealth underwater. They gave tons of money to the tailor, but nothing to me. I pleaded with them with tearful eyes to give me some, but still they declined. If perchance they give me some, I will give it to father. Father then will not upbraid me, nor will brother abuse me.'

The milkwoman said, 'O my dear child! What a beastly father is he who wants to marry off such a gem of a daughter to Jonardon Choudhuri! Wait, if ever I meet that fellow, I will give him a sound talking-to that will exorcise his ghost of greed.'

Konkaboti answered, 'No, masi, don't be rude to my father. You know, masi, father is an unhappy man. He has to feed many every day. How can he run his family unless he sells me?'

It was then decided that Konkaboti would reside for some days in the milkwoman's house.

Konkaboti said, 'Masi, I know you go out to my locality every day. Please narrate to me the day-to-day happenings there.'

Konkaboti thus stayed back in the milkwoman's house. The milkwoman reported to her what she saw and heard while selling milk in her locality.

One day, the milkwoman told Konkaboti, 'Aha, Khetu's mother has taken seriously ill! The chances of her survival are slim.'

Konkaboti was mortified to hear this, and with a tear-choked voice, she eagerly asked her, 'What's her ailment, masi? Please tell me what it is.'

The milkwoman answered, 'I have heard that she has a delirious fever. Khetu went to call in a *boidyo*. But he refused to come. He reportedly said, "I can't go, for if I do, I will have to lose my caste!"'

Konkaboti said, 'Masi, she loves me a lot! She is like my own mother to me! That I am not being able to do something for her at such a critical moment of her life is breaking my heart.'

Konkaboti started to weep profusely.

Next day, early at dawn, Konkaboti said, 'Masi, please go to my locality early today. And come back soon to let me know how she is.'

The milkwoman did as told and reported back to Konkaboti, 'Aha, what mournful news, Khetu's mother is no more! She has passed away! Khetu is going from door to door to take his mother to the *ghat*, but none is willing to help him out. Everyone is saying, "You have eaten 'borokh', you have lost your caste. If we take your mother to cremate, we too will lose ours." Shnareshwor Chakraborty, Gobordhon Shiromoni and, Konkaboti, your father too are going around forbidding everyone to take part in the funeral procession.'

This news simply felled Konkaboti. She started to wail inconsolably. The milkwoman tried to console her. She said, 'Konkaboti, please stop crying. Konkaboti, please get up, and take some food.' But, Konkaboti did not get up, did not cook, and did not take her food that day. She lay on the ground and just wept ceaselessly.

In the evening, Konkaboti said, 'Masi, please go to my locality once again. Find out what is happening there right now, and report everything to me quickly.'

The milkwoman went as instructed. The evening darkened to night, but the milkwoman did not return. It was already one prohor of the night, but still she did not come back. Konkaboti wept her eyes out, looking at the road and lying on the ground.

As the first prohor of the night got over, the milkwoman came back.

The milkwoman said, 'Konkaboti, the news that I have heard is really heart-rending! None came forward to take the corpse of Khetu's mother to cremate. What could Khetu do in such a situation? In the evening, he collected bundles of sticks for fuel and carried those on his head to the riverbank. Aha, how could he carry so many faggots at one go! He had to repeat this three times. Now, he is carrying his mother's corpse to the bank. A dead body is heavy. The burning ghat is quite far. Carrying her alone, he has to stop often to rest. It is a dark night all round. I have watched all this from a distance.'

Hearing this, Konkaboti took to thinking for a little while. Then she got up slowly, went forward to unbolt the door, stepped outside the house, and started running post-haste.

The milkwoman kept asking, 'Konkaboti, where are you going?'

But to no avail. Today, Konkaboti was not a great queen, this Konkaboti was a mad woman. She was not clad in any royal robe, she wore a shabby piece of cloth belonging to the milkwoman. Today her face was not radiant like a full moon, but dark as a storm cloud.

Bolting out of the milkwoman's house, the dowdily-clad, dishevelled-haired, grief-frenzied Konkaboti rushed towards the burning ghat.

The milkwoman followed her up to a certain distance, saying, 'Konkaboti, wait, Konkaboti, listen to me!' But Konkaboti had no ear for her words, and did not once look back.

Like an eclipsed full moon, Konkaboti soon disappeared into the engulfing darkness of the night. The milkwoman lost track of her. She came back home, weeping.

5

The Burning Ghat

The hysterical Konkaboti dashed towards the burning ghat, oblivious of everything else. Having gone a certain distance, she saw that Khetu had laid his mother's corpse on the ground, her head on his lap. Khetu was staring at his mother's face, and crying. Tears were coursing down incessantly from his eyes.

Konkaboti stole up and stood by his side quietly. The night was dark, so Khetu could not see her.

Khetu looked at his mother's face, and said 'Ma! You too are on your way, then? When Konkaboti went away, I thought that I would end this inconsequential life. Ma, it was only for you that I had been living so long. Now, ma, you too have departed! Now, of what use is this life to me? I am absolutely out on a limb now. For whom, and for what, will I live? Useless it is to live in this songsar, useless to plough a lonely furrow. It is too full of sins and sorrows! Konkaboti, you were absolutely right to have deserted it! And, ma, you too have made the right choice to turn your back on this sinful earth! I too will soon follow you and Konkaboti to the place you are now in. This earth hemmed in by oceans has turned into a cremation ground for me. I now have none to call my own in this songsar. Don't worry, ma, I'll soon be following you to your place to soothe my parched soul. Ma, tell Konkaboti that I'll meet her soon.'

Konkaboti stood before Khetu with bowed head. Khetu was startled, but failed to recognise her in the pervasive darkness.

Konkaboti sat at his dead mother's feet. She took up her feet on to her lap. She rested her head on those feet, and wept silently.

Khetu was amazed, and gazed at her face for a long time.

At last, Khetu said, 'Konkaboti! I have never wished ill for anybody in all my days on earth; rather, I have wished everyone's well-being. I have never lied consciously, have never deceived anybody, and have never done a wrong deed. For what grievous sin am I then subjected to this retribution? Why have I been through such hell? I have borne everything, including persecution by my village folk, the death by drowning of the darling of my heart, which was you, Konkaboti, and also ma's death, ma who was more precious even than life to me, but I have never dreamt in my wildest dreams that at such a critical time of my life, you, Konkaboti, would come and be my tormentor. I can no longer carry my mother's corpse. Because of her sickness, I have neither been able to take a bite of food for three days running, nor sleep a wink. For three days now, I have not sipped even a drop of water. I don't have any strength left, I am at the end of my tether. I cannot move even one inch forward with ma's body. I am at my wit's end about what to do. And at this moment of crisis, you, Konkaboti, have come to me as a ghost to scare me? My cup of misery is now full! I cannot take it any longer.'

In a tear-choked voice, and with bowed head, Konkaboti replied, 'I am not a ghost. I have not died. I am alive.'

Khetu, astonished, asked, 'You are alive? You were drowned, and we made a thorough search for you. But we found no trace of you. I thought about taking my life too. So I dived into the water. Although I know how to swim, I resolutely refrained from swimming, and stayed put under the water. I held out long enough, but after that, I fainted. Some fishermen picked me up in that unconscious state, and saved my life. When I came back to my senses, I found ma crying. I went on living for her sake. Konkaboti, how were you saved?'

Konkaboti replied, 'That is a long story. I will tell the details later on. I was in the milkwoman masi's house. It was from her that

I heard about this crisis of yours. I could not stay back, and so came running here. Now come, let us take your ma to be cremated. You hold one side, I will hold the other.'

Thus, Konkaboti and Khetu took the corpse to the burning ghat. The two of them arranged the pyre. They bathed the body well, and wrapped a new sari around it. Then they laid it on the pyre. They wept long at the feet of the corpse.

Khetu said, 'So, ma, you are on your way to heaven. Please bless this poor child of yours so that I do not deviate from the path of truth. Bless me so that truth be my goal, truth be my knowledge, and truth be my work. Bless me so that desire for wealth or pleasure does not deflect me from the path of truth and of dharma, so that I do not shy away from my duty like those timid and base people, scared of the scowls and frowns of an ignorant and deceitful society. O ma, bless me so that I, being a man, do not turn a coward even in the face of death.'

Konkaboti said, 'Ma, you are on your way to heaven. Please have pity on this orphaned Konkaboti. Bless me so that dharma be my thought and dharma be my vocation whether I am awake or asleep or dreaming. What else shall I say! You know everything about what is in Konkaboti's mind. Even if she loses her life, Konkaboti will preserve her dharma. Even if the sun does not rise in the east, but on some other side, even if a cataclysm occurs, none will be able to make Konkaboti stray from the path of dharma, if she be a chaste woman. This has been the resolve of my mind all along, and today, I once again make this resolve and speak it out touching your feet. O ma, your Konkaboti is now out of her mind, please forgive her faults.'

Khetu said, 'Konkaboti, how can I possibly ignite the pyre? How shall I bring myself to bid farewell to ma for good! I shall never see her again. Come, Konkaboti, let us gaze long at ma's face once again.'

Khetu stood near his mother's body, and ran his fingers through her hair. Konkaboti stood by, and kept on shedding tears.

Khetu said, 'See, Konkaboti, how calm and peaceful ma's face looks! It is as if she is sleeping happily. Konkaboti, do you remember when, in your childhood, you would play about with the cat, and could not read the first part of your primer and I would scold you, ma would get cross with me? Ma loved you as much she did me. Aha! Konkaboti! What a mother we have lost!'

Bemoaning like this, and circumambulating the pyre, Khetu lit it. The pyre started burning with leaping flames.

Khetu and Konkaboti sat near the pyre, wept from time to time, uttered words of lamentation and exchanged words on other matters. Konkaboti told Khetu the story of how she was saved from drowning in the river water. Khetu thought to himself that grief had unhinged Konkaboti's mind. It was as if the streak of sorrow never ends! Khetu now had a new source of agony. But he did not speak his mind.

When they had done with his mother's last rites, Khetu and Konkaboti went to the river to bathe.

Then Khetu said, 'Konkaboti, come, I'll escort you to your home.'

Konkaboti answered, 'How shall I go back home again? For if I do, father will certainly give me a mouthful, and brother will tell me unkind things. Let me go back underwater and live with the fishes, or return to milkwoman masi's.'

Khetu said, 'Konkaboti, one should not do such things. Go home you must. No matter how much you suffer, you have to put up with everything, living at home. Pay attention to my words! Talking like a small girl will not do now. We are driven about by this songsar like two flimsy boats tossed and buffeted by tremendous waves in the vast expanse of a turbulent ocean. So, Konkaboti, now we will have to talk sense, and act responsibly. I want to hear from you prudent and solemn words like those you spoke when you sat clasping ma's feet. Maybe man doesn't have total control over things to come, still he does have *some*. Otherwise, why do farmers sow seeds for future crops? Why do men put in work in this songsar with so much industry and gusto? Due to man's ignorance, he enjoys varying degrees of control over future events. This wait for the result of the work done is what constitutes man's hope and faith. Relying on that hope and faith, today I'll be taking leave of you. Come, let me escort you to your home. Because you stepped out of your house, Jonardon Choudhuri will not marry you now. And it is not possible for your father to quickly arrange your marriage elsewhere. For one year, put up with whatever harassment your father and brother mete out to you. I have heard that in the western part of the country there are better-paid jobs. Now, I'll be leaving for the west. I will perform ma's shraddho in Kashi,[1] and then look for a job. Whatever I manage to earn in the next one year, I will offer to your father. If I do that, I am certain your father will be only too glad to fulfil the desire of my heart. It is only a matter of one year, Konkaboti. Time will fly. Stay this one year at home somehow, whether in sorrow or in happiness.'

Konkaboti said, 'I will do what you command me to.'

The two slowly made their way towards their village. It was not dawn yet when the two arrived at the door of Tonu Roy's house.

Khetu said, 'Konkaboti, let me take leave then. Take care.'

But Khetu could not quite leave that spot even if he intended to. He could not move his feet, as it were. Tears shed by both of them drenched Tonu Roy's door.

Khetu plucked up some courage and went some distance away, but returned soon, and said, 'Konkaboti, I forgot to tell you one thing well enough, that is—"Be extremely careful."'

Once again the two started talking. With the dawn breaking, people's noises could be heard all around.

Then Khetu said, 'Konkaboti, now I must go. Take extreme care of yourself. Do not give way to tears. I will come back after one year if I manage to stay alive. Then our sorrow will come to an end. Tell everything to your mother, but you need not let the others know anything.'

Khetu departed this time. Unblinkingly, Konkaboti gazed at the way in which he went as far as she could see. Then tears blurred her vision, and soon it was darkness all round. She stood leaning against the wall by the door, lest she should swoon and collapse. Khetu turned round and saw Konkaboti standing like a painted image. And then he lost sight of her altogether.

Khetu thought, 'O my lord, how hard is the human heart! I have left that pale, lustreless image of the golden goddess behind, but my heart is not yet rent asunder!'

Note

1. Kashi: A neighbourhood in modern-day Benaras in Uttar Pradesh in modern India. One of the oldest Indian cities, called the city of temples, and in common Bengali parlance often deemed synonymous with Benaras.

6

The Tiger

When Khetu went out of sight, Konkaboti stood leaning against the wall by the side of the door for a long time, weeping profusely. She did not have the courage to push the door open. Then she braced herself and pushed the door gently.

By that time, Tonu Roy had left his bed, and was smoking tobacco. He went out to see who it was that was pushing the door. And he saw that it was Konkaboti!

Seeing her, Tonu Roy said, 'What, Konkaboti, is it you? Have you not died? But this is understandable. How are you supposed to die, after all! Where were you all this while? And where did you come from now? Go back to the place where you had stayed so long. I can accommodate you no longer in my house!'

Konkaboti did not step inside. In her faded, wet clothes, she stood by the side of the door, and went on weeping. She gave no answer to what her father said.

Hearing his father rumble and grumble, the son too came to the spot.

Her brother addressed Konkaboti, 'O, the damnable sinner is back again! Where else will you go, after all? But we are in no position to take you back; we can no longer feed you, dear! Don't think that Jonardon Choudhuri will marry you! Father, before the neighbours get wind of her coming back, drive this sinful black sheep away this very moment!'

These angry words of the father and the son brought Konkaboti's two sisters out. And her mother came too. She saw that the sorrow-laden Konkaboti, clad in pale, tattered clothes, was crying, standing by the door, and her husband and son were about to drive her away with cruel words.

Konkaboti's mother did not speak a word to anybody. She did not cast a single glance at her husband or son. She clasped Konkaboti to her bosom, and said softly with great affection, 'Come, dear child, you're back home. Where have you been so long, forgetting your woebegone mother?'

Konkaboti rested her head on her mother's bosom, and that soothed her parched soul. The terrible blaze that was raging in her heart was now largely doused.

Then her mother took Konkaboti by an arm. And with the other hand she held the arm of another daughter of hers. Addressing her husband and son, she said, 'You have a plan to chase Konka away? You won't accommodate her in your house? Indeed! Tell me what grievous wrong has this child committed that she will have to forfeit her place with her parents? Very well then, you two stay in ease and luxury here with all your honour and social prestige, and let us four hapless women get out of this place. Come, child, let us all move out. We will beg for alms from door to door, but never touch the food offered by these sages and saints.'

The mother, with the three daughters, did look set to troop out. Now, Tonu Roy felt afraid.

He said, '*Grihini*, O wife, what's this you are up to? Have you gone out of your mind? Just think what am I supposed to do with this girl? Will she ever get married? That is why I say, let her go wherever she likes, and let us have nothing to do with her.'

Tonu Roy's wife said, 'Konkaboti will not get married, is that what you said? Okay, you needn't bother about that, leave the matter of her marriage to me. But the fact is, you are not really worried about that. What pains you is that you have lost the money that Jonardon Choudhuri promised. Anyway, we don't want to be a thorn in your side. We will go we don't know where. Holding my daughters' hands, I'll beg for alms from door to door.'

Seeing this inflamed image of his wife, Tonu Roy thought, 'What calamity!' He tried to console his wife with coaxing and cajoling. When his wife calmed down considerably, Tonu Roy said, 'Don't rave like a crank. Go inside the house. And Konkaboti, child, you too go in.'

Konkaboti went inside the house along with her mother and sisters. She resumed living with her parents. She gave her mother a full account of what had happened to her after leaving home. Neither Konkaboti nor her mother shared these tales with anybody else.

Tonu Roy never missed an opportunity to castigate Konkaboti, or to make snide remarks about her. She did not retort, and swallowed all those insults with lowered head.

Tonu Roy said, 'I set your marriage up with such a kingly bridegroom. It was your ill luck that failed you, what could I do? I tried so hard to get Jonardon Choudhuri round to marry you, but he was adamant not to. Now what can I do with this daughter of mine? None is prepared to pay even fifty rupees to marry her.'

Tonu Roy and his wife had tiffs over this from time to time. His wife said, 'You needn't worry about my Konka's marriage. Just stay put for one year. I myself will marry her off. But in case you do not pay heed to my words, and try to bring matters to a head, I will simply march out of your house with these three daughters of mine.'

Tonu Roy had grown old. He feared his wife these days, and now did not dare to chastise her as before.

One year passed like this. But Khetu did not come, nor was there any news of him. Konkaboti's face turned paler with each passing day, and her mother was worried sick. If perchance her husband told her a thing or two about Konkaboti's marriage, she now did not venture to answer arrogantly back. As the days wore on after that one year, Tonu Roy's censure became more strident.

Konkaboti's mother maintained an embarrassed silence in the face of all that.

One evening, Tonu Roy said, 'This girl is now grown up, what will I do with her? Let alone good grooms, even bad grooms are difficult to come by.'

Konkaboti's mother replied, 'You have waited for one year, now wait for a few more days. A good bridegroom will be there for the taking.'

Tonu Roy said, 'You have been harping on the same theme for more than a year now. I don't know where you expect your "good bridegroom" to emerge from. It is because I listened to you that I have now ended up in the soup. If, on the day of her return, I had shooed away this tarnisher of our family pride, I wouldn't have had to face the music. Now I see I will have to do what the kings of olden times used to. In case I don't find a Brahman, I will marry her off to a *chondal*. In case I don't find a human, I will have to marry her off to an animal. My whole body is seething with rage. To speak the truth, if a tiger from the forest approaches me now, wishing to marry Konkaboti, I will agree even to that marriage. If this very moment the tiger comes, and says, "Roy mohashoy, open the door, please," I will at once do so.'

No sooner had he uttered these words than a dreadful roar was heard outside. Somebody growled out, 'Roy mohashoy, will you then really open the door?'

That sound sent a shiver down Tonu Roy's spine. He had no clue as to what it was that was growling. He opened the door gingerly, and, to his consternation, found a humongous tiger standing outside!

The tiger said, 'Roy mohashoy, this very moment you have promised you will willingly marry Konkaboti off to a tiger if it comes in, wishing to marry her. That is why I have come, now marry her off to me right at this moment, or else I will devour you.'

True, Tonu Roy was frightened out of his wits, and absolutely flummoxed, but even so, he did not forget his business.

Tonu Roy said, 'Once I have promised, I will surely marry my daughter off to you. I never go back on my word. But I suppose you know my terms and conditions regarding marrying off my daughters. If you take care to preserve my family pride, I do not object to the proposed wedding at all.'

The tiger asked, 'Exactly how much do you need to preserve your family pride?'

Tonu Roy said, 'I am a Brahman of prestigious lineage. I do not take water before I perform my evening prayers.[1] To become the son-in-law of such a devoted Brahman is a matter of great honour. So if you cherish the desire of becoming my son-in-law, you should be prepared to preserve my prestige. You have to spend a decent amount.'

The tiger replied, 'I know that well. Now come clean on the amount you have to be paid.'

Tonu Roy said, "My daughter's marriage was fixed with Jonardon Choudhuri, the honourable zamindar of this village. By some accident, that marriage failed to materialise. Choudhuri mohashoy had agreed to pay two thousand rupees. He was a human, and a Brahman and of my own caste. You must admit that you are no match for him. So you need to pay a little more.'

The tiger said, 'Let us go inside the house. I will give you so much money that you have never seen, nor have ever dreamed of.'

Saying this, and growling thunderously, the tiger entered the house. Tonu Roy's blood now ran cold. He thought that the tiger would now gobble up the entire family. But he was helpless, so he followed the tiger into the house.

After they heard the tiger's roar, Konkaboti, along with her mother and sisters, had been sitting numbed with fear. Tonu Roy's son was not at home then, he had gone out for a stroll! He was a man with qualities, and so he never came home till late at night.

The tiger came to the spot where Konkaboti sat with the others. And there, it threw down a fat purse.

The tiger said, 'Open it, and see what is inside.'

Tonu Roy untied the bundle, and saw that it was filled with gold coins. He picked those up, and examined them thoroughly in the light by adjusting his glasses time and again. At last he was convinced that they were not fake. Everyone was bemused as to how this wealth had come to this tiger's possession. Tonu Roy's heart leapt up in joy.

He thought, 'Now, at long last, I have found a really good bridegroom.'

He went near the lamp, and started counting the coins.

Meanwhile, the tiger slowly approached Konkaboti and her mother, and told them, 'Don't be afraid.'

Konkaboti and her mother were startled. They instantly knew whose voice it was. That voice gave them courage. Not only courage, an ecstasy filled their hearts. Konkaboti's mother murmured, 'O my God, I wish it were all true.'

The tiger said this, then went back to Tonu Roy again and sat placing its paws on the ground. Tonu Roy counted three thousand gold coins from the purse.

The tiger asked, 'So, what now?'

Tonu Roy said, 'What else? When I have given my word, I will marry my daughter off to you tonight itself. You needn't worry about that. And never think that I have any disregard for you because you are a tiger. O no, I am not that type of a man. I know pretty well how, and to whom, to show respect. Let alone Jonardon Choudhuri, even if his father comes to me, and bows and scrapes, pleading with me to marry my daughter off to him, I'll stand my ground stoutly, and refuse to offer my daughter to him instead of you.'

Then Tonu Roy told his wife, 'Don't attempt to oppose my words, for if you do, there will be hell to pay. I am obliged to offer my daughter to him. A bridegroom like him I will never come across in this universe. I will heed nobody's words in this matter. In case you weep, I will ask the tiger mohashoy to devour you all.'

Tonu Roy's wife said, 'Do whatever you wish. I will not be in the way.'

Those who have money have no reason for anxiety. Tonu Roy sent for his son right at that moment, the neighbours trooped in then, the barber and priest came in too,[2] all arrangements were made for marriage in that instant.

That very night, the tiger and Konkaboti tied the knot. Who does not feel elated having a ferocious tiger of the forest as one's son-in-law? So Tonu Roy was virtually on top of the world that night.

He told his neighbours, 'Make merry with my son-in-law, and make sure that he has his fill of enjoyment.'

Tonu Roy told the bridegroom, '*Babaji*, you will have to sing in the *basor*. Have you rehearsed your song? Mere roaring and growling won't do here. Your sisters-in-law will then twist your ears.[3] They won't let even a tiger go scot-free.'

A bridegroom or a captive! The tiger sat with lowered head. Whether he really sang in the basor only his sisters-in-law and grannies can tell. How are we supposed to know all that?

Before daybreak, the tiger told Tonu Roy, 'Mohashoy, I must go back to the forest from this human habitation while it's still dark. So send your bedecked daughter to go along with me without delay.'

The female neighbours coiffed Konkaboti's hair. And Konkaboti's mother pulled out her daughter's choicest clothes from the wardrobe.

Noticing this, Tonu Roy told his wife with bloodshot eyes, 'I have never seen a fool like you. One who has such a spendthrift wife in his house can never prosper. Tell me, what does the tiger lack? He will roar his way into a cloth merchant's shop, the shopkeeper will turn tail, and the tiger will carry away the bundles of clothes. He will growl into the goldsmith's, the poor chap will dash off hell for leather to save his life, and the tiger will carry off the jewellery. When I've found such an excellent bridegroom, why then pack so many rich garments for her? That is why I say that you are the stupidest person in the whole world.'

Tonu Roy was a frugal fellow; he was the last person to brook waste. Before his mother shuffled off her mortal coil, she had lain in bed. When she was gasping, Tonu Roy laid her on a tattered mat. His mother then wore a not-too-old sari. When she was about to breathe her last, Tony Roy took that piece of cloth off from her body, and wrapped a shabby, shredded one around her. As he was busy with this strenuous activity, Tonu Roy failed to put even a drop of water into his dying mother's mouth.[4] When he laid her down finally with deep respect he found that his mother had long since expired.

Reproached by her husband, Tonu Roy's wife tied a bundle or two of rags and scraps. She handed those bundles over to Konkaboti, and then bade her adieu with tearful eyes, repeatedly invoking the names of deities.

Notes

1. 'I do not take water ... evening prayers ...': This is a must-do for devout Bengali Brahmans even now, and is called '*ahnnik*'.
2. '... the barber and priest came in too ...': They are two important personages for Bengali Hindu weddings. The barber cuts nails and shaves, while the priest performs rituals and chants mantras.
3. '... Your sisters-in-law ... your ears ...': This jesting gesture on the part of the sisters-in-law of the bridegroom was common in Bengali Hindu weddings, especially in the nineteenth century.
4. '... failed to put ... dying mother's mouth': Putting a drop of water into a dying parent's mouth is deemed among Hindus to be a solemn duty of a son.

7

In the Forest

Carrying those bundles, Konkaboti came near the tiger and stood by him with bowed head. The tiger said in a pleasant tone, 'Konkaboti, you are a girl. I am afraid you cannot travel far. Get on my back so that I can carry you. This will not trouble me even a wee bit.'

Konkaboti tied the end of her sari around her waist tightly, and then got on the tiger's back. The tiger said, 'Konkaboti, hold tight to the hair on my back. Take care that you do not fall.'

Konkaboti did just that. The tiger now sprinted towards the forest.

When he reached the middle of it, the tiger asked, 'Konkaboti, do you feel the jitters?'

Konkaboti answered, 'Why should I when I have you for company?'

Although Konkaboti spoke these words, the fact was that she was not absolutely unafraid. Never had she ridden a tiger before. No wonder she would have butterflies in her stomach on her first tiger ride.

The tiger said, 'Konkaboti, I will tell you later why I have become a tiger. Soon I will get rid of this state, and you should not worry about that. But for the present, do not ask me any question.'

Conversing like this, the two went along. At last they came to a large and towering hill.

The tiger said, 'Konkaboti, please close your eyes. Don't open them until I tell you to.'

Konkaboti closed her eyes at the tiger's bidding. And the tiger ran at the double. A little while later, the noise of a horrible loud giggle pierced Konkaboti's ears.

Konkaboti said, 'Oh what dreadful, blood-curdling laughter! Who laughed like that?'

The tiger replied, 'I will tell you that later on. There's no need to know it at this moment. Now you can open your eyes, you needn't fear any more.'

Konkaboti opened her eyes and found that they had reached a grand mansion. It was an exceedingly elegant building, made of white marble and encrusted with priceless gems and pearls. The inner chambers were plush and spick and apan, filled with treasure and adorned with various designs. Konkaboti was amazed to see diamonds, pearls, gems, gold and silver piled high all over the place. The mansion was inside the hill and not visible from the outside. Only a densely dark tunnel from the side of the hill opened on to it. The light from the top of the hill entered the mansion. But even that path of light was so cleverly hidden and skilfully located that neither could a flying creature or land animal slide into it, nor could anyone from inside the mansion go out. Within the mansion, robes and ornaments, beds and cots lay scattered aplenty. Only articles of food were lacking.

Entering the mansion, the tiger said, 'Konkaboti, now get down from my back. Sit here for a while; I'll be coming back soon. But careful, do not touch or pick up anything. Take only those things that I will hand over to you, never touch anything on your own.'

Having cautioned Konkaboti in this manner, the tiger left the place. A little while later, Khetu came there and stood before Konkaboti. Khetu asked, 'Konkaboti, can you recognise me?' Konkaboti sat, her eyes downcast.

Khetu asked again, 'Konkaboti, do you feel afraid having come to the middle of this dense forest?'

Konkaboti said mildly, 'No, I do not. On seeing you, I should have covered my head with a veil,[1] and should also have been bashful.

But I am unable to do it in this situation. So I am wondering what you will think of me.'

Khetu said, 'No, Konkaboti, you do not need to wear a veil, nor feel shy in front of me. Rest assured that I won't think ill of you. Moreover, in this place there is no one except you and me, so what's there to feel embarrassed about? But even so, we should not think that we are completely safe here, for there are plenty of perils lurking.'

Konkaboti said, 'What are they?'

Khetu replied, 'You needn't know of all that right now, for if you do, you'll be frightened. Don't ask me questions about that now. But this much I can tell you that unless you touch any material here, you will be in no danger. Take only what I put in your hand, and don't touch anything on your own. We will have to put up in this place for one year. Thereafter, this raft of wealth and riches will be ours. We will take along all this wealth to our land. Well, Konkaboti, tell me one thing—could you recognise me when I married you?'

Konkaboti answered, 'Yes, I could. For one whole year I had been waiting eagerly for your arrival. When the year was over, and you didn't show up, mother and I got terribly disappointed. What shall I tell of the tears that we two shed then! When father said last night, "I will marry Konkaboti off to a tiger," and, hearing those words, you said, "Okay, mohashoy, open the door," I discerned a known voice in the tiger's growl. And later, when you came near mother and me, and whispered, "You needn't fear," I was sure that you were not a tiger.'

Khetu said, 'We have suffered a lot, Konkaboti, both you and I. Only for one more year we need to stay here, bearing pain. Then, God willing, happy days will arrive for us. This one year will elapse in no time. After that, all this wealth will be ours. Dear O dear, ma is no more! What will we do with this huge wealth? I wonder. Had ma been alive, I would have her attend and perform all holy ceremonies. Anyway, this world is teeming with the poor and the destitute, with the sorrowful. Konkaboti, together we will spend our lives trying to remove the miseries of the world as much as we can.'

Konkaboti asked, 'When you had done with your ma's funeral, and escorted me to my house, where did you go? And what did you do then? Why did it take more than a year for you to return? Why did you take the shape of a tiger? Won't you tell me all that now?'

Khetu said, 'No, Konkaboti, not now. Let one year pass, and then I will tell you everything.'

Konkaboti asked no more questions.

Konkaboti and Khetu started dwelling in that mansion inside the hill. Konkaboti would not touch anything stored in the mansion. She took only those things that Khetu handed over to her.

Inside the mansion, there was everything except food. Khetu went out every day to collect fruits and roots from the forest, and they both ate them and spent their days. While venturing out, Khetu took the form of the tiger. He never went out in any other guise. Having entered the mansion, he again turned into a human. Konkaboti had no clue why Khetu assumed the look of a tiger while going out. Since Khetu had forbidden her to ask questions about this, she had no option but to refrain from it.

Ten months passed like this.

One day, Konkaboti said, 'It has been long since I last saw ma. I yearn to see her. Ma too has not heard from us. Probably, she too is worried. She does not have the faintest idea about where we went and what we did after that night we got married.'

Khetu answered, 'I did not give them any news because we will soon be returning home. What is more, I will have to travel to the human locality in the guise of a tiger, which is why I feel disinclined to go there. Who can tell what peril waits? Anyway, since you desire to visit your ma, I will ensure that. Tomorrow evening I will take you to your ma's. Konkaboti, it is now only two months for the year to end. You may stay with your parents for these two months if you so wish.'

Konkaboti said, 'No, I don't want that. How can it be that you will stay all alone in this forest beset with perils, and I will stay at my ma's? I'm anxious to see ma, I will go and visit her once, and then come back.'

Note

1. '... On seeing you I should ... a veil ...': It was customary for a Bengali Hindu wife in days of yore to hide her face behind a veil called 'ghomta', 'gunthon' or 'obogunthon' in front of her husband, especially during their first close meeting. Such a gesture of bashfulness was deemed becoming of a bride.

8

The In-laws

The next evening, Khetu, in the form of a tiger, asked Konkaboti to ride on his back. He took oodles of money from the mansion for Konkaboti, and said, 'Give this to your mother, father, brother and sisters.'

Stepping out of the mansion, the two went along the dark tunnel. While coming out of the tunnel, Khetu asked Konkaboti to shut her eyes. She again heard that blood-curdling laugh. Entering the forest, Khetu asked her to open her eyes. The tiger now dashed towards the village. During the first prohor of the night, the daughter and son-in-law reached Tonu Roy's house.

On seeing Konkaboti again, her mother was in seventh heaven. Konkaboti's sisters too were delighted. Offering a lot of money and gold coins, the tiger saluted Tonu Roy. He gave enough money to his brother-in-law as well. The tiger became everyone's blue-eyed boy.

Konkaboti's mother fed her sumptuously on a five-course dinner. Tonu Roy now started wondering, 'What shall I feed my son-in-law?'

Tonu Roy pondered hard on it, and then said, 'Babaji, you have travelled such a long distance! You must be starving now. But we have only rice and byanjon in our house; I know full well that this stuff is not your food. So I am wondering what to serve you. I suggest you do one thing. I have an old cow in my shed. It was once a milch cow but now it does not calve, so it gives no milk. It is useless, and simply eats. You go and devour it. In that case your stomach will be filled, and I too will feel gratified for treating my son-in-law to a grand dinner. We will not have to collect hay for the animal needlessly.'

The tiger said, 'No, mohashoy, I have already had my fill in the daytime. I am not at all hungry. I am in no position to eat that cow.'

Tonu Roy said, 'Okay, in that case you can do something else. Go and eat Nironjon Kobirotno. That fellow is my arch enemy. He does not know the shastras, but dares to argue with me. I can't stand the sight of him. He, however, has moved out from this village. He has gone to his maternal uncle's, which is six kroshes away. I will give you the details about where to find him; you can easily go and eat him up.'

The tiger replied, 'No, mohashoy, I am not at all hungry tonight. I cannot eat Nironjon Kobirotno.'

Tonu Roy said, 'Okay, if you are loath to travel that far, I can arrange a lavish feast for you here in this village itself. There is a milkwoman living here. That *magi* is extremely wicked. She comes here twice a day, and harangues me. She abuses me for having offered my daughter to you. That magi tells me, "You greedy old rascal, how could you barter your daughter for money?" You are my son-in-law, so you have to redress this. You break her neck, and drink her blood. I am certain that her blood is tasty, and you will feel contented.'

The tiger again said, 'No, mohashoy, I cannot eat her tonight, for I am not hungry.'

Tonu Roy reasoned, 'Sons-in-law are usually shy. They have to be repeatedly entreated before they can be persuaded to eat. When they sit to eat, the people around must beseech them, "Eat this, eat that, eat a little more," otherwise, they do not eat their fill, but get up leaving food on their plates. Their stomach churns with the fire of hunger, but their lips speak, "My hunger is sated, I can eat no more." This is the usual custom with sons-in-law.'

Thinking in this vein, Tonu Roy said, 'Does it look fair if you don't take any food at your in-laws'? If you do this, it will give me a bad name, will it not? And what shall I tell you of the people of this locality? Each one of them is an avatar, as it were! They all like *tamasha*s when somebody is in trouble, and hate to see anybody prosper. That you have become my son-in-law, and that you are quite well off, have made people green with envy. Everyone will be keen to say tomorrow, "Tonu Roy's son-in-law came, but he did not treat him cordially at all. He did not give him even a drop of water to drink." That is why I have been entreating you so persistently to eat a morsel or two. Come, let me show you the hut of that milkwoman. She consumes milk and ghee. Her flesh must be tender. You will find her meat tasty. Can I ask you to eat worthless food!'

The tiger replied, 'Pardon me this time, please. When I come next, I shall see.'

Tonu Roy was slightly put off. A son-in-law is always a person held in affection. If in-laws do not have an opportunity to show their fondness for their son-in-law, they are mortified. Tonu Roy had proposed three scrumptious items of food, but his son-in-law had rebuffed all three. He had the right to be offended, didn't he?

Tonu Roy said, 'One should not come to one's in-laws' with a full stomach. The in-laws find this difficult to accept. If the son-in-law does not take a bite of food, a father or mother-in-law gets deeply distressed. Your mother-in-law will surely chastise me because you haven't taken any food here. She will say, "You didn't entreat our son-in-law well enough, which is why he didn't eat anything." When you come next time, please do not come having eaten your fill. You will dine here. And I have fixed up these three food items for you. Next time you will have to eat all three. If you don't, I will not let you go back to the forest, and will hide your umbrella and wrap to prevent you from going. O no, I am mistaken! You don't have an umbrella or a wrap after all. Okay then, if you don't eat them, I will be angry with you.'

Konkaboti talked to her mother and sisters all night. She told her mother who the tiger really was. She also told her that after two months they would return home with a huge amount of wealth.

Tonu Roy called Konkaboti, and told her confidentially, 'Konkaboti, I have a gut feeling that our son-in-law is not really a tiger. He is that kind of a tiger which a human turns into when he wears a special root from the forest. I offered him so many delicious food items—I asked him to eat the old cow in my cowshed, to eat Nironjon, and also to eat the milkwoman, but he desisted from eating any of them. Had he been a real tiger, would he have been able to resist these tempting offers? That is why I feel that he may not be a real tiger. You have to check whether there is any kind of root on his head. If by chance you find one, burn it down immediately. If somebody had cast a spell on him, he will be all right once that root is burnt. Whatever might be the reason for his turning into a tiger, burning the rogue root will purge him of the curse. After that, he will be able to come to any human habitation in his usual human form.'

Having received this piece of advice from her father, Konkaboti came back to her mother, who asked her, 'What did your father whisper to you?'

Konkaboti divulged her father's advice to her mother.

Hearing this, her mother said, 'Konkaboti, never ever do such a thing. If you do, you will court danger. Khetu is a level-headed and quick-witted lad. Whatever he is doing, he is doing for everybody's good. Don't ever attempt to overrule his words. Careful, Konkaboti, remember what I have just told you!'

When the night was about to end, Khetu and Konkaboti once again started for the forest. When they came near the mountain, Khetu asked Konkaboti to close her eyes as before. Near the entrance of the tunnel, Konkaboti heard that spine-chilling laughter yet again. Having gone inside the mansion, they started spending their days as before.

9 The Root

One more month passed.

Khetu said, 'Konkaboti, just another month remains. We will be free after that. Once this month gets over, we will no longer be forest-dwellers. With this stupendous wealth, we will return to our land.'

With each passing day, Khetu said, 'Konkaboti, we need to spend just twenty-nine days more! Konkaboti, twenty-eight days to go! Konkaboti, twenty-seven days remain!'

Twenty days passed like this. Only ten remained. After these ten days, he would go back to his village with Konkaboti—this thought filled Khetu with boundless joy. His face was always beaming.

Khetu said, 'Konkaboti, do one thing. Scratch ten lines on this wall with a piece of charcoal. Every morning we will wipe out one such line, and thus we would know exactly how many days remain.'

Konkaboti thought, 'My husband is now falling over himself to go back home. I have marked ten lines on the wall, with each passing day I will erase one—this arrangement makes sense all right. But what if I erase all those lines at one go? Can I not rescue my husband in a single day? What's wrong in trying what my father advised? If my husband gets an opportunity to go back to his village today or tomorrow, he will surely be overjoyed.'

In these two months, she had recalled her father's advice several times. The suspicion that some crook had cast an evil spell on her husband crept into her mind time and again. But since her mother had forbidden her, she never attempted to remove that charm. But now, seeing her husband so very eager to return to his homeland, Konkaboti became rather restless.

Konkaboti thought, 'Father is a male. As such, he is supposed to know more about these hills and mountains, woods and forests, tigers and bears, roots and sprigs, charms and spells than mother. Ma is, after all, a woman, and she never ventures out. How can she possibly know how to remove the charm of a root? Father said that if the root is burnt down, the danger will be weeded out. Now, it is ten days more to go, and my husband is counting these days down. If perchance he gets to go home tomorrow itself, how jubilant he will possibly be!'

The whole day Konkaboti contemplated in this vein. Once she thought, 'What if my well-meaning attempt yields bad results? O my God, that will be a real disaster! Better to stubbornly stay put for the next few days. What father advised, mother forbade.'

But then again, she reflected, 'Some scamps cast an evil spell on my husband. I will extricate my husband from their evil designs. If I succeed in doing that, how pleased will he be with me!'

Konkaboti kept on weighing these thoughts in her mind. She could not decide what she should ideally do. She gave way to such thoughts even at night. She remembered the fairy tale of Tiloksundori and Bhushkumro.

The story runs like this. A prince became enamoured of Tiloksundori's beauty. He wished to marry her. But Tiloksundori's stepmother made her wear a root. The charm of that root transformed her into a bird. She flew away and perched on the branch of a tree. The stepmother guilefully arranged the prince's marriage with her daughter Bhushkumro. The prince started to caress her. Seeing this, Tiloksundori cheeped from the tree, 'Bhushkumro is on the lap, Tiloksundori her wings flap.' The prince wondered what it was that the bird chirped.

He beckoned to the bird to come to him. The bird flew in to perch on his hand. Moved by her beauty, the prince ran his fingers over the bird's head. And the movement of his hand flicked the root off. The bird was instantly morphed to Tiloksundori again.

The prince now came to understand the stepmother's wicked ploy. He buried Bhushkumro alive by making her wear thorns all over her body. Then he lived with Tiloksundori happily ever after.

Konkaboti now remembered the Tiloksundori tale. She also remembered stories of this sort in the *Arabian Nights.* She thought, 'This is the way crooks do harm. Let me go and see whether there really is any root on my husband's head.'

Thinking thus, she went to another room and lit a lamp. Carrying that lamp, she came back to search for a root on her husband's head. Khetu was then fast asleep, and had no inkling of all this.

Calamity! While searching, Konkaboti found a root on Khetu's head. She thought, 'Father's guess was absolutely spot on. What an odiously evil design of some rascals this is! Luckily I have found this root, otherwise who knows what would have happened?'

Konkaboti tried to pick up that root from Khetu's head. But the root was so entangled with his hair that she failed to remove it. She could not employ more force lest Khetu woke up. She went to the other room again to get her scissors. Now she cut the strand of hair with which the root was fastened. And she instantly burnt the root down in the flame of her lamp.

The moment the root went up in flames, a pungent stench filled the room. That odour nearly choked Konkaboti. She was now overpowered by fear. Her entire body started trembling.

Khetu suddenly woke up, startled. Putting his hand on his head, he found the root missing. Then he saw Konkaboti standing in front, nonplussed and shuddering, on the brink of swooning.

Just at the moment Konkaboti was about to pass out and fall, Khetu caught hold of her. He took the lamp from her hand, and made her sit. Sprinkling water on her face, Khetu tried to restore her senses.

Feeling better, Konkaboti said, 'I now realise what terrible wrong I have done. Please pardon me.'

With these words, Konkaboti started crying, lowering her head.

Khetu said, 'Konkaboti, it's not your fault. First, it all seems to have been destined, otherwise why should all this befall us after so many days? Then, I erred. If I had revealed everything from the beginning to you, without concealment, you would certainly not have done this, and this accident would never have taken place. Did you burn the root in the flame of the lamp?"

Konkaboti said with a nod, 'Yes, I did.'

Khetu said, 'Okay, you will have to pluck up courage now. You cannot afford to cry like a girl any more. You are all alone in these desolate woods. It is for your sake that I am filled with anxiety. Konkaboti, men of mettle are not scared to die! They worry only for their soon-to-be-widowed wives, or other dependants.'

Alarmed, Konkaboti asked, 'Why? What peril will befall us? Tell me what danger lurks ahead of us.'

Khetu replied, 'If I had enough time to conceal all this, I would. But now, I have no time left to keep these things a secret. You will have to go back home from this place all alone. Getting out of the tunnel, go straight north. Once the sun rises at dawn, keep walking with the sun to your right and you will reach your village.'

Konkaboti asked, 'And you?'

Khetu said, 'I shall have to stay here. I have touched the things of this place, and also have taken money from here, so I cannot leave this place. I have to remain here. That is why I had asked you not to touch anything in this place. Now, get up, and don't delay. After going out of this mansion, walk through the tunnel. Having stepped out of that, spend the night under some tree. When the sun rises, you will easily know which side is north. Walking northward, you will reach your village. Konkaboti, get a move on.'

Konkaboti said, 'I will leave this place all alone? Do you want me to go away from here, leaving you to your fate? How could you say this? I know that I have committed a serious blunder. True, I am a culprit, and ill-fated too. But should you banish me for that? I am a young girl, and ignorant; what wrong I have done I have done unwittingly. I have done wrong having intended to do well. Don't I deserve forgiveness at all?'

Khetu replied, 'Konkaboti, I am not vexed with you. It is not out of resentment that I asked you to go away from this place. A terrible danger lurks here; it is something appalling. How will I describe all this to you? Konkaboti, you must leave this place and that too at this very instant. Delay is out of the question. Go back to your father's house. Come back here, escorted, after ten days. You can then take away the wealth that you see scattered all over. If you take all this after ten days, you will be in no danger, and none will come in your way. Then, divide the wealth into four parts. Give one share to your father, one share to Ramhori dadamohashoy, one to Nironjonkaka, and take the remaining share yourself. Spend the rest of your life by performing charity, dharma and penance. Human life is short, isn't it? Konkaboti, before you realise it this brief life will be spent. After that, you too will go where I am going now; there we two will meet again.'

Konkaboti said, 'Your words have cut me to the quick, and my heart is about to burst. *Hai,* alas, what have I done! How terrible does all this seem! Where will you go now? Please, tell me everything right now.'

Khetu said, 'Okay, then listen. Whatever wealth you see here is guarded by a hideous long-nosed ghostess called Nakeshwori.[1] She always guards the entrance to the tunnel. The horrendous giggle that you heard was Nakeshwori's. She will eat up whoever touches her wealth. I have taken this wealth. But the root that you have burnt down was what protected me so far from her. Otherwise, I would have long ago been devoured by Nakeshwori! She probably is yet to get a whiff of the root being destroyed. But she will find out soon. And the moment she does, she will come and kill me. No way can I escape her clutches. There is no escape route from here. Even if there were any, it would be of little help to us. Wherever I go, whether to forests or underwater, whether to villages or to towns, Nakeshwori will chase me down and slay me.'

Hearing this, Konkaboti clasped Khetu's feet, and lay prostrated there.

Khetu said, 'Konkaboti, do not cry. How will crying help? Whatever was there in our destiny has come about. It is the divine will. Get up, and go through the tunnel. Nakeshwori will come here in no time. Her sight will make your blood run cold. Get up and go home, the company of your mother will calm your mind somewhat.'

Konkaboti sat up with a flushed face and eyes reddened with tears. Her gentle and captivating beauty had now turned wild with a harsh edge, exuding a different charm.

Konkaboti said, 'Do you suppose I will leave you here to your fate? Do you believe I will escape from Nakeshwori to save my life, leaving you here? If I do that, then cursed be my life! Konkaboti may be a dim-witted girl who has disregarded your advice because of her stupidity, but she is not a worm from hell for all that. If I can rescue you from the clutches of Nakeshwori, all's well. Otherwise, we will embrace the same fate together. If you die, I will too. Konkaboti is not scared of death. And she does not want to live in this world without you. This is Konkaboti's resolve, and she will preserve it through thick and thin.'

Khetu looked at Konkaboti's face. Her face suggested that she was full of grit, and that her resolve was unwavering. Khetu found that Konkaboti's eyes were no longer moist with tears, and that her face did not have a trace of fear. Khetu thought, 'It will be futile to ask Konkaboti to go away from this place.'

Note

1. '... ghostess called Nakeshwori ...': 'Nakeshwori' literally means 'goddess of the nose'. She is so named because of her long nose.

10

The Theft

Khetu said, 'Konkaboti, if you are that determined not to leave this place, let me tell you everything. You are but a slip of a girl, we live in this desolate forest, and Nakeshwori keeps vigil at the door—considering all this, I refrained from unravelling the story. But now I shall tell you, listen. I, however, have grave doubts I will manage to finish the tale in time. The moment Nakeshwori sniffs the odour of the burning root, she will conclude that I no longer have it. She will then come and kill me. I fear that she may come in before I can finish my story.

'Having concluded ma's funeral, I set off for Kashi. I have already narrated why I travelled towards the western parts instead of coming to Kolkata. Reaching Kashi, I performed all the rituals related to the shraddho ceremony. Then I started looking for a job. And fortunately, I soon found a reasonably good one. Though the work was harrowing, and I had to keep my nose to the grindstone, the salary was handsome. I hoped that within a year, I would be able to save a lot of money. I spent only that much needed to keep body and soul together, and the rest I saved for your father. Konkaboti, to speak the truth, I lived more or less on water. After the day's labours, I felt such a pang of hunger some evenings that I could barely stand, and my head reeled. Still, I would not eat anything at night. No food, but water, plain and simple, filled my hungry stomach. This device would soothe me a little, and the bite of hunger was somewhat abated. After that I used to lie down, and the moment I did that I was dead to the world and turned oblivious to the demon of hunger. I didn't pay a single paisa to anybody for getting me water. I bought a large tumbler. Once the evenings would set in, I would go to the bank of the Ganga to fetch water, for then there was very little chance of somebody recognising me. The banks at Kashi are rather high. Once, while fetching water in the darkness, I fell. I was grievously hurt in the hands and feet. I got up, straining every nerve, and sat on a step. Konkaboti, how will I describe how profusely I cried then! I thought to myself, "O God, what sin have I committed to deserve such punishment!" I understood why people desert their songsar and embrace monkhood. Only he who lives solely for his own self can hope for some solace in this world. Can those who live with or for other people hope to find peace? How can I know what wrong is done by the person whom I have loved and bound my life with, and for whose good I have always prayed? I have no claims on the fruits of the work that person has done, but their unhappiness hurts me sorely. Even if they have done no wrong themselves, or have not caused their own unhappiness, still they may be afflicted by some others. Maybe I am unable to protect them from that torment. So I have no option but to helplessly see that person, who is dearest to my soul, suffer. Take, for instance, the torment inflicted on you by your father and brother. What could I do to prevent it? Sitting on that riverbank, surrounded by the sacrificial fires enkindled by ascetics, I was troubled by these thoughts. Then again I mused, "This songsar is a battleground in the truest sense. So many vices and so many sorrows stalk here. A legion of living souls is being fevered and weighed down by these vices and sorrows every day, and is suffering enormously. Will I, whose eyes of wisdom have now opened more widely than many others, and who is now more equipped than them to combat these vices and sufferings, beat a retreat from the arena? Will I retire to a deep, desolate forest without putting up a fight against the ills for the sake of the world's good, and conceding defeat like a coward?" Konkaboti, what shall I tell you of the many strands of thoughts like this that crossed my mind that evening?

'I got up and went slowly back home with my water container. One year passed this way. I managed to save about two thousand rupees in this period. I thought that your father would be pleased if he got this money, and that I would have your hand in marriage. I set off for home with that money. All the money was in coins; I did not take currency notes along because the people of my village had no faith in them. I put all those coins in a purse, and boarded a train. I kept that bag with me and was very careful about it. I never got down from the train lest somebody should steal it. In the evening, the train pulled up at a big station. There the train was scheduled to stay long. Though I was famished, I did not disembark to buy snacks. In the compartment I was travelling, in there was just one man, a stranger, and none else was around. That man went to buy his food, courteously asking me, "Mohashoy, if you want something, tell me, I can get it for you." I told him, "If you do that, it will be a great help." Saying this, I gave him some paise to buy my food. And with that, he brought food for me. I ate that. A little while later, my head started reeling. I thought that maybe the heat of the train had got into my head, triggering that trouble. I lay down for a while. And the moment I did that, I was overtaken by a deep slumber. I was out for the count. At daybreak, I came somewhat back to my senses. But I had a splitting headache, in fact my head felt so heavy that I could barely lift it. However, when eventually I got back my full consciousness, I came to realise that the bag containing coins, which had been near my head, was missing. I looked around, but failed to locate that man either. I was thunderstruck. Slowly I got up, and made a hunt in every nook and cranny of the compartment to trace that bag. Nowhere could it be found! It was well and truly lost. Now I was certain that I had been utterly ruined. Now I realised that the money that I had saved by such gruelling privation, having lived for days on end only on water, had gone for ever! Konkaboti, can you feel what excruciating agony ate into my heart at that moment? Can you tell me, Konkaboti, how can man be so cruel? If such cruelty is not hell itself, then what is? Konkaboti, can you tell me why man inflicts such pain on a fellow being? Doesn't the tormentor feel any compunction?'

Now, after a long time, tears welled up in Konkaboti's eyes. She started crying. Konkaboti said, 'So much the better for us. No use living in this world! Come, let us go away from this pain-laden world. Nakeshwori now no longer seems to be our enemy; on the contrary, she seems to be our dearest friend.'

Khetu said, 'Listen carefully. Do you hear any noise made by Nakeshwori?'

Konkaboti did what Khetu bade her do, and then said, 'No, I don't hear anything.'

Khetu said again, 'Now I'll tell you what happened thereafter. Let me narrate the complete story before Nakeshwori barges in.

'When I realised that my money had been stolen, I knew for certain that all my hopes were dashed. I concluded that the very fellow who was with me in the compartment was the thief who had made me a pauper. He must have mixed some drug with my food. When I was unconscious after having consumed that food, he stole my money and decamped. How could I know when and in which station he had got down? There was little chance of catching the man. Even so, I told the railway personnel of my misfortune. They searched all the compartments with me for company. But the search drew a blank. And then I felt an abysmal void all round me. Konkaboti, the human world that you see around you is composed only of some aspirations and disappointments! What could I do then, Konkaboti! I thought, "Should I go to Kolkata, or go back to Kashi, or to my village?" Then I remembered that I had nothing with me except the ticket for Raniganj station[1] and some coins. However, destitute though I was, I decided to come back to my village, because I had promised you to come back after one year. I knew you would be waiting eagerly for me. I guessed you might have had to suffer loads of humiliations, embarrassments and diatribes in the period of my absence. I persuaded myself that I would fall at your father's feet, sign him a bond of two thousand rupees, and start paying off in instalments every month.

'Konkaboti, referring to your father time and again is itself disturbing. Whatever his nature may be, he is after all your father. It is unfortunate that whenever I come to speak about him I end up vilifying him. I thought that I would give him so much wealth from this place that he would come to despise it very soon. This is another malady of this world—everyone is crazy about wealth, everyone lusts for it. How much do we eat, Konkaboti, and what do we wear? Why should we long so much for wealth? Yes, we need to earn an income for it helps us serve relatives and friends, shelter the poor, feed the starving, bail people out of financial straits, and remove the world's sorrows to a large extent.

'He who serves humanity at large, who desists from luxury and pomp, and who spends time to earn money or knowledge for the welfare of the world is a real deity in this universe enveloped with darkness all round. But, Konkaboti, one should not hanker frantically after wealth. If one gets frenzied for acquiring knowledge or dharma, that is okay. The rumbling of the clouds and the howling of winds are heard at the lower altitudes. At the higher, in the great blue firmament, it is all calm and serene. Similarly, in this human world, there are lower and higher strata. Whatever clamour you get to hear about wealth, honour, caste, dharma, etc., rises from among the ignorant masses given over to low thinking. Now, at this hour of death, Konkaboti, I can hardly help laughing at the wrangling and jangling of these befuddled and infatuated masses grovelling basely on earth.

'Anyway, I decided to come back home instead of going to Kolkata or Kashi, and so I disembarked at Raniganj. There are two paths from Raniganj leading to our village. One of these is a highway trodden by innumerable scurrying feet. The second one is through a forest. Since this path is infested with tigers and bears, it remains usually unfrequented, but it is shorter. While it takes five days to reach our village if one takes this route, it takes six if one chooses the highway instead. When I got down at Raniganj, I had barely four paise. I wished to reach the village at the earliest, and so I took the forest route. On the first day itself, the four paise were spent. I crossed hills and mountains, woods and groves, streams and fountains on my way. Whatever fruits I could gather, I ate. At night if I found myself in a village, I lay at somebody's door. And if I found myself in the wilderness itself, I lay under the trees. I thought to myself, I am safe from tigers and bears. If these creatures eat me up, who will be there to suffer all the misfortunes which are exclusively my share?

'Four days passed like this. In the evening, I reached the base of the high hill which is visible from our village. That one is this very hill in which we are now. From here, our village is one day's walk. I had turned very feeble after having starved for a few days. I thought in the morning I might get even weaker, so I decided to walk on in the night to reach the village at dawn. Thinking thus, I took no rest, but simply plodded on. After the first prohor of the night, the moon set, pitch-black darkness engulfed the forest, and I lost my way. I strayed into the deeper part of the jungle, and could not find my way out. I advanced a little, then retraced my steps, wandered to the right, then to the left, but I found no way out of that tangle. For a long time, I traipsed in the forest, but was not able to discern an escape route. In the end I was fagged out, my feet felt too heavy to move, and my chest felt so parched that it was about to split open, as it were. At this moment, a temple loomed in front. Seeing that, I felt life coming back to my body. I thought there must be people in this temple; at least I could hope to have water to drink there. With this idea, I rushed towards the temple like a thirsty chatok bird. But woe is me! Having stepped inside the temple, I found that it was absolutely deserted, that there was neither an idol nor a human being about. The temple was ancient, a tumbledown affair, both its inside and outside were swathed in creepers and thick foliage. It was clear that it had lain untrodden by human feet for eons. "O God, let me see what more you have in store for me!" I uttered these words, sighed and lay down there.'

Note

1. Raniganj station: Raniganj is now an important colliery town in Burdwan district of West Bengal.

11

The Ghost Company

Khetu continued, 'It was nearly the second prohor of the night, and over-exhaustion was just about to make me fall asleep. Suddenly, I heard a clattering noise on the steps of the temple. I looked up, and lo and behold, there was a macabre white skull! It was jumping up from one step to another. Konkaboti, I have never been chicken-hearted, but still I had an eerie feeling when I saw that skull behaving in that manner. I got up. That skull hopped up all the steps, and then rolled towards me like a disc. Having come near me, it leapt up, and then remained suspended in the air right in front of my face, staring hard at me. Stationed like that in the void, it gaped from ear to ear to bare its rows of teeth.

'With that hideous gape, it asked me, "Babu, is it true you don't believe in ghosts?"

'I replied, "O mohashoy, some respite, please! It will be the limit if you and your tribe too begin pestering me. I am overwrought with many troubles and worries. Go away, please! Stop bothering me."

'My words angered the skull even more. It screamed while asking me again, "Babu, is it true you don't believe in ghosts? You have studied English enough not to believe in ghosts! Am I right?"

'I said, "Has the fact that English-knowing babus do not believe in ghosts driven you up the wall? Do you feel humiliated if people disbelieve in ghosts?"

'The skull answered, "Should we not see red if people refuse to believe in us? Should we feel soothed instead? If people ignore our existence, should we not feel insulted? Could such a gesture enhance our sense of dignity? Why should people say that ghosts do not exist, pray? What have we done to those English-knowing people that they should simply dismiss us like this? You have already banished your godheads, now if you succeed in blasting away spirits like us, your triumph will be complete, won't it?"

'Even at that moment of crisis, I could not suppress a smile. I knew that gods feel offended if people do not honour or worship them, but had never heard that ghosts go ballistic or feel disgraced if people do not believe in them. I felt like laughing.

'I said, "Yes, mohashoy. This really is a reprehensible act on the part of the English-knowing babus!"

'My words mollified the skull's wounded sentiments to some extent, and its rage was greatly mitigated. The skull said, "You, young man, seem to be a good, sensible fellow. You, I think, are not a dyed-in-the-wool atheist like those English-knowing babus. Do you have a *tiki* on your head?"

'I said, "No, mohashoy, I do not."

'The skull said, "Okay, when you go back home this time, start sporting a tiki. And listen, we will not spare those English-knowing babus all that easily. We have arranged so that they will come to believe in ghosts all over again. We will try to win them over. We will start lecturing and haranguing, publishing books and booklets, and bringing out newspapers. With that end in view, we have already set up a company. We have named that company, 'Skull, Skeleton and Co.'"

'Konkaboti, I think you remember what the words "skull" and "skeleton" mean. What the skull said meant that ghostly entities like skulls and skeletons had joined hands to reclaim people's respect for, and belief in, ghosts.'

'The skull repeated, "Our new company is named 'Skull, Skeleton and Co.' Can you guess why we opted for an English name? It is because such names bring both money and prestige, and instil trust in people. Otherwise, everybody would have considered us frauds. Haven't you noticed when the Mukhopadhyays,

Bandyopadhyays, or Chattopadhyays set up shops for footwear or ham, they name their shops 'Longman and Co.' and the like?[1] In fact, having been swindled on hundreds of occasions, people do not give any credence to natives. They trust English or Portuguese shop owners more than their own brethren. Then again, talking about the shastras, and the Vedas, these scriptural texts are deemed to have merit only when Bilati sahibs extol them. None cares a hoot for what native scholars say. Thinking in this vein, we have given the name 'Skull, Skeleton and Co.' The skeleton, my dear friend, stands over there. Come, skeleton chum, come here, please."

'The skeleton came to me, rattling its bones. The whole bony framework of the human body is called a skeleton, but the one which came to me was headless.

'The skull asked me then, "Come, do you now believe totally in ghosts!"

'I answered, "I have always believed in ghosts, because it is thanks to ghouls that I have been suffering so long. But those are another category of ghosts. From now on, I reverently accept ghosts of your type as well. How can I not accept what I have seen with my own eyes? So I think you have no reason to lose heart. Please, get back home now, because it is late at night. The members of your family will start to worry about you. Besides, I need to sleep a wink or two. I shall have to set out early tomorrow morning."

'The skull then told the skeleton, "Have you noticed, dear skeleton, how immensely rewarding is this setting up of a company? This babu has studied English, so his wits had gone completely awry. With a few words we have succeeded in bringing him back to his dharma. Now, let us go and seek out other babus who have gone astray. Let us try to make them believe in and revere ghosts."

'The skeleton rattled its bones. I cocked my ear, and understood that it was not merely the rattling of bones. It did not have a head, so it could not open its mouth and speak. That was why it shook its bones, and the clatter was a substitute for speech. What was amazing was that I could easily follow what it said.

'The skeleton said, "Since this fellow has become a devotee of ghosts, he should be rewarded. If you want people's devotion, you need to offer them money. If one gets money, one does not object to being devoted and dharma-minded. So, dear skull, pay him. When he goes back to his land, and narrates this story of his, people will pay obeisance to ghosts because of the lure of money."

'I said, "I am indeed in extreme need of funds now, but I am not greedy. You needn't pay me to make me fawn on ghosts. I won't take your money."

'Hearing this, the skull became even more pleased. It said, "Come with me. If we give you our money, I am sure it will fall in good hands, and this money will be used for good purposes. So we have decided to give you all our accumulated wealth. We did not make good use of money when we were alive. If this money is now used by you for some noble purpose, you'll be doing us a good turn."

'The skeleton too implored me. I at last consented to accompany them. The skeleton walked, while the skull hopped and rolled forward. First, they took me to some orchard. I found many fruits like mangoes, bananas, jackfruits, mangosteens, nuts, etc., which had ripened. They asked me to eat those fruits. I ate to my heart's content. Then they pointed out a crystal clear waterfall to me. I drank its water and slaked my thirst. From there, we advanced further. A little while later, we came near this hill. Having approached a particular place of that hill, the skull said, "We need to clear this area. For a thousand years nobody has trodden these paths." We three started tidying the place up. After it was somewhat cleared, a structure on the side of the hill became dimly visible. The skull, the skeleton and I detached stone slabs of that rocky structure after strenuous effort. Once the structure came loose, this tunnel became visible. At the entrance of the tunnel, I glimpsed that terrible Nakeshwori. She let out a squeal of chilling laughter. But the moment the skull looked daggers at her, dilating its eye-sockets, her laughter stopped. We entered this mansion through that tunnel. I marvelled at the treasure stored up here.

'The skull said, "A thousand years ago, we ruled over this place. We battled with our neighbouring kings and amassed this immeasurable wealth. While alive, we performed no rituals of dharma; we spent life only skirmishing and acquiring wealth. We had no children. But we were not sorry for that; rather, we were delighted, for children cause expenses. We derived heavenly pleasure from counting, handling and shuffling money. Lest somebody took our money after us, we employed a '*jok*' on our property, that is to say, we appointed a ghostess to keep vigil over it. In order to employ a jok, in our case we built this gorgeous mansion inside the hill. We brought here money, gems, pearls, clothes and ornaments from our palace. We performed *joggo*, and sacrificed a nine-year-old girl with the instruction that she would have to stand guard on this property for one thousand years. We told her that she would have to immediately kill anybody who touched even a speck of this wealth. We also said that she could go anywhere she liked after a thousand years, for after that period of time whoever would come upon this wealth could take it. Having instructed the girl thus, we lit a lamp in that mansion, and shut the door of the tunnel. The moment the lamp went out, the girl died. After her death, she became a terrible-looking, long-nosed ghostess. For her long nose, she came to be known as 'Nakeshwori' in the ghost community. The horrid ghostess whom you just saw at the entrance of this tunnel, and whose laughter you just heard, is none other than Nakeshwori, who has been keeping vigil here for a thousand years. On some occasions, people employ a boy instead of a girl to stand guard on property; that boy turns into a spirit once he dies. However, some days after we made this arrangement, we got killed in a battle. The enemy's sword severed my head from my body. I was a single individual in life, but after death I became a pair of ghostly entities in the form of this skull and this skeleton. Now I, here, am the skull, and the torso and limbs are this fellow—brother skeleton. We employed 'jok' on this property 999 years ago. It is only one year to go before the jok's tenure terminates. Then Nakeshwori will no longer watch over this treasure. In the last month of *Poush*,

Nakeshwori tied the knot with a ghost called Ghanghon. Once the coming year is over, Nakeshwori will go to her in-laws'. If you take this property then, you will be in no danger at all. But never ever touch even an iota of this property within this year, for if you do, Nakeshwori will eat you up. We two are the actual proprietors of this property. And we offer this treasure to you. But beware, never touch this wealth within this year, we repeat!"

'I replied, "Mohashoy, I am hugely obliged for your kindness. If you have given me this property, please devise a ploy so that I can take at least a small part of it. I need money badly now. If I manage to get some of your property now, I'll be immensely served, or to tell you more precisely, my life will be saved. If I don't get this now, I doubt whether I will be living at all for the whole of next year to enjoy your property."

'Hearing this, the skull and the skeleton were locked in a long discussion. But I could not understand what they discussed.

'The skull said, "Come out of this cave with us." We all exited again, and again we started travelling through the forest. The skull was looking out for something. At last, finding a tree bearing herbs, it told me, "Extract the root of this tree." I pulled that root up. At the skull's behest, I stuck that root to my hair with the gum of another tree. Then we all came back to this mansion once again.

'Having returned, the skull told me, "Listen carefully to what I'll tell you now. For the present, take as much money as you need to meet your requirements. The root we gave you has the special property that if you have it on your head, Nakeshwori will not be able to kill you as long as you are within this mansion. The root has another virtue which will enable you to take the shape of any animal as long as it is on your head. The tiger is Nakeshwori's adored deity. So whenever you travel out of this cave, don't forget to assume the form of a tiger, for in that case, you will be perfectly safe from Nakeshwori. When you come back again into the mansion, you can re-assume the human form at will. Remember these two things; never forget them under any circumstances. First, never ever let this root drop from your head within this one year, for that will cost you your life, no matter where you are, and second, do not ever venture out without assuming the form of a tiger, never roam as a human, for if you do, death is inevitable at that very instant. After one year, you can burn down this root, and go home taking possession of this treasure. If you do not take this property within this one year, all these arrangements will not be called for. This is because Nakeshwori does not, rather cannot, do harm to anybody if he has not taken the riches under her vigilance. However, after one year, Nakeshwori will go to her in-laws', leaving this property behind. When her marriage was being settled with Ghanghon the ghost, so many people tried to spoil the party!"

'I asked, "Why did people try to prevent the marriage, mohashoy?"

'The skull said, "You do not know, and so ask such stupid questions. When one succeeds in queering someone else's pitch in marriage, one derives such immense pleasure from this effort that it can hardly be obtained from any other enterprise. Fix a bride or a bridegroom for a marriage, and then ask your relatives or acquaintances for their opinions; they will inevitably say, 'Okay, let them marry, if you like, but ...' In that word 'but' resides a shipload of meaning. Anyway, I must admit for all that that they brilliantly spoilt Ghanghon's party. It really merits acclaim."

'I queried, "How can something be 'brilliantly' spoilt, mohashoy?"

'The skull said, "You might have read seven *kando*s of that book which we do not want to name,[2] but you are an ignoramus in the matters of ghosts. Now, listen to what I will narrate. When Ghanghon's marriage was settled, Nakeshwori's aunt sent a ghost to see the bridegroom.[3] When that ghost came to Ghanghon's, Ghanghon took great care to be hospitable and cordial to him. When lunch was being prepared, that ghost went to take his bath in a nearby pond. There, the neighbouring ghosts of Ghanghon's locality too went, having hatched a conspiracy. One among those neighbours asked the guest ghost, 'Where do you live, mohashoy?' The stranger ghost replied, "I live in a mango tree called 'wife-forgetter', beyond where the single-leg ghost community dwells." Ghanghon's neighbour now asked, "May I know the purpose of your visit here?" The stranger ghost replied, "I have come to see Ghanghon as the prospective bridegroom of a girl." The neighbours asked in unison, "Mohashoy must be a physician, then?" The stranger ghost asked in astonishment, "Why should I be a physician? Do you mean Ghanghon is ailing?" The neighbour ghosts were a bit put out, and replied hesitantly, "Ailing? O no, that's nothing serious. He has a slight cough, and his spittle has a wee bit sprinkling of tar, and he runs a mild temperature in the afternoons. But that is nothing to be made much of. That must have been caused by this summer heat; he will surely recuperate if he takes proper food and bath in the next few days." These words flummoxed the stranger ghost. He did not return to Ghanghon. Leaving the pond, he headed straight for the place beyond the habitation of the single-leg ghost community. He relayed the whole story to Nakeshwori's aunt. And consequently, the marriage plans ran aground. Nakeshwori is a beautiful ghostess. Ghanghon had been spellbound by her beauty. For a long time thereafter, he meandered from one tree to another, bemoaning this loss and ruing his ill luck. Then, for some days he took a vow of silence, and lived in a dark well. However, in the end, the marriage took place, and we all rejoice at this happy union of souls."

'I asked, "What is this sprinkling of tar in the ghost's phlegm that you have just spoken of?"

'The skull said, "Just as you have blood in your body, we have tar. Violent coughs cause us to spit out phlegm mixed with tar."

'I asked, "If ghosts contract diseases like humans, they also die like humans, I suppose? Well then, if humans turn into ghosts after death, what do ghosts become?"

'The skull answered, "Ghosts turn into marbles. You know, those little globules with which kids play."

'I said, "Ghosts become marbles! Why, of all things, do they turn into marbles?"

'The skull retorted, chagrined, "O, I am mistaken. From now on we ghosts will die after consultation with you! That settles the matter, I presume."

'I said, "Mohashoy, please forgive me. I am asking you questions because I am ignorant in such matters. If you permit me, I will ask just another question. If it is true that ghosts become marbles after death, then playing with marbles must be a dangerous business, isn't it?"

'The skull answered, "What danger can there be in playing with dead ghosts? In case these ghosts were alive, then, I admit, it would have been really dangerous playing with them."

'The skull continued, "I cannot afford to waste time talking with you. We have set up a company; I must go now to perform the official duties of that company. We are 'Skull, Skeleton and Co.' We are no ordinary ghosts! Take care to remember what we have told you. If you don't, you are in for serious trouble. Now we'll take leave. Never will we meet you again."

'Having said this, the skull and the skeleton left that spot. I sat all alone in that mansion. What I did thereafter is known to you, I needn't speak on that. So, Konkaboti, now you have heard all that I had to tell you.'

Konkaboti said, 'Okay, then let me go and take Nakeshwori's wealth, because in that case she will kill us both together. What better fate can a devoted wife think of?'

When, with these words, Konkaboti was just about to get up, a frightening yell rent the air. The mansion started shaking violently. Doors and windows began rattling. The entire place was immersed in darkness. Though the lamp that was guttering was not extinguished, a pall of shadow descended over it.

Khetu said, 'Konkaboti, Nakeshwori must be approaching us.'

Till now, Konkaboti had sat on the edge of the bed. Now she quickly got up and bolted the door, and leaned against it with all the resistance she could muster. She would not allow Nakeshwori to force an entry.

A gut-wrenching stench, an impenetrable darkness, and frequent rumblings filled the chamber.

Gradually the noise died down, the darkness was dispelled, and the light of the lamp once again illumined the room.

Then Konkaboti came to see that Khetu lay there in deathly stupor with eyes shut, and beside him stood Nakeshwori, the hideous-looking ghostess. Konkaboti ran up and fell straight at Nakeshwori's feet.

Konkaboti said, 'Ogo, please don't kill my husband, please be kind. O dear ghostess, I am a wretched beggar-girl. Having suffered immense hardship, I have got back my husband, who is my very life. I have none in this world except my husband. O you noble soul, please kill me instead of my husband. I throw myself at your feet and beg of you to spare my husband's life. We do not want your treasure, we want nothing. Give my husband back to me, let me take him home. Whatever money of yours I have taken, I promise to refund it. In case you desire to taste human flesh, eat me up and drink my blood. But please do not harm my husband, let him go back home.'

In this manner Konkaboti wailed, clasping Nakeshwori's feet, and beseeched her to be merciful. Her wailing could have melted a stone. But Nakeshwori did not feel pity; she turned a deaf ear to all the pleading. The more Konkaboti cried, the more Nakeshwori lifted her left hand, and said, 'Go away, out!'

Konkaboti said, 'Ogo, I will never go away leaving my husband behind. Give my husband to me, I will leave straight away. O dear husband, please get up, let us go away from here!'

The more Konkaboti cried and every time she pleaded, Nakeshwori raised her hand, and said, 'Go away, get out!"

Konkaboti got to her feet, and wiped her tears. Then, with crimson eyes she defiantly declared, 'You won't give me back my husband, nor eat me up? You will only say, "Go away, get out," and nothing else—that is what you are up to? Indeed! Whether you be Nakeshwori or whoever, let us have a showdown then right here, let us see who triumphs!'

With these words, Konkaboti made a frantic effort to catch hold of Nakeshwori. The latter did not say a word, but simply exhaled once. The gust of that breath blew Konkaboti away to the door.

Konkaboti got up once again, and made another desperate attempt to grasp the ghostess. Nakeshwori exhaled once more, which blew Konkaboti away outside the mansion itself.

Then Konkaboti slowly picked herself up again, and told Nakeshwori, 'Ogo, I will no longer attempt to grab you, nor will I attempt to kill you. I no longer want my husband back. My only desire is that you do not tear me away from my husband. I implore you to let me die clasping my husband's feet. If you want to kill, kill us both together, if you want to eat, eat us both together. Nothing else do I pray of you. Please grant this sole prayer of mine. Don't deprive me of this."

With these words, Konkaboti once again rushed towards the chamber. Nakeshwori did not utter a word, but released another breath, which blew Konkaboti away beyond the hills and landed her in the middle of the forest.

Notes

1. '... Mukhopadhyays, Bandyopadhyays, or Chattopadhyays ...': These are common Bengali Hindu surnames among Brahmans.
2. '... that book which we do not want to name ...': The reference is to the epic, the Ramayana. The name of Rama is believed by Hindus to be anathema to ghosts. Hence the skull, being a ghost, cannot name the book.
3. '... sent a ghost to see the bridegroom ...': It is customary of 'arranged' marriages among Bengali Hindus that one or more elderly persons go to 'see' the prospective groom in his surroundings before the negotiation may progress.

12

Frog Sahib

Inside the forest, Konkaboti lay in a stupor. Repeated falls and efforts to rise had lacerated her body. She was bleeding from wounds all over, and now she did not have the strength to rise. And having risen, what could she do, after all? If she approached her husband at all, Nakeshwori would once again blow her away with another blustery breath. She started weeping profusely, sitting all alone in the forest. That she could not sacrifice her life at her husband's feet was what now gnawed at her heart. Continued sobbing wore her down. She thought to herself, 'Okay then, so be it. Let my husband be inside, I will lay down my life here outside the mansion, contemplating his feet. All-merciful God will surely have mercy on me. I will surely find him after my death.'

Thinking thus, Konkaboti started meditating on her husband's feet. She could, as it were, almost see those bright, fair feet with toes like *chompok* buds.

While she was contemplating the feet with rapt attention, a new idea crossed her mind. She thought, 'If ghostesses, spirits or witches do harm to people, there are ways to fend them off. There are exorcists who know the mantras to cure their spells. Why cannot they then save my husband? And if perchance my husband's life cannot be saved, I will get his corpse at least. If I can burn myself to death in the company of that corpse, I will get some peace of mind. Whatever may be the consequence, I will strive to save my husband from Nakeshwori; I will not sit idle here. Maybe I am a woman, so what? Am I not a human being? For the well-being of my husband, I regard the whole world simply as blades of grass, I dread none and nothing.'

Having so reasoned, Konkaboti got up and wiped her tears. She braced herself to go where people lived.

But alas, she did not know in which direction habitations lay. Khetu had told her to move towards the north. But then, which side was the north? In the pervasive darkness of the forest, it was never easy to determine the direction. Night was over, the morning sun was not yet out, how then was she supposed to know which direction was the north, and which the south?

So she thought, 'I will go in any random direction. Surely I will reach one village or another if I do that. I will make a search for a good physician in the locality. It will not be wise to waste precious time. If I dawdle, whatever hope I have may fizzle out.'

Konkaboti, like a lunatic, staggered across woods and forests, hills and caves. She travelled far and wide, but failed to sight any village. The night ended, the sun rose, and the day wore gradually on, but Konkaboti did not come upon a single human soul.

Konkaboti was thinking, 'Now what should I do? In which direction should I go? Whom shall I ask my way?'—and at that moment, she found a frog right in front. The frog was so ravishingly graceful! His exquisite looks bowled Konkaboti over! He wore a hat on his head, a coat on his body, and pantaloons to cover his legs. He was sporting a sahib's attire! He was almost unrecognisable. Only his complexion had not changed into a sahib's, despite the persistent use of soaps. And the only other thing missing were shoes. He was yet to buy a pair, but would surely buy one afterwards. At present, he was striding away proudly in a sahib's outfit with his hands tucked in his pockets.

Seeing the appealing grace of the frog, Konkaboti allowed herself a faint smile even in this hour of distress. She thought, 'Let me ask this fellow the way out of the forest.'

Konkaboti asked, 'Frog mohashoy, which way leads to the village? Will you tell me in which direction I should go to reach some human habitation?'

The frog answered, 'Hit mit fat.'

Konkaboti said, 'Frog mohashoy, I could not quite make out what you said. Say it more distinctly, please. I am asking you in which direction should I go to reach a village.'

The frog rejoined, 'Hish fish dam.'

Konkaboti said, 'Frog mohashoy, you are speaking English, I see. But I have not studied English, and therefore I can hardly make sense of what you say. If you do me the favour of speaking in Bengali, I will be able to understand.'

The frog looked around to see whether he was being watched, and found that he was not. He feared that if he was heard speaking Bengali he would lose his caste, and would be looked upon as a 'native'. When he found that no one was around, he mustered the courage to speak in Bengali.

The frog glowered at Konkaboti, and spoke in high dudgeon, 'What an obnoxious slip of a girl you are! What nonsense is all this! You see that I am a sahib, but still address me as "Frog mohashoy"! What prevents you from calling me a sahib?'

Konkaboti answered, 'Frog sahib, I was grievously mistaken, please pardon me for my fault. Now, will you please tell me in which direction I should go to reach a village?'

Hearing this, the frog was livid, and spoke to her with greater fury, 'What rubbish! This girl does not know her manners! She keeps doing what I forbid her to. Why, girl, do you keep parroting the word "frog" disgustingly? Why? Can't you call me by my name? My name is Mr Gomes.'

Konkaboti said, 'Mohashoy, I have committed a serious offence. But I have done that unknowingly, so please forgive me. Now, Mr Gomes, will you kindly tell me the way that will lead to some human habitation? For your information, my name is Konkaboti, and I am in deep waters. I have lost my husband, whom I loved with all my heart. I am now looking for a physician who can restore his life, and so I need to reach a village. I cannot afford to wait even for an instant. Please, have pity on this poor soul, and show me the way.'

That Konkaboti had called him a sahib, and addressed him as Mr Gomes calmed down the frog, and his wrath abated.

He now asked Konkaboti rather affectionately, 'Do you know why I have turned into a sahib?'

Konkaboti replied, 'No mohashoy, I do not know that. Please tell me the way to the village. Do you know how far it is?'

The frog said, 'Lonkaboti, listen.[1] You said your name is Lonkaboti, didn't you? Listen, Lonkaboti. One day I was sitting in this forest. An elephant was passing this way. I thought to myself, the elephant would respect my dignity, and pass round me fearfully. But will you believe its impudence? That wicked elephant did not go past me, but crossed over. My entire being was trembling in rage. When I feel hot under the collar, I take leave of my senses. That is why people always dread me. I thought that the elephant had to be taught a good lesson. So I let rip at the beast, "You bumpy-headed comb-toothed elephant, dare you cross me!" Lonkaboti, didn't I speak well?'

Konkaboti said, 'I am not Lonkaboti, but Konkaboti. Yes, you spoke really well. But you have not told me how I can reach a village, have you? Anyway, I must go now, for I can afford to wait no longer.'

The frog said, 'O, listen, please. Why do you hurry so much? Just listen to what that rascal elephant retorted. That I was so very incensed did not scare him at all! The elephant replied, "You blunt-nosed frog, God has saved thee!" Now Konkaboti, what do you say, am I blunt-nosed?'

Konkaboti thought that once the crab had had hard feelings regarding the aspersions cast on his nose, now this frog too was being touchy about his nose in a similar fashion.

Konkaboti said, 'O no, who says that you are blunt-nosed? Your nose is so very bewitching! Mohashoy, is this the way to the village?'

The frog was immersed in thought for a while. Konkaboti felt that the frog was pondering on the way to the village so that he could guide her properly. She looked at his face agog with the anticipation that he would soon come out with an answer.

Having pondered long, the frog said at last, 'I suppose he said this for the sake of rhyme. Take note how my words and the elephant's rhyme as a couplet:

> You bumpy-headed comb-toothed elephant, dare you cross me!
>
> You blunt-nosed frog, God has saved thee!

'Konkaboti, will it be a bad idea if I publish this couplet in a newspaper? But this couplet contains a slander on me and on my "blunt nose". No, I will not publish it. So now, Konkaboti, you have heard everything. Now, I think, you have got a measure of the elephant's haughtiness. I reasoned that people do not respect anyone who is not a sahib. That is why I have donned the sahib's attire. Am I not looking a pucca sahib? From now on, everybody will hold me in high esteem and awe, and do me salaam. When I board the third class compartment of a train, no one else will dare embark on that. Wearing a hat, I will stand near the gate. Everyone will peep into the compartment, and say, "Look, there is a sahib in that compartment!" What do you think, Konkaboti, is this not a good idea?'

Konkaboti said, 'An excellent idea. Now please do me the favour of telling me the way to the village. And in case you don't, I shall take leave of you.'

The frog cocked his ear, and said, 'What is that you said?'

Konkaboti said, 'I asked which way leads to the village, and how far it is. I also wanted to know how long it would take to reach there.'

The frog asked, 'Do you know the rule of three in arithmetic?'

Konkaboti replied, 'Yes I do, but only a little bit.'

The frog said, 'Okay, then take a slate and pencil.'

Konkaboti said, 'Mohashoy, do not mock me in this hour of crisis. Now I am immersed in a sea of sorrow. Intense suffering has almost knocked the stuffing out of me. You have already spoken a great deal, but enough is enough. This is not the time for gossip. Tell me the way, and I will go, and strive to save my husband's life.'

The frog replied, 'I was not mocking you. How, without working out the sum, am I supposed to tell the time you will need to reach the village? However, if you don't have a slate and pencil, don't worry, you can work that out mentally. Now, take a leap, please do. Let me see how far you go with one leap. All these are the figures of the rule of three. Calculating these figures I will be able to tell you how long you will take to reach some habitation. The simple reason for this observation is that everybody doesn't leap the same distance.'

Konkaboti said, 'Mohashoy, we humans do not leap our way through like you. I do not know how to leap.'

The frog said, 'That is the problem. How then shall I get figures for the rule of three? Konkaboti, do you know where to find them? Are those not in the burrows under the earth? Or in the hollows of the trees? Konkaboti, will you go and find those numbers?'

Konkaboti said, 'I know nothing about that, please tell me the way.'

The frog said, 'Well then, work this sum out. If two men build a one-arm-long wall in two days, in how many days will two thousand men build a one-arm-long wall?'

Konkaboti thought a little, and answered, 'In the 500th part of a day, that is, one part of a day of five hundred parts.'

The frog said, 'Wrong! If I take one day to comprise twenty-four hours, going by your calculation the answer should be approximately three minutes. But, you know, the wall is merely one arm long, so where will these two thousand men stand that they will accomplish the task in three minutes?'

Konkaboti thought, 'True, where will those two thousand men stand to build the wall?'

Then the frog said, 'Since you have not been able to work out this sum properly, try to do another one. Suppose I have one fifty-paise coin, and suppose I lend it to someone. It was settled that the debtor will pay back in instalments, and that the repayable amount will be calculated every day, and the debtor will pay off the remainder in *halves*. Now, Konkaboti, tell me, in how many days will the borrower pay off my loan?'

Konkaboti said, 'This is a simple problem. The entire loan will be paid off in six days.'

The frog said, 'I too thought in a similar vein. But now, having delved deep into the problem, my mind has given way to some doubts. Okay, please explain to me how the loan can be paid off in six days.'

Konkaboti said, 'Half of a fifty-paise coin is four annas, so the borrower will pay four annas on the first day. Now four annas remain to be paid off. On the second day, he will pay half of four annas, that is to say, he will pay two annas. On the third, he will pay half of the remaining two annas, that is to say, he will pay one anna. Half of one anna is two paise, so on the fourth day he will pay two paise. Now two more paise remain. Half of two paise is one paisa, so on the fifth day the borrower will pay one paisa. Now just one paisa remains. On the sixth day, the borrower will pay that one paisa, and the loan will be paid off entirely.'

The frog said, 'How can that be? Why should he pay the full one paisa on the sixth day, pray? The condition is that the borrower will pay only half the remainder on the following day, is not that so? One paisa is equivalent to five *gonda*s, which again is equivalent to twenty *kora*s. So on the sixth day the borrower will pay ten koras. The next day he will pay me five koras. The day after, he will pay two and a half koras. Next, he will pay half of that; the next day, he will pay half of that half; the next day, he will pay half of the half of that half; and the next day still, half of the half of the half of that half ...'

The frog now started a full-throated wailing in his enchanting croaking voice, 'Ogo, O dear, I see that my loan will never be repaid. Where shall I go now? I have lost everything to a thug, O dear me! I have nothing in this world except that coin! Ogo, man cracks jokes at that coin of mine, I know![2] People get green with envy for that coin that I have. O ma, what misfortune has befallen me!'

The frog wailed loudly in this manner in his mellifluous voice. Konkaboti tried to bring him back to his senses.

Konkaboti said, 'Mohashoy, don't cry like that. Restrain yourself, and have patience.'

The frog once again started crooning, 'Ogo, I have nothing in this world except that coin.'

Konkaboti said, 'Chhi, mohashoy, shame! Please stop wailing. It does not become you. You are a sahib. You will surely earn lots of such coins.'

But the frog kept wailing in a singsong manner, 'O I have lost everything to an imposter! That fraud has ruined me! O what disaster! O ma, O dear me!'

Konkaboti sprinkled water on his face and hands; she had a trying time calming him down.

At last the frog said, amid sobs and blubberings, 'Ogo, O dear girl, I thought I would chat with you for some time. Ogo, that was not to be! Ogo, dear O dear, my ocean of sorrow has swelled. Ogo, you follow that path, that will lead you to a human habitation. Ogo, that is quite a far way off. Ogo, it is impossible for you to reach there tonight. Ogo, you people cannot leap like me! Ogo, you only walk and plod slowly! Ogo, your gait makes me laugh! Ogo, your gait does not make me cry. Ogo, you are such a good girl! Ogo, education has not made you androgynous! Ogo, you are so gentle, so demure, so modest, so very devoted to your husband! Ogo, you are not a precocious girl! Ogo, my fifty-paise coin is lost for ever! Ogo, what has happened to me! Ogo, ma!'

Notes

1. 'Lonkaboti': It is a misheard distortion of Konkaboti's name, the Bengali word '*lonka*' meaning 'chilli'.
2. '... man cracks jokes at that coin of mine ...': The reference is to a common Bengali idiom ('*byanger adhuli*', literally, the fifty-paise coin of a frog) that implies 'the meagre means of a poor man that makes him vain', used in a slighting and facetious sense.

13

Putrid Water

Konkaboti thought, 'I am already over-laden with my own sorrows, and now to cap it, a pest has emerged out of nowhere! Well, now the frog's wailing has stopped for a while, now it is time for me to go.'

Konkaboti went along the path the frog had instructed her to. She walked on and on, but could not cross the forest even when dusk set in. By then, Konkaboti had grown extremely travel-weary; her numbed legs refused to proceed further. She sat down on a piece of rock, and started weeping.

While Konkaboti was sobbing, someone whispered in her ear in a quiet, euphonious tone, 'Who are you, please? Whose girl are you?'

Konkaboti looked in all directions. At last, she noticed that a teeny-weeny mosquito was whispering in her ear. Having scanned the mosquito thoroughly enough, Konkaboti realised that it was a young female mosquito.

Konkaboti answered, 'I am a human girl. My name is Konkaboti.'

The girl mosquito said, 'A girl of humans! Our food, isn't that so? It is the blood of humans that father flies out to collect every day. We drink human blood, but so far I have not seen any human beings. I do not know on which tree humans grow. Well, let me see how humans look!'

Having said so, that girl mosquito child started flying round Konkaboti to have a good look at her.

After scanning her, the mosquito girl asked at last, 'You are not an adult human, but a child, I suppose?'

Konkaboti replied, 'I am not a mere child, but people still call me a girl.'

The mosquito girl asked, 'What did you say your name was?'

Konkaboti repeated her name.

The mosquito girl said, 'O that's splendid! My name is Roktoboti.[1] When I was just a toddler, I drank blood so much that my belly swelled taut, and so my father called me 'Roktoboti'. Now our two names rhyme, I see—Konkaboti and Roktoboti! Come, let us call each other by a pet name.'[2]

Konkaboti said, 'I am now greatly distressed. A profound grief weighs down my heart. I am now a devoted wife who has lost her husband. You are only a child, and so you will not comprehend these matters. This is not the time for me to call each other by a pet name.'

Roktoboti said, 'You are a devoted woman who has lost her husband! What is there to worry about? Let my father come. I will tell him. He will get you numerous spouses, that's for sure! Now come, please, let us be sworn buddies by calling each other by a pet name. But what will that name be? I like putrid water. Wherever there is putrid water about, I fly about happily—I frisk and gambol flying round that spot. So let 'Putrid Water' be our pet name! You are my 'Putrid Water', and I am yours. Now, how do you feel about it? You like the name, don't you?'

Konkaboti thought, 'Useless it is to argue with these creatures. I was so very hard put to explain things to that old fogey of a frog, and here I have a small mosquito girl to contend with! She is yet to mature! Let her do whatever she wishes, I will simply keep mum.'

Sighing heavily, Konkaboti said, 'Okay, let that be, I am "Putrid Water" to you, and you are the same to me. O my husband, O my soul mate! Just to think where you are and where I am! To imagine the condition you are in there and that I am in here!'

Saying this, Konkaboti kept breathing hard, and weeping profusely.

The grief of her 'Putrid Water' saddened the mosquito girl too. But it baffled her to figure out why her Putrid Water was weeping buckets. She flew about, humming and droning round Konkaboti, and tried to find the reason.

Roktoboti said, 'Putrid Water, where are your two other legs? You have two upper legs, I see, and I can also see your two lower legs, but where are the middle ones? Those are broken, I presume? Is that the reason why you are crying? Now I understand! But, Putrid Water, this, I am afraid, is too small a matter to shed tears for. While playing, I too broke one of my legs once. But look, that leg is growing anew! Your legs too will grow back on; come on, don't cry.'

Konkaboti said, 'For your information, none of my legs is broken. My legs are not like yours, human legs are like what you see me with. It is not for my legs that I am crying.'

The mosquito girl started droning round once again. She circumambulated Konkaboti, and surveyed her body parts and limbs closely.

At last, she flew near Konkaboti's nose, and said, 'What's this, Putrid Water? O what a disaster is this! Where is your nose? Who has cut that off? Alas, how will you eat and drink without your nose?'

Initially, Konkaboti could not follow what the mosquito girl was saying. But then it was clear she meant the antennae. Konkaboti felt, 'This mosquito girl really is a mere child, she has no knowledge at all.'

Konkaboti replied, 'Putrid Water, human noses are like this. Your snouts are long, but not ours. We do not eat and drink with our noses, but with our mouths.'

Roktoboti said, 'Aha, Putrid Water, you humans are really a wretched lot because you do not have long noses like ours. See how beautiful I look with these antennae of mine! When I see my reflection in the water, how very delighted do I get! Mother says, "My Roktoboti will be ravishingly beautiful when she grows up." Dear Putrid Water, I will make you beautiful too. When my father comes back home, I will ask him to pull your nose to make it long. Then you will look really fetching.'

Konkaboti thought, 'O dear me, once again that talk of noses! I don't know why all these creatures have such a fetish about noses. Crab mohashoy spoke about his nose, Frog Sahib did too, and now this little mosquito girl too is toeing their line. And then, to think about Nakeshwori's nose! O how dreadful!'

Konkaboti thought further, 'I find I am really in a fix in this hour of crisis. I was supposed to go to a village and find a physician at the earliest. But here, first the frog, and then this mosquito girl, have really tested my patience. No sooner did I escape the clutches of that frog than I was in the grip of this mosquito. This little girl has already got under my skin; who knows what is in store for me when her father comes back home?'

Roktoboti said, 'Putrid Water, can you see that leaf with a shrunken corner? We dwell in that corner of the leaf. My mothers live in that hut. I have three mothers. My father has gone out to roam and find food. Very soon he will be back with a lot of choice food items. Now let me go and inform mother that Putrid Water is our guest today.'

With these words, Roktoboti flew towards their hut.

She came back soon, and said, 'Putrid Water, mother is calling you in. Now get up please, I want you to meet my mother.'

What else could Konkaboti do but comply with this request? She got up slowly. She moved towards that crumpled corner of the leaf that was the mosquitoes' dwelling.

A young mosquito woman peeked out of that rumpled corner, and said, 'Dear child, have you become friends with Roktoboti with the pet name "Putrid Water" for each other? Well done! Roktoboti is our darling. My husband is a wealthy fellow, and this Roktoboti is his only child. O yes bachha, Roktoboti said something about your husband. Will you tell us what happened to him?'

Konkaboti spoke through sobs, 'I am a terribly grief-stricken woman. Tragedy has struck me. For me, the universe is dark. If I lose my husband for good, I will sacrifice my life too. Nakeshwori has ended my husband's life. I am travelling to a village to restore his life. I will try to find a good physician in the village for my husband. I can hardly afford to delay. I will start walking again this very night. But I do not know the way, and in the dark I will not be able to find it anyway. If you can show me the direction, I will be much obliged.'

The mosquito woman said, 'You are a young girl, and that is why you are talking out of turn. We are but womenfolk, and on top of that, we are the wives of a respectable and aristocratic mosquito, and besides, we live behind the veil. Custom decrees we cannot step beyond this threshold, child. How can we know the paths through the forest? But cry no more. Let our master come back home. I will explain everything to him. You have become our close relative as Roktoboti's Putrid Water, and so our master will do what's best for you. Just wait for a while.'

The woman who was talking to Konkaboti was Roktoboti's mother, and the master mosquito's youngest queen. Now the master's eldest queen peeped out by her side.

The eldest mosquito wife said, 'That is a human child, I presume? I want to keep her as a pet. I am childless, for long have I cherished the desire of keeping some animal or other as a pet. Well, well, now that this human child has come here on her own, I will keep her as a pet. Yes, she is a bit grown up, but there is still time for taming her. I have heard that humans keep animals like sheep, goats and pigeons as pets, and eat them too. But if I keep this human child as a pet, I will come to love her, and I will refrain from drinking her blood.'

Now the second of the mosquito's wives peeped out from another side, and said, '*Didi*, the things you say! If you ever keep a human child as a pet, do so in a way that she is of service to us. Maintain her just as the humans keep cows for milk. Our master brings blood from far-off places. The blood often goes stale by the time he brings it home. If we have a human as a pet in our home, we will taste fresh blood whenever we wish to.'

Roktoboti's mother said, 'O you always talk like that! Do only considerations of necessity matter to you! Roktoboti is only a child, she has found this human girl as a foundling, why will she allow you to eat her, or keep her as a pet? You want to snatch her away from my child! Is this what you call prudence? Let the master come. I will let him know everything. I no longer want to live in this songsar, I want him to send me to my parents'. I have parents and brothers to look after me, why should I care for others? I am not a barren, rootless woman of poor lineage. I am of respectable descent, remember that!'

The eldest mosquito queen said, 'Fie on you, rascal woman! Puffed up with pride for your parents and brothers! Let your parents and brothers rot!'

In this manner, the three co-wives of the mosquito broke into a fierce bickering. Konkaboti was taken aback. She thought, 'What an idea! These creatures want to keep me as a pet like an animal!'

The quarrel among the mosquito queens gradually became less vociferous. Konkaboti waited there eagerly for the master mosquito to come back home. Time passed, hours elapsed, but the master mosquito was still not in sight.

Konkaboti asked, '*Hna ga*, O listen, why is your master so late in getting back?'

The youngest queen said, 'Maybe he has collected oodles of blood, so he has been delayed cutting bamboos, making poles, and using porters, and will probably bring blood soon.'

Konkaboti continued to wait, but still the master mosquito was not sighted.

Konkaboti asked again, 'When will your master return? It is getting much too late.'

Now the second mosquito queen answered, 'The husk-burnt smoke, fanned by a *kulo*, has perhaps made him retire to a corner.'

This meant, 'The master might have sneaked into somebody's room. That fellow might have burnt husks and fanned the smouldering fire by a kulo. As a result, the room might have been filled with smoke. The master mosquito might have hidden in some corner of the room, unable to come out. This may have deterred him. When the smoke dissipates, he will come out of hiding.'

Konkaboti sat quietly for some more time. Then again, she asked, '*Koi ga*, O dear mistresses of the house, can you tell me how long I will have to wait?'

Now the eldest of the mosquito's wives answered, 'A sharp sting, and a slap, he has probably been killed.'

This meant, 'The master might have sat on someone to suck blood. The moment he gave him a bite, that fellow might have smacked him hard. And that slap might have killed the master mosquito.'

'—has probably been killed'—these ominous words made the youngest queen fly into a rage. She hissed out at the eldest, 'What, dare you speak such dreadful words! Let the master come; I will tell him, "If you die, your eldest wife will heave a sigh of relief!" He will paint your face black and white, shave your head, pour whey on it, and show you the door.'[3]

Notes

1. 'Roktoboti': The word 'rokto' means 'blood', and the name literally means 'carrying, or filled with, blood', referring to a female.
2. '... let us call ... a pet name ...': A reference to a custom, especially in nineteenth-century Bengal, and particularly rural Bengal, in which two girls or women, while becoming friends, assigned each other a pet name to call her by. This was known as '*soi patano*', literally meaning 'befriending'.
3. '... paint your face ... and show you the door': A reference to a common especially nineteenth-century custom in Bengal, which decreed such modes of punishment for an errant individual who committed a disgraceful act.

14

The Master Mosquito

The three wives of the master mosquito once again broke into a terrible squabble. Roktoboti started crying loudly. The mosquito household was aflutter with a real racket. At that moment, the master mosquito made an entry. The kerfuffle made him bristle in anger.

The mosquito said, 'I can put up with this nuisance no longer! The din of your quarrels does not give a chap a moment's peace.[1] Mother Lakshmi deserts a place where such discords and hubbub rage all the time;[2] blood in human bodies dries up in such a strife-ridden place. I can no longer take this, sometimes I feel like hanging or poisoning myself to death! Yes, I swear that suicide is my ultimate fate! The other day, I had a real close shave. I squatted on an opium-eater. O how shall I describe how bitter his blood tasted! I sucked in one antenna-ful of blood, and then ejected it. I had to rinse my antenna time and again, and that was how I was saved on that occasion. I thought to myself that it would be unfair to suffer an accidental death. So I strove so hard to save my life. But you have tormented me so much that I no longer nurse one bit of desire to live longer.'

In this manner, the master mosquito kept berating his wives. Finally, when his ire was somewhat abated and he was a bit composed, Roktoboti went and sat on his lap.

Roktoboti said, 'Father, see, here is my Putrid Water.'

The mosquito asked, 'Putrid Water? What do you mean? What is Putrid Water?'

Roktoboti's mother answered, 'Ogo, O dear husband, she is a human girl. She has been sitting here the entire evening. Roktoboti is friends with her, with the pet name "Putrid Water". Aha, that girl has been crying since she came here. She says, "I am a devoted wife who has lost her husband. Nakeshwori has devoured my husband. I will go to some human habitation, get a physician, and make my husband whole again." I told her, "Child, wait for a while. Let my master come back, I will consult with him about your problem, and try to find a way out. Since you have become my Roktoboti's Putrid Water, we will surely try to remove your sorrow." But your other two wives cannot bear that my Roktoboti will have her Putrid Water, and have fun with her. They wanted to have that human child as their pet. And since I objected, they assailed me with invectives. I no longer desire to stay here, please make arrangements to send me back to my parental home. You can live happily with your other two wives. I have become a thorn in your side, so it is better that I leave this place.'

The master mosquito asked, 'Where is that human girl?'

Roktoboti's mother said, 'She is sitting over there.'

Roktoboti said, 'Father, please come with me, I will show you where my Putrid Water is.'

The master mosquito and Roktoboti flew out together. They droned their way to the spot where Konkaboti sat in a sulk and with tearful eyes.

Roktoboti said, 'Putrid Water, look up and see, my father has come to you.'

Konkaboti got up reverently, and saluted the mosquito. The master mosquito flew out to sit atop a blade of grass to have a better view of Konkaboti. By his side, on another blade of grass, sat Roktoboti. Konkaboti stood before the master mosquito with joined palms.

With great humility, Konkaboti said, 'Mohashoy, I am an imperilled and orphaned girl. I am roaming alone in this desolate forest. I am a chaste woman who has lost her husband. I am Konkaboti, the grief-stricken girl. My husband, who is my very soul, is now under a ghostess's control. Please do me the good turn of rescuing my husband. I seek your help.'

The master mosquito asked, 'I must know to whom you belong.'

Konkaboti replied, 'Mohashoy, I was my father's property before. Human girls are their father's property in childhood. The father enjoys the right to sell or give them away to any blind, crippled, old or diseased fellow he wishes. Parents are relieved by selling or giving away their daughters even before they mature. This is the custom that prevails in our society. My father sold me to my husband for three thousand gold coins. Now I am my husband's property, and, having lost that husband I am forsaken now, and am crying and wandering in the forest. I was my father's property earlier, but am my husband's now.'

The master mosquito said, 'O no, I don't want to know all that. My question is—which mosquito's property are you?'

Konkaboti answered, 'Which mosquito's property! I don't have the foggiest notion. I don't think I am any mosquito's property.'

The master mosquito said to his daughter, 'Roktoboti, your Putrid Water seems to be raving mad! She has taken leave of her senses. How can I help your Putrid Water if I don't get right answers to my questions?"

Roktoboti said, 'Dear Putrid Water, answer truthfully to my father's questions, please.'

The master mosquito said, 'Listen, human child, all men and women in India are the mosquitoes' property. You have perhaps escaped from the mosquito mohashoy who owns you. Maybe, to cover up your crime you are not speaking the truth, rather, you are trying to conceal it from me. But you needn't fear, give truthful answers to my questions. I ask you, which mosquito's property are you? Which mosquito sits on your body to drink your blood? What is his name? Where does he live? How many wives does he have? How many sons? How many daughters? Has he any grandsons and granddaughters? Do his kith and kin and friends enjoy any rights to your blood? Do they regard you as common property, or have they already divided your hands and feet among themselves? In case you have been divided, where are those documents? Have you been divided by a middleman, or at the behest of a supervisor employed by the court? You need to answer all these questions because I desire to buy you. There are so many people in my land; there is no dearth of people here. The blood in the bodies of humans who are my property is enough for me to drink. But you have hit it off with Roktoboti with the pet name Putrid Water, which is why I want to purchase you. Unless I do that, your proprietor mosquitoes may arraign me in court. They may even take you back again from here. My Roktoboti will cry if they do that. And let me tell you another thing—Indians should not be travelling about from one village to another in this manner. Indians ought to stay put in their own villages. If they do that, there can be no disputes among the mosquitoes over property. In that case, the mosquitoes may enjoy their own property without trouble. However, very soon we will devise a way for ensuring this. Now, please answer my question. What is the name of your mosquito proprietor?'

Konkaboti replied, 'Mohashoy, I swear that I do not know. To this day I did not know that humans are the property of mosquitoes. I did not know that humans are distributed, sold, and divided among the mosquitoes. I do not even know that mosquitoes have names. How can I tell you the name of my mosquito proprietor?'

At this, the master mosquito was infuriated. His eyes turned bloodshot in violent rage. He said, 'O, you know nothing, is that so? You are a toddler, I suppose? Have you never seen a mosquito land on your body? You do not know them! Their names are unknown to you! Acting coy! You only know how to go about as a chaste woman weeping for her dead husband!'

These cruel words of the mosquito so upset Konkaboti that she started crying. Roktoboti winked at Konkaboti. That wink meant: 'Putrid Water, do not cry. My father has a mercurial temper. Now that he is ruffled, he'll get even angrier if you cry. Stop crying, father's anger will soon subside.'

What Roktoboti had signified happened. Konkaboti's sobs irritated the master mosquito even more. He said, 'What an irksome, whining girl is this! She only knows how to sniff and snivel! You said that you have no answers to the questions I asked! Now try to answer this question, will you? Tell me why these people whom you see around you, these crores of people who live in India, exist at all. Why were they created? Now, come on, answer that.'

Konkaboti said, 'Why have men been created? I do not know the answer.'

The master mosquito said, 'Oh, this girl is a dolt, a nitwit in the truest sense! She is insane. She knows nothing! Really, these Indian people are idiots of the first water! They are deplorably devoid of common sense. Roktoboti is just a child, but even so, she is a thousand times better in terms of common sense. Now Roktoboti, dear child, will you tell me why Indian people have been created?'

Roktoboti said, 'Why father, they have been created so that we can drink their blood.'

The master mosquito said, 'Did you hear that? Now, have you understood why the Indian populace was created?'

Konkaboti replied, 'Yes, now I have understood. Human beings were created so that mosquitoes can feed on them.'

Roktoboti said, 'My Putrid Water is a mere human child. Every mosquito knows that humans are numskulls. That is why foolish mosquitoes are called 'humans'. Mosquitoes say, 'O that mosquito is not a mosquito at all, he is a human.' No wonder, my Putrid Water, being human, is not as sensible as us. So father, please scold her no more.'

The mosquito thought, 'It is true that it's no use snubbing this human child. I will have to look into the matter on my own.'

The mosquito said, 'Hello girl, in which village do you live? You can tell the name of your village, I suppose?'

Konkaboti answered that the name of their village was Kusumghati. The mosquito immediately sent his attendants and emissaries to Kusumghati. He ordered them to fetch Konkaboti's proprietor mosquitoes. The emissaries reached Kusumghati, and learnt after much inquiry that Konkaboti's proprietors were three in number—Elephant Cheeks, Large Skull and Broken Snout.

Roktoboti's father's name was Long Antenna. The emissaries learnt that Konkaboti's proprietors lived in a *sal* tree called 'Akashmukh' meaning 'facing the Sky'. So they went to inform those proprietors what they knew about Konkaboti. They came immediately with the emissaries to Long Antenna. After much chafing and haggling, Long Antenna purchased Konkaboti for three *chhotak*s of human blood. Having purchased her, he said to his daughter, 'Roktoboti, now Putrid Water is yours. From now on, this human child is our own, we are her proprietors.'

Long Antenna then addressed Elephant Cheeks, Large Skull and Broken Snout and other mosquitoes, and said, 'O great souls, I find that we are faced with a grave danger! All the mosquitoes of the world have so long been drinking the Indians' blood, and living in clover. India is surrounded by seas and oceans on three sides, and the other end is blocked by a towering mountain range. Humans keep their livestock within an enclosure, and we did the same with the Indians. And the Indians too, confined within their country, have been humbly serving us, and nourishing us with their blood. But regrettably, some Indians have become adventurous enough these days to set sail on oceans and to surmount mountains. You all know that those who do such things and deprive us of our right to drink their blood commit the most heinous of sins. Now we must dissuade Indians from committing such reprehensible acts. Besides this, Indians are showing a disturbing tendency to travel from this village to that. This very evening, a human child hailing from Kusumghati has darkened my door. That human child was your property. Today your property has fled, tomorrow mine will. If these humans continue to travel from one village to another in like manner, we the mosquitoes will be at loggerheads with each other over our property. Then again, imagine the disastrous effects of going places. Travelling gives man exposure to various forms of knowledge, it makes him wise. If the scales fall from the Indians' eyes, they will be loath to be under our thumb. Further, commerce will make them rich. Then they will employ devices like mosquito nets and other such items to prevent us from drinking their blood.

So, comrades, we need to find ways to stop Indians from crossing the seas, and also from travelling from one village to another.'

Long Antenna's speech mesmerised the audience. All the listeners started extolling him to the skies. They said that Long Antenna was a sagacious mosquito, and that no mosquito as far-sighted, as sapient, and as sharp-witted as him existed in the whole world. Everybody agreed that Indians must be prevented from travelling from one village to another. After much deliberation, the mosquitoes decided that pundits should be called in to deliver a mandate on this matter. They felt that only that mandate, and nothing else, would be acceptable to the masses. Having agreed on this, the mosquito assembly invited pundits from all over India. When the pundits arrived, Long Antenna requested them to bring out shastric commandments approved of by the mosquito community. Having discussed the shastras, the pundits decreed that from then on, Indians were forbidden to travel from one village to another. They ruled that if somebody ever disregarded the decree, he would commit a dreadful sin. And that sin would be inexpiable. What, then, were the Indians supposed to do in this age of Koli? They need not worry. The pundits had the verdict ready for them in the form of a Sanskrit fiat, whose essence was: in the age of Koli, Indians would sit immobile with blinkered eyes and joined palms inside a dark well, and mosquitoes would come in droves to suck their blood.

This arrangement gave the mosquitoes a world of satisfaction. The pundits got their due remuneration, and went back to their own places. And the other mosquitoes too returned to their respective lands.

Notes

1. '... does not give a chap a moment's peace ...': The colourful idiom in the original is '... *kak chil boste pare na*', meaning that 'crows and kites [birds] can't remain perched (on the branches of trees near homes of people who always quarrel)'.
2. Mother Lakshmi: The goddess of wealth, noted for her beauty, revered by Hindus.

15

Khorbur

Long Antenna said, 'Roktoboti, this human child is now yours. You can do with her whatever you wish.'

Roktoboti said, 'Father, she is like a sister to me. I call her Putrid Water. Now my Putrid Water is in danger. Her husband has been devoured by Nakeshwori. Putrid Water is crying her eyes out. Father, please do something so that my Putrid Water gets her husband back.'

The master mosquito wished to listen to the entire account of how Nakeshwori had taken the life of Konkaboti's husband. Konkaboti narrated her jeremiad from beginning to end.

Having pondered long over the matter, the mosquito said, 'Since you are my Roktoboti's Putrid Water, I have developed a soft spot for you. We will not drink your blood. We will bring you up with affection. We will try heart and soul to get you reunited with your husband. There is a man called Khorbur moharaj in my territory. I have heard that he is well-versed in herbal medicine, and in magical mantras. If it does not rain for a long time, he can utter chants to drill holes in the clouds. When hail threatens to fall, he can prevent it. If he comes across an old woman, he can declare with conviction whether she is a witch or not. Even ghosts take to their heels if they catch sight of this fellow. Another man as virtuous and capable as him is not to be seen in the world. I am sure that this fellow will be able to rescue your husband from Nakeshwori.'

Konkaboti said, 'In that case, mohashoy, I beg you not to tarry. I suppose we need to go to this man at this very instant. Mohashoy, my bereaved soul is bleeding for my husband, and I see void all round. I am alive only in the hope that my husband will ultimately be saved. Had it not been so, I would have sacrificed my sinful life long ago.'

The mosquito said, 'It is late at night, and you look tired. My locality is not very near. But wait, I am sending for my younger brother. We will all go to Khorbur moharaj, riding piggyback on him right away."

So the mosquito sent for his younger brother, who came in a short while. The mosquito queens called him 'elephant-the-brother-in-law' and greeted him cordially, while jesting and pulling his leg.

Roktoboti told his brother, 'Uncle, I have found a human child. And I befriended her with the pet name "Putrid Water". I love my Putrid Water very much, and my Putrid Water too loves me with all her heart.'

Konkaboti was amazed. The younger brother of the mosquito was an elephant—an enormous one! Everyone in the forest called him 'elephant-the-brother-in-law'.

Roktoboti's father told the elephant, 'Dear brother, I am in deep trouble. Roktoboti has made friends with a human girl with the pet name Putrid Water. And that girl's husband has been devoured by Nakeshwori. For this, that girl has been roaming around and weeping in the forest. Roktoboti is a kind-hearted girl, and she is greatly distressed by her friend's sorrow. That is why I have decided to leave no stone unturned to rescue her husband. This can be done only by Khorbur moharaj. But this girl is fatigued after walking and weeping for long. She is dead on her feet, so can hardly move. Now, brother, we appeal to you to do us a favour. We request you to carry us on your back.'

Elephant-the-brother-in-law agreed to the proposal. Konkaboti saluted the mosquito queens, and took leave of them.

Konkaboti wound her arms round Roktoboti's neck, and said, 'O dear Putrid Water, you have done me a great service. I cannot forget your love and kindness in my life. In case I get my husband back, we will meet again. And in case I don't, you see your Putrid Water now for the last time.'

Roktoboti's eyes moistened and tears dripped from her eyes on to the ground.

The mosquito rode on the elephant's back with Konkaboti for company. Elephant-the-brother-in-law ambled on. The night passed. In the wee hours of the morning, they reached Khorbur's. They found that Khorbur had just left his bed and was sitting at his door with a sullen face. The darkness of the night was yet to be dispelled fully. The waning moon of the dark fortnight was yet to go down. But the moon sported a mirthful face upon seeing Khorbur's morose expression. The moon was, as it were, smiling from ear to ear. And that lunar smile got Khorbur's goat. Nettled, he resolved to himself, 'I must take the moon to task. If I cannot teach this moon a lesson, my magical roots and mantras are all useless.'

The mosquito, the elephant and Konkaboti appeared at Khorbur's door. Seeing the mosquito, Khorbur got up quickly to greet him.

With joined palms he said, 'Mohashoy, what is the purpose of your visit at dawn? You usually visit us in the evening. Why in the daytime today? Is some kin your guest? Have you come with your younger brother to take lots of blood in order to treat your honoured guests to a sumptuous spread?'

The mosquito replied, 'No, I have not come for that. I will tell you about our purpose presently, but now let me ask you why you sit here in brooding silence. You should never be in such a despondent mood. I forbade you several times to mope, or to be in low spirits. Unless people are hale and hearty, their bodies do not form blood, and even if blood forms, it is never tasty. If you do not live cheerfully, and do not eat nutritious and invigorating food, what will we suck out of your bloodless bodies? If you continue to perform such misdeeds, how are we supposed to sustain our families? Don't you ever get scared that if the mosquitoes, your lords, are not able to drink your blood plentifully and properly, they will get extremely annoyed?"

Khorbur said, 'Lord, it is true that I am getting thinner. I know that unless you get a good quantity of delicious blood out of my body, you will be offended. But what can I do? My wife has driven me to this desperate state.'

The mosquito asked, 'Why, what is the matter? What kind of torture does your wife inflict on you?'

Khorbur said, 'Lord, we have endless tiffs. And very often, we even get locked in scuffles a couple or more times a day. But, O lord, what shall I say of my misfortune? I am three arms in height, but my wife is seven. When we come to blows, my wife smacks my scalp hard with *nagra* shoes. I cannot get up to her head, and so my strikes fall on her back. No wonder, my wife's beating easily wears me down, but mine has little effect on her. So every time my wife wins hands down. With such bashing, coupled with the mental affliction, I am getting emaciated, and I have turned anaemic. My lord may take umbrage at this, and there is no doubt about that. But what can I do? I am blameless.'

The mosquito said, 'Well, now I understand your plight! Okay, I advise you to do one thing. Today you get on my brother's back, and fight with your wife.'

With these words, the mosquito offered the elephant to Khorbur. Khorbur got on his back, went into his house, and started quarrelling with his wife. The spat soon snowballed into a brawl. Khorbur, sitting pretty on the elephant's back, gleefully brought the nagra shoes down on his wife's head time and again. And his wife's blows landed lightly on Khorbur's legs. When the fight climaxed, the mosquito went into raptures. He had no hands to clap with, no nails to rub together, and so he started dancing, raising one and, sometimes, both his legs, humming, 'Narod, Narod'.[1] Within a short while, Khorbur's wife had to bite the dust. And Khorbur brimmed with joy. Blood started coursing through his veins and arteries at a rate of knots. The mosquito tasted that blood a little, and said, 'O how very scrummy! How sweet!'

Khorbur moharaj heaped thanks on the mosquito mohashoy for his assistance, and asked him the reason for his untimely arrival. The mosquito then put Khorbur wise to the entire account involving Konkaboti and Nakeshwori.

Having listened to the whole story, Khorbur said, 'You needn't worry. I will salvage this girl's husband from the clutches of Nakeshwori. The whole tribe of ghosts, ghostesses, spirits and witches dread me. Now please take me to Nakeshwori's alcove, let me see what power she wields.'

The mosquito said, 'Yes, come, let us travel together. But all this travelling will soon come to an end. You people have all started going to places like Rangoon or *Bilat* in big ships of late! Travelling by train to this country and that. Just you wait, let the new shastra be promulgated; you will then face your day of reckoning!'

Khorbur asked, 'Does the new shastra prohibit our travelling altogether? May we not travel even to search out medicinal roots?'

The mosquito answered, 'No, not at all! The new shastra decrees that you people cannot venture out of your rooms at all. Everyone will have to dig a dark well and crouch in that well with blinkered eyes. If someone steps out of that well, or removes the blinkers, it will be a serious sin. This will not be any ordinary sin, but what people describe as a cardinal sin. Not only a cardinal sin, but what people describe as a great cardinal sin. Not only a great cardinal sin, but what people describe as a great and grievous cardinal sin. Now, what do you feel, poor mortals! Boarding ships and trains for travelling, getting educated and using such detestable objects as mosquito nets, are now all well and truly put paid to! Serves you right! Now put that in your pipe and smoke it!'

Khorbur said, 'You are our honourable lords. Whatever shastras you make for us we are bound to obey. You are our lords and masters, our gods. You can do whatever you deem fit.'

The mosquito, along with Konkaboti and Khorbur, rode on the elephant's back towards the forest. Around the second prohor of the night, they came near the hill that was Nakeshwori's dominion.

Note

1. "... legs, humming, 'Narod, Narod'.": Narod is a mythical sage who is a *veena*-player and Lord Vishnu's devotee. He is believed to enjoy instigating people to quarrel by reporting one's private talk to another.

16

The Ogre

When Nakeshwori had Khetu under her control, he was out cold, absolutely dead to the world. He had no idea that Nakeshwori had blown Konkaboti away with a vigorous blast of her breath.

With Khetu about to breathe his last, Nakeshwori thought, 'I have been starving for long. At last, when thanks to the tiger, my deity of devotion, I have got this delicious food, I must cook it well and eat it. Such toothsome stuff does not give enough pleasure if relished by oneself alone. Let me go and invite my aunt in.'

Lest the food turned stale before her aunt came in, Nakeshwori did not kill Khetu, but kept him alive in an unconscious state.

Nakeshwori went to call in her aunt. Nakeshwori's aunt lived far off, beyond the seven seas and the thirteen rivers,[1] on the other side of the place where the community of ghosts with single legs lived. It took quite some time for Nakeshwori to go that distance and come back with her aunt.

Nakeshwori's aunt was an old woman. She was completely toothless. Having seen Khetu's soft flesh, the aunt turned ecstatic and started to salivate.

The aunt pinched and poked Khetu's body, and said, 'Aaha, what soft flesh! At this old age, I can hardly chew the rope-like stiff meat that I usually get in the place of the single-leg ghost community. Today, I will have my fill chomping the meat of a biped. Let us make a broth of his head, fry the sliced flesh from off his back, make *chochhori* of his fingers, and make *ombol* of the rest of the meat, which will not go off even if we eat it over two days.'

When the aunt and niece were engaged in such conversation, a noise was heard outside. An elephant's trumpet, a mosquito's drone and a human voice drifted into the mansion from beyond the hill.

Nakeshwori was alarmed, and said, 'O aunt, a disaster is round the corner. I think we are going to lose this scrumptious food. That girl has probably come back with an exorcist.'

The aunt said, 'Come then, let us stand above the door, with our legs wide apart.'

Nakeshwori and her aunt straddled above the door of the mansion.

Arriving near the tunnel by the side of the hill, the mosquito, Konkaboti and Khorbur alighted from the elephant. Elephant-the-brother-in-law stood outside, and got busy swatting flies with the snapped branch of a tree. At times, he sucked in the dust with his trunk and sprinkled it on his body like talcum powder. When he felt like rocking, he started swaying his bulk to and fro quite merrily.

The mosquito, Konkaboti and Khorbur entered the tunnel. Walking along it, they stepped inside the mansion. While entering they slipped in under the feet of Nakeshwori and her aunt.

Once inside, they approached Khetu. Khetu lay unconscious. It was doubtful whether he was still breathing at all. Konkaboti sat near his feet, clasped them to her bosom, and started wailing. Khorbur began examining Khetu in various ways.

At last, Khorbur said, 'Konkaboti, don't cry. Your husband is alive, and he will soon come round. I will begin curing him this very instant.'

Saying this, Khorbur started chanting mantras, blew over Khetu's body several times, and administered different drugs. But to no avail. Khetu lay in a faint as before. Not a single limb of his moved.

Khorbur was surprised, and said, 'Strange! My magical mantras never fail like this. Even if the patient is not fully revived, the mantras at least have some effect. What can be the reason for the inefficacy of my mantras and roots?'

Khorbur was perturbed, for he failed to figure out the cause.

Finally, he said, 'Lord mosquito, come, let us get out into the open. I need to find out what's going on.'

They came out of the mansion. Konkaboti was now totally crestfallen. She thought it was only natural that an ill-fated girl like her would lose her husband, otherwise why should all these events have taken place? But the thought that now she was in a position to get possession of her husband's body, and to sacrifice her life at her husband's lotus feet,[2] comforted her somewhat, even when immersed in an ocean of sorrow.

After going out once, they again made their way back through the tunnel. While walking, Khorbur kept surveying all sides minutely, casting sharp glances above and below, in front and behind, and sideways. When he came near the mansion, he found the ghostesses straddled above the entrance. Khorbur chuckled, and thought to himself, 'Well, well, well, so you have played a clever trick, haven't you?'

Now Khrobur started intoning chants outside the mansion. The chanting had an immediate effect, for the ghostesses rose higher and turned tail in no time. Now Khorbur re-entered the mansion, and resumed his magic ritual. Gradually, the magic spell drew Nakeshwori in to possess Khetu's body. Khetu started talking, but it was the ghostess who spoke through Khetu's mouth. Khorbur administered many drugs, and muttered many chants, commanding Nakeshwori to desert that place. But Nakeshwori was not ready to oblige. She said, 'This man is a great sinner. He plundered the treasure that I had been watching over so long; no way can I let him go scot-free. I will and I must devour him.' Khorbur chanted more spells to torment Nakeshwori, who in the end, being unable to bear that pain, decided to beat a retreat. But although she agreed to leave Khetu's body, in reality she did not do so. Repeatedly, she said, 'O yes, now I will go, yes, surely I will,' but she stayed on. Nakeshwori's hypocrisy got on Khorbur's nerves. His lips trembled in fury, and his eyes turned bloodshot. He said, 'So, you won't go, is that so? Okay, let me see who triumphs!' With these words, he brought a gourd. He chanted spells to solemnise it, smeared it with vermilion, and prepared to subject it to ritualistic sacrifice. He put the gourd on a piece of broken earthenware, and lifted his curved knife to cut it into halves. Just when the knife was about to strike, Nakeshwori screamed in a terrified voice, saying, 'O save me, please do! Don't bring down that knife, don't cut me up. Give me a chance to speak the whole truth. I will not lie, I swear.'

Khorbur said, 'What do you want to say? Say truthfully why you are not leaving the place. Unless you do that, I will cut you up.'

Nakeshwori said, 'Even if I go away, that will not yield the desired results. The patient will give up the ghost right at this moment. I wrapped this fellow's life-span in an arum ['*kochu*'] leaf and kept that on the top of a palm tree. I thought when my aunt arrived, we would grind that into chutney, and slurp that stuff up. Now, that leaf containing the life-span has been swept down by the wind from the top of the palm tree. And ants have already eaten that up. Now where will I get that life-span so that I can restore it to the patient? That is why I say that the moment I desert this fellow's body, he will breathe his last.'

Khorbur made some magico-astrological calculations to judge the veracity of Nakeshwori's statement. He found that her words were indeed true. Khorbur thought to himself, 'Now I see serious trouble afoot! How to get round this? If the life-span is lost, none can give it back.'

After long contemplation, Khorbur commanded Nakeshwori, 'You search out those little ants which have eaten up the life-span.'

Nakeshwori went under the palm tree, and started looking for the ants in the crevices of mounds, the fissures of the soil, and the hollows of trees. But her efforts were fruitless. Those little ants were nowhere to be seen. Nakeshwori and her aunt came upon large black ants, wood ants, tickling ants, bait ants and some other species of ants, and asked them, 'Do you know where those little ants have gone? Have any of you seen them?' But none could give them a clue. The predicament of the niece pained the aunt, and so, she too made an extensive search. But she soon lost her breath due to overstrain, and her legs ached. Then the old ghostess thought, 'I came here to savour the succulent meat of a human biped, and now I am left fending for my life! What a quirk of fate, really!'

After an arduous search, Nakeshwori bumped into a one-eyed ant whom she asked about the little ants. That one-eyed ant said, 'Yes, I know what happened to those little ants. They had licked the sweet human life-span entirely out of the arum leaf, washed and wiped their hands and mouths, and were returning home. Just at that moment, a frog in a sahib's attire burst on the scene out of nowhere, and devoured those homebound ants one by one.'

Returning to the mansion, Nakeshwori shared this news with Khorbur. Now Khorbur sent Nakeshwori once again to search the frog out. Nakeswori rued, 'What a splendid arrangement! This damned fellow has robbed me of my food, and on top of that, is making me slog hard.' However, she had no option but to carry out Khorbur's command. If she did not comply, Khorbur would sacrifice that vermilion-smeared gourd. The moment he cut up the gourd, Nakeshwori's head would be severed from her torso.

So Nakeshwori and her aunt went looking for the frog in forests, hills, ponds and ditches. But how were the ghostesses supposed to know in which hole the frog, having gorged on his meal, was having his siesta? The frog could not be traced. Nakeshwori came back and informed Khorbur, 'Kill me or cut me if you so wish, but the fact is that I have failed to run that frog to ground.'

Nakeshwori's words plunged Khorbur once again into deep cogitation. Having thought long and hard, he took up a fistful of mustard seeds. Casting a spell, he scattered those seeds about. Those fallen seeds rushed in all directions at lightning speed. They raced and galloped across countries, villages and towns, valleys and dunes, seas and oceans. Frog mohashoy was having his forty winks in a snug, cool hole beside an old hyacinth-filled, mucky pond. The charmed mustard seeds sneaked into that hole. The needle-sharp edges of those seeds penetrated the frog's skin and flesh, and weighed heavy on his head. At this, the hat slipped off from the frog's head. The frog started screaming shrilly in pain. The seeds pushed him out of the hole. And they kept pushing him up towards the mansion. They pushed him into the tunnel as well. Having come to the mansion, Frog mohashoy knocked on the door.

The mosquito opened the door. Frog mohashoy entered the mansion, and went to the spot where Konkaboti and Khorbur sat. Konkaboti recognised him as the very frog she had come upon, and the frog too recognised Konkaboti as *that* girl.

The frog said, 'O bright girl, I had such a long conversation with you, and you came here and shared the story of my fifty-paise coin with each and everybody. Chhi! Shame! That was a disgraceful act on your part. Does anybody in her senses share an account of wealth with pickpockets? Especially with that flat-bottomed sneak thief! Now I beseech you to take whatever remains of that coin, and divide that among yourselves, and let me go. And, you flat-bottomed mohashoy, these seeds are all your attendants, I see! Now, please ask your charmed mustard seeds to dismount from my head. I am about to kick the bucket in pain.'

Khorbur said, 'We have nothing to do with your coin. This girl is known to you. And maybe you also know that she is faced with a crisis. That youth on his deathbed that you see in front of you is her husband. He had been assailed by Nakeshwori. She took away his life-span, and kept it hidden on the top of a palm tree. But that span was blown down to the ground by a gust of wind, little ants licked that up and you ate those ants. Now please make it convenient to bring out those ants from your stomach. I will then squeeze that span out of those ants and try to save Konkaboti's husband. Once you regurgitate those ants, the seeds will let you go.'

The frog replied, 'Yes, I know this girl, and I am ready to do her a good turn.'

Having said so, the frog poked one of his fingers into his throat in order to throw up, but in vain. Then he thrust a feather into his throat so that he could vomit, but even this effort came to nought.

At last, Khorbur made him consume various emetic drugs, but still he did not manage to disgorge the food ingested.

Khorbur thought, 'This is a new tangle! How will I unravel this?'

Khorbur then felt the frog's pulse with great care. He thought, 'Now I have got the moon in a tight corner.' The fact is that at that moment, Khorbur came to remember the moon. The main root of the moon was a sure-fire remedy for this disease, and the frog would vomit the moment he munched it down.

Addressing the mosquito, Khorbur said, 'Mohashoy, there is no drug in this universe that can make this frog throw up. With one exception. You need to get a slice of the main root of the moon that you see in the sky. The frog needs to consume that slice made into a paste with seven globules of black pepper in order to vomit. Nothing else will work.'

Hearing this, the mosquito was dejected. And Konkaboti was overcome with despair.

Konkaboti said, 'Mosquito mohashoy and Khorbur moharaj, you have laboured hard and long for this ill-fated girl. But what can you do? This unfortunate girl who stands in front of you has been doomed unredeemably. Who can go up in the sky and cut the main root of the moon? It is impossible to do that, and so no way can my husband be revived. Now, all of you go back home please, do not feel anguish over my fate. With your assistance I have at least possessed my husband's corpse, and I believe that is good enough for me. Let me now take refuge at my husband's feet, and lay down my life. All of you, please return home.'

The mosquito said, 'It's true that I can fly far, but I lack the power to fly as far as the moon. So I now fear that all our efforts have gone up in smoke. Aha, Roktoboti, my dear child, is awaiting my return eagerly. What will I tell her?'

Khorbur said, 'You need not fret so much. Can you find me an ogre cub? If you do, one can ride it and soar to the sky at a canter. But listen, an adult ogre will not do, because taming it will be impossible! You need an ogre *cub* for the purpose.'

The frog said, 'I know where an ogress gave birth to a cub. But how will you catch it? Its mother will simply gobble you up if ever you attempt to do that, will she not? And even if you manage to seize it, how will you ride it and soar to the sky? You will have to take your life in your hands to do that. There is a formidable sepoy in the sky. He is the sentry. He is deaf, but for all that, he is a terrific sepoy. The inhabitants of the firmament live in fear of this sepoy. He patrols all sides of the sky, and if you run into him, your game is up. So I wonder who will dare go up to the sky to cut the main root of the moon.'

Konkaboti said, 'That is not a worrying matter at all. If I get an ogre cub I am prepared to ride piggyback on it up into the sky. What do I fear now? In case I run into the sepoy, he will at worst kill me; what more harm can he do to me? I am resolved to lay down my life in any case if I do not get my husband back. So why should I be scared to die?'

Thus, it was decided that the ogre cub had to be seized and tamed. The frog gave the directions to the cavity by the side of a hill in which that cub could be found. The mosquito said, 'We need to seize the cub by some strategem.'

Their scheme entailed the frog and Khorbur keeping watch over Khetu within the mansion, while the mosquito, Konkaboti and the elephant would go to capture the ogre cub.

Before setting off, Konkaboti took the dust off Khetu's feet on to her head.

The mosquito asked Konkaboti once again, 'Konkaboti, how about it? Do you think you will manage to soar up to the sky? Won't you be afraid?'

Konkaboti said, 'Afraid? What do you mean? What is there to fear? If ever I manage to get up to the sky, I will see how the moon manages to save his main root. And I also want to see how many swords and shields that deaf sepoy has! Today I will demonstrate to the inhabitants of the sky the prowess of a devoted wife.'

Notes

1. '... beyond the seven seas and the thirteen rivers, ...': Literal translation of a common Bengali idiom, often used in fairy tales, to indicate a vast distance, dating from the time when it was mythically believed this was the number of seas and rivers on earth.
2. '... sacrifice her life ... lotus feet ...': 'Lotus feet' is a common metaphor, especially in nineteenth-century Bengali literature, indicating the target of one's devotion—as, in this case, of a wife towards her husband.

17

The Wife of the Stars

Nakeswori and her aunt heard everything about the plan to capture the ogre cub, and Konkaboti's proposed flight to the sky. Now they conspired, 'If we can prevent this venture, Khorbur cannot blame us, and on the other hand, we will not have to lose our food.'

The aunt said, 'I have grown old, and I have developed a distaste for most of the food of the world. I long to eat such soft, succulent flesh as this fellow's, but though by some chance we had a windfall, it is going to slip away. O, what misfortune!'

Nakeshwori said, 'Aunt, do one thing, please. Sit in this basket and soar up to the sky. Please whitewash the entire sky. Whitewash well so that not a single gap remains. Go wearing your glasses, so that you can spot the openings. If the sky is whitewashed perfectly, that girl will not be able to find her way through it, nor will she sight the moon and cut his main root.'

Having schemed so, the aunt went out and sat in the basket. The basket whooshed up to the sky. And Nakeshwori's aunt whitewashed it entirely.

While emerging out of the mansion, the mosquito found an abandoned drum and picked that up. Coming out, the mosquito and Konkaboti rode on the elephant's back. Now they went towards the forest where the ogre cub nestled. After evening had set in, they reached the burrow of the ogress.

The mosquito looked up at the sky, and said, 'What's the matter? Today is the second day of the bright fortnight, but the moon is not yet out! The sky is not overcast, where are the stars then? And why does the sky look so very white?'

The ogress was keeping tight vigil over her cub. It was night, and the forest was dense. From afar, the ogress smelt Konkaboti.

The ogress shouted fiercely, '*Haom*, *maom*, *khaom*, I smell a human! Who are you, approaching this way?'

The mosquito yelled back, 'Who on earth are you?'

The ogress said, 'Don't you know who I am? I am an ogress.'

The mosquito said, 'You want to know who we are? We are a bunch of *quogresses*.'

The retort gave the ogress the creeps. She said, 'O dear me, you are no footling creatures then! My name starts with an "o" and yours with a "q", which means you are two notches above me. Well, give me proof that you are really "quogresses". Let me hear you cough.'

The mosquito beat the drum a couple of times.

Hearing that 'boom!' the ogress said, 'O my goodness, how terrible is the noise of your cough! It gave me a real fright, and nearly ruptured my eardrums. I accept that you really are quogresses.'

But the ogress was still a little sceptical. Even that irrefutable proof did not convince her fully. So she asked, 'Well, throw down a strand of your hair, will you?'

The mosquito now dropped the cord used to tether the elephant. The ogress picked that up, and examined it, turning it over in her hand. After quite a while, she said, wonderstruck, 'O dear, is this a strand of your hair! When one strand of your hair is so thick and strong, who knows how hefty and brawny you yourselves are! It will be a tall order to stand up to you.'

But even so, the ogress did not believe fully what she said. Having pondered over the matter, she said, 'Well, in case you are quogresses, just chuck down a louse from your head and let me look at it!'

The mosquito said, 'Konkaboti, get down fast from the elephant's back. Be quick!'

Then the mosquito told the elephant, 'Now elephant, my brother, it is your turn...'

Having said this, the mosquito dropped the elephant in the ogress's burrow. The elephant slid down, and wound his trunk round the ogre cub. And the cub, with its shrill, prolonged scream, rent the heaven, the earth and the nether world. The ogress herself was frightened to death on seeing the mountain-size louse with a trunk! She thought, 'Their louse has come here to seize my cub, now what if they themselves barge in and capture me!' In a tizzy, the ogress took flight, leaving her cub behind.

Then the mosquito and Konkaboti approached the burrow.

The mosquito said, 'Konkaboti, now ride this creature. Ride your way right up to the sky. Having cut the main root of the moon, come back to this very place. We will be waiting for you here. When you come back, we will return this cub to its mother, because it is still a suckling, and how are we supposed to take care of it? However, now you have your job cut out to elude the clutches of the formidable sepoy of the sky. Word goes that he is a fierce, redoubtable and awesome fellow. So, Konkaboti, be on your guard!'

The mosquito then cast his glance towards the sky, and said, 'Konkaboti, the sky baffles me tonight. Today is the second day of the bright fortnight; the time of moonrise is long past. But I can see neither the moon nor the stars. The sky is not enveloped in dark clouds, but rather has been varnished white. I cannot make out what this means. What can be the reason behind this phenomenon? You may get some clue when you reach the sky. Proceed carefully to achieve your goal.'

Konkaboti now rode the ogre cub, and steered it towards the sky. The cub flew pretty fast. Konkaboti reached the sky in a short while.

Having gone near her target, Konkaboti found that the entire sky was whitewashed. Konkaboti muttered, 'What's this? Who has whitewashed the sky?'

Konkaboti was unable to pick her way through the sky. Whichever direction she went was whitewashed without a chink. She moved from one end to another, but failed to find a way in. White paint pervaded each and every corner. Konkaboti thought, 'What a calamity! Now, how shall I go up into the sky?'

A distraught Konkaboti traipsed round the sky to find a way. Having searched thoroughly enough, she suddenly discerned a tiny chink in a corner. The wife of the stars was peeping through that gap. Konkaboti approached it. Having seen her approach, the stars' wife hid herself, and then again fearfully took a sneak peek.

Konkaboti said, 'Ogo, hello, wife of the stars, you needn't be scared. I am a woman like yourself. What is there to be shy about?'

The stars' wife answered, 'Who are you, girl? Your words sound really sweet. I have been watching you for a long time. You have been hanging about here, so I felt that I should ask you what you were looking for. But, as you know, I am a wife after all, and so I cannot talk to anybody just like that, can I?[1] And on top of that, it is night-time. Please speak softly, girl. My children have all turned in. Your voice may rouse them from sleep, and if it does, they will nag me with whines and whimpers.'

Konkaboti said, 'O wife of the stars, my name is Konkaboti. I am a woman who has lost her beloved husband! I am a hapless girl. I am looking for a path that will lead me into the sky. But, dear woman, what is all this that I see? Why is there not a single route visible? If I can get into the sky even for once, my husband's life will be saved. Dear woman, if you tell me which path I should take to get into the sky, I will be hugely obliged.'

The stars' wife replied, 'Dear girl, how will you possibly find a route? A nasty, old ghostess came here this evening to whitewash the entire sky. Be that as it may, I am opening up the postern of the sky for you. Please enter through that gate.'

Having said so, the stars' wife surreptitiously opened the back door for Konkaboti. And through it Konkaboti managed to step into the sky.

Note

1. '... I cannot talk ..., can I?': A pointer to the interned and highly regulated domestic existence of women in the orthodox nineteenth-century Bengali society.

18

The Formidable Sepoy

Konkaboti stepped into the sky and tied the ogre cub to the branch of a cloud. Then she started roaming the meadows of the sky. She looked round and saw stars of various hues twinkling. They lit the sky up. The moon, at a distance, was lodged like a disc.

The moment Konkaboti entered the sky, the moon heard through the grapevine that a human being was on her way to cut his main root; a woman armed with a pick and a shovel was approaching him with a wild manner about her. The bad news gave the moon the shock of his life. He started to tremble.

The moon thought, 'Why did I have to be so beautiful? That is why people nurse such a grudge against me. Had I not been handsome, nobody would have come to cut my main root! Rahu always bays for my blood, and now on top of that, a human is on my trail.[1] O, how shall I live! If I had a neck, I would hang myself. O my God, this damned body is like a disc. Why don't I have a neck? Where shall I tie the rope?'

Moaning thus and being frightened out of his skin, the moon sent for the sepoy of the sky. The sepoy was otherwise quite efficient, though a little hard of hearing. You had to really yell to make him hear something.

The sepoy came, and the moon shouted out what he had to say.

The moon told him, 'A human being is coming to cut my main root.'

The sepoy thought that the moon took him to be stone deaf and so was yelping with his mouth agape. He was miffed.

The sepoy said, 'You needn't open your mouth that much. Chances are that you will be split in half.'

Now the moon opened his mouth less wide, and repeated, 'A human being is approaching to cut my main root.'

The sepoy said, 'O, don't whisper like that, are you planning a heist that you need that much secrecy? Anyway, in case you do commit a robbery somewhere, I'll not let go of my share.'

The moon thought, 'It's hopeless to talk to a person like this. He loses his cool so easily.'

The moon said again, 'O no, I'm not talking of robbery, I'm going nowhere to loot. What I'm saying is that a human being is approaching me to cut my main root.'

And now the sepoy managed to hear what the moon was saying.

The sepoy said, 'A human being is approaching you to cut your main root? All right, let it happen. What's wrong with that?"

The moon said, 'You are the sepoy of the sky. Won't you save me from the imminent danger? If you don't, why do you get paid?'

The sepoy said, 'Don't talk about my pay! I'm ready to give up the job. I'll go to the earth and be a constable instead. If they get a formidable sepoy like me, they will welcome me heartily. They don't have all this cutting of roots. Yes, riots and strife do take place there, but I'll give all turmoil a wide berth in troubled times. When the riots subside, and the rioters go back home, I'll pick up some innocent fellows from the streets and produce them in court. But now I'll be off. Suppose that human being comes here and drags me into it! Who knows?'

With these words, the terrific sepoy briskly made himself scarce. And the helpless moon thought, 'I'll face the music if I have to,' and leaned against the sky.

Meanwhile, Konkaboti was marching rapidly across the skyfield towards the moon.

Word got round that a human being was approaching to cut the main roots of all inhabitants in the sky, ranging from children to women to the old. All sky-dwellers cautioned their children and bolted their doors. But the poor stars had nowhere to escape, so they sat in groves and gardens wherever they were, and kept gleaming. And the moon too had no chance to flee, for he would be fined if he escaped without giving light to the earth, so he strolled on the streets of the sky with a sullen face and a heavy heart.

Finally, Konkaboti came near the moon.

The moon thought, 'O my God, now I'll have to part with my main root. Only if I myself am not robbed whole, I'll be thankful. But I don't trust this woman. Even in case she says, "O what a beautiful moon, I'll take him wrapped in my sari!" there's nothing I can do. No use messing with her. Let me lie still with eyes closed, without breathing, and play possum. The woman will think, "This is a dead moon. I've no use for a dead moon," and not take me along.'

The clever moon, thinking thus, closed his eyes and held his breath.

As she found the moon wan, morose and seemingly dead, Konkaboti thought, 'Oh! The moon is dead? He gave up the ghost in fear that I would cut his main root? Dear O dear, how beautiful was the moon! How he did give light, how charming was the full moon night! Nothing of that will ever happen again. From now on, the earth will always be dark at night. People will blame me so much for that.'

Konkaboti made a careful inspection, and then spoke to herself, 'No, the moon hasn't died. Maybe he has swooned. So be it. While operating, doctors first benumb the patients with anaesthetic drugs, and then they sever their limbs. It is good that the moon has lost his senses on his own, which means I don't need his assistance to cut his main root. But I'll not cut it completely, for then the moon will die. I need to cut only a slice of its bark, so I'll scrape only that much off.'

Thinking on these lines, and after circling round, Konkaboti at last found the main root of the moon. Then, with a knife she set about scraping the skin off it just from the surface.

For some moments, the moon endured the pain with pursed lips and gritted teeth. Then he gave in. He groaned, 'Ouch, it hurts!'

Konkaboti assured him, 'Don't fear. I'm nearly done.'

Swiftly enough, Konkaboti sliced a bit of skin off the moon's main root.

The moon asked, 'Sure my root will grow again?'

Konkaboti said, 'Definitely it will. It won't be like this forever. Smear it with a little mud, to prevent it being poisoned by the evil eye of malicious fellows.'

The moon queried, 'If it festers?'

Konkaboti answered, 'In that case, administer *luchi*-frying ghee on the wound.'

The moon asked, 'You are a lady doctor, I presume. Do you know any drug for the roots of teeth? The roots of my teeth tingle.'

Konkaboti said, 'I'm not a lady doctor. But I have seen and known a lot already at my age, so I've learnt the use of a drug or two. But I don't think the root of your teeth will ever be cured. Teeth do not hold forever. Try to remember how old you are. It has been ages since you emerged out of the sea. Now if you want to be a child moon once again, how can that be?'

The moon said, 'I don't want to be a child moon. I have quite a few children at home. Bless them so that they live long, and then you'll see how many moons shine in the sky! Moons will then rise all round the sky. Even now my children say, "Papa, you get tired on new moon nights, and cannot get out of the bed in the evening. Please allow us to go and rise in the sky." But I don't let them go. One end of the sky is a long distance from the other. They are mere children, how can they roll that far?'

Konkaboti said, 'How old are your children?'

The moon said, 'My eldest daughter has grown up to be like a *kansi*. What a shining kansi does she look like! Even if you scrub your kansi with tamarind, you won't get that colour. The next son is like a cymbal. There are a few others in between. The youngest is a baby now; she is slightly dark-skinned. She is like that stone insect *tip* you people used to wear once on your foreheads. She is dark all right, but winsome. When she grows up, and you see a black moon in the sky, you will admit, "O yes, she is startlingly beautiful!" Her dark light will make the earth shimmering black, cloaked as if in varnished leather. Well, anyway, what will happen to the roots of my teeth now? I can eat nothing. It hurts badly when I chew plant stems.[2] If you know some medicine, please prescribe it for me.'

Konkaboti said, 'Okay, moon, you can do one thing. Come with me. I've got your root, now my husband will get better. He lives in Kolkata, where there are so many dentists about. They will pull out your decayed teeth with pincers, and supply you with dentures.'

These words frightened the moon. He said, 'My main root hurts badly now, so in this condition I can't roll and go that far with you.'

Konkaboti said, 'What's there to worry about? I'll take you along wrapped in my sari.'

The moon's heart sank at this. He thought, 'I feared as much. Why did I talk to her at all! I should have kept silent with my eyes shut.'

The moon said, 'The roots of my teeth have been cured. I no longer feel pain. You needn't take trouble for that. I'm too heavy for you to carry along. Go home now. The members of your family will worry if you are late.'

Konkaboti answered, 'What did you say? You're heavy! At my parents' I used to carry many heavy *thala*s larger than you to the riverbank to scrub. Just see how I carry you along.'

With these words, Konkaboti spread the end of her sari on the sky. She was just about to wrap up the moon with that end when the moon's wife barged in with their children, wailing loudly and rolling over on the road. The lady moon's cry rent the sky. The children's cry all but deafened Konkaboti.

The lady moon wailed, 'O dear, the formidable sepoy brought me the news that a woman will cut your main root. Have I ever given a raw deal to that ignoble woman that she will be so cruel to me? If I have to be a widow because of her, her condition would be like mine. She will spell doom to her father and brothers.'

The moon's children pulled Konkaboti's sari, and said, 'We fall at your feet! Don't cut papa's main root, don't take papa with you.'

The youngest child, the girl who was like a stone insect, cried in fits and starts, fumed on and off, and called Konkaboti names, 'You wretched woman, nasty creature, *shaala*.' She bit and scratched Konkaboti, and pinched her. Her pinching tested Konkaboti's patience.

Konkaboti said, 'O dear lady moon, please control your daughter. This youngest one of yours is tearing my skin off.'

The lady moon said, 'You really think I'll control her! You ruin my life, and I'll keep her in check! Why, darling? What harm have I done to you to deserve such treatment? Why will you kill my husband by cutting his main root?'

Konkaboti said, 'O no, I'll not kill your husband. I needed just a little bit of the root skin, and I've scraped only that much off superficially. He has not bled much, nothing really has happened. Better ask the moon, if you like. Then your husband has said that his teeth have come loose. So I proposed to take him to Kolkata, get his teeth cured, and send him back to the sky again. Now I think, that is no longer needed, you people just stop howling, please. And ask your daughter not to pinch me any more.'

These words assured the lady moon. The moon's children stopped crying.

The lady moon said, 'In case you're done, please go home now. The entire sky is at sixes and sevens in fear. The panic-stricken sky-dwellers are all behind bolted doors. Everybody is on tenterhooks.'

Konkaboti said, 'True that I'm done with, but I need a basketful of stars. Aha, in our earth, there are no stars! How beautifully they shine here all around! I've decided to take a few from here. My ogre cub is tied at quite a remove from this spot. How shall I carry these stars that far? Where shall I find a porter, please?'

The lady moon said, 'Dear girl, people haven't ventured out today in fear of you, so how do you hope to get a porter? All shopkeepers and vendors have pulled down their shutters. All streets are deserted. Only I, because it was a matter of life and death, have come out.'

When these words were being exchanged, Konkaboti noticed a man peeking out from behind a piece of cloud. Konkaboti thought, 'Let me ask that man to carry the stars to where the ogre cub is.' Thinking thus, Konkaboti called out to him. Konkaboti said, 'Hey you, listen, I've something to ask you.'

The moment Konkaboti uttered these words, the man ran away for dear life. Konkaboti gave chase. She went on pleading, 'Hey, man, please stop. Listen to me. You needn't fear me.'

But her words had no effect. The more Konkaboti chased him, the faster the man ran with even more desperation. Konkaboti thought, 'What an amazing sprinter this man is! It is as if he is flying, like the wind.'

Konkaboti would have had no chance to catch up with the man if he had not stumbled over a mound of cloud. He fell, and tried to rise again, but before he could do that, Konkaboti caught hold of him.

Konkaboti touched his body and found it was without bones, flesh, in fact, without anything. His body was extremely light. With two fingers Konkaboti lifted him up.

She brought him up near her eyes, and saw that his body was made up of two or three palm leaves. He had palm leaf hands, palm leaf legs, and a palm leaf nose and face. He wore a shirt over those palm leaves. His body left Konkaboti absolutely bewildered.

Konkaboti asked, 'Who are you?'

The man answered, 'Who else but the formidable sepoy of the sky? Leave me, I'll go home. Don't press me with your fingers like that.'

Konkaboti asked, 'Is your body made of palm leaves?'

The formidable sepoy answered, 'What do you suppose it is made of except palm leaves? Would it have been made by cementing bricks, stones, lime and gravel? You've travelled so widely, and accomplished so much, and yet you've never heard of the palm leaf sepoy?[3] Who doesn't know me in this universe? Whenever people come across any brave and strong man, they compare him to me. Now release me, I'll go home. I've had enough of this cutting-the-main-root business!'

Konkaboti now realised that the palm leaf sepoy she had heard of in her childhood lived in the sky, and not on earth. And that it was he who was the formidable sepoy of the sky.

Konkaboti said, 'Formidable sepoy, listen! You need to do me a favour. Otherwise, I'll not let you go. From here I'll carry away a bundle of stars. You need to haul that bundle a certain distance.'

The sepoy had no other option, so he had to agree. But Konkaboti's sari could barely accommodate a handful of stars. Konkaboti started thinking about how to tie the stars together.

The sepoy said, 'What's there to mull over? Let's go to the great granny[4] of the sky. She has spun so many cloths on her *chorka*. Let's borrow a gamchha from her.'

Konkaboti and the sepoy went to the sky-granny to borrow a gamchha. After a great deal of grumbling and mumbling, the granny gave them one. Konkaboti started plucking stars in the fields of the sky. With a fair deal of discretion, she gathered some blossoming stars, some in full bloom, and stars of varied colours. Wrapping them up in the gamchha, she put the load on the sepoy's head.

The sepoy thought, 'In my long period of service in the sky, I never had to do a porter's job. Fortunately, all the sky-dwellers today are indoors. If anybody had chanced upon me today in this distress, I would have died a thousand deaths in humiliation.'

Carrying the load, the sepoy walked in front. Konkaboti followed him. After a while, the two of them reached the place where the ogre cub was. Taking the load off the sepoy's head, Konkaboti said, 'Now you may go, I need you no longer.' No sooner had the words been uttered than the sepoy darted off and vanished into thin air.

Konkaboti thought, 'It is only because he is a palm leaf sepoy that he can run so fast.'

Konkaboti got on the back of the ogre cub with the load and started descending from the sky to the earth.

Notes

1. 'Rahu': A demon god without a torso in Indian mythology; he devours the moon, who escapes through his throat. This is the mythological explanation for the lunar eclipse.
2. '... chewing plant stems ...': Stems of some edible plants are a favourite food item for middle-class and lower-middle-class Bengalis in their lunch menu, chewed leisurely.
3. '... palm leaf sepoy ...': A child's toy once sold and purchased in fairs. It has come to acquire the status of a Bengali idiom ('*tal patar sepai*') as a facetious reference to a thin person acting brave or strong.
4. '... great granny of the sky ...': In Hindu mythology, the dark spots on the body of the moon are interpreted as the silhouette of an old lady spinning fabric on a wheel. She is called '*Akashburi*', that is, old woman of the sky.

19

The Sati on the Pyre

Konkaboti soon returned to where the mosquito and the elephant had been waiting for her. On learning that she had succeeded in getting the root, the mosquito and the elephant were overjoyed. Restoring the ogre cub to its burrow, the mosquito and Konkaboti rode on the elephant's back, and set off for the mansion inside the hill.

On reaching the mansion, Konkaboti handed the main root over to Khorbur. He picked a tola from it after weighing, and rolled it with great care into a paste on the mortar with seven globules of black pepper. Then he made the frog swallow that paste. After consuming it, the frog started throwing up immediately and copiously. Whatever was inside his stomach came out. The frog said, 'All the things I ate since I was a tadpole wriggling in the water have been disgorged. There is nothing left inside my stomach.'

And those little ants too were ejected. Khorbur picked them up from the frog's spew. Then he took the ants one by one, and with a delicate stick scooped out Khetu's life-span in dribs and drabs. When the whole life-span was scrubbed out, Khorbur said, 'What is this? Only a smidgen of the life-span has been squeezed out. Of what use will such a minuscule life-span be? I don't think it will be of any help to us.'

Khorbur was dejected, the mosquito too was in despair, the frog started shedding tears, and Konkaboti sat still, as if petrified. Only Nakeshwori and her aunt, who were invisible, were on a high.

However, Khorbur held that tiny amount of life-span near Khetu's nose. Khetu got up with a start.

Khetu said, 'I was in such a deep slumber! Konkaboti, why didn't you wake me up? Look, it is already so late in the day.'

Konkaboti said, 'Do you think I would not have woken you up if I could?'

Khetu then looked around. He found that tears were coursing down Konkaboti's eyes. He also noticed Khorbur, the mosquito, and the frog sitting glum-faced. Khetu asked, 'Konkaboti, why are you crying? And who are the others?'

Konkaboti did not answer.

Khetu thought a little, and said, 'Now it's all coming back to me. Nakeshwori ate me up because the root was not there on my head. Konkaboti, you called these people in here, and brought me round, I suppose? Why do you cry, then? I am fully cured now. Only my head is aching a trifle. Let me lie down once again. Konkaboti, please massage my head, will you? It is paining now. Oh, it is now aching unbearably! Maybe my life will be snuffed out now. All of you, please look after my Konkaboti! Please take her back to her mother. O my God!'

Khetu breathed his last.

Everybody sat there with bowed head. They were speechless. Tears rolled down their faces. Only Konkaboti sat quietly, composed and serene.

After a long while, Khorbur said, 'Now it's all over. Our efforts have all been futile. Nothing can be done now. When his life-span fell from the top of the palm tree, most of it was blown away by the wind. The ants ate only a modicum of it. But how long can a man live with that meagre life-span?'

Saying this, Khorbur started crying, the mosquito too was crying, the frog was wiping his tears with his handkerchief, and the elephant outside blew dust with his trunk. Only Konkaboti spoke not a word, nor did she shed a tear.

At last, the mosquito said, 'Dear child, get up, please. Lamenting will be of no use. Now we will cremate your husband as befits him.

Then you will go with me to Roktoboti. When you see her, your mind will be soothed.'

The mosquito, along with Khorbur and the frog, tried hard to console and counsel Konkaboti.

Khrobur said, 'Life is ephemeral. Nothing on earth is certain. None can be sure how long someone will live, or when someone will depart. Get up, dear child. After your husband is cremated, stay with Roktoboti for a few days. After that, I will take you to your mother's.'

Konkaboti said, 'Mohashoys, you have done so much for me. The efforts all of you put in for me have been tremendous. That your Herculean labours did not succeed is only due to my miserable destiny. God will always be good to you. Now, since you left no stone unturned to help me, I beseech you to do me another small favour. Having done that, please go back to your respective homes. I have dedicated my life at my husband's feet. This body of mine is little more than an inert mass. I intend to burn this mass to ashes along with my husband's body, right at this moment. Please do this little favour of arranging all the ingredients required for this sacrifice.'

The mosquito said, 'Chhi, child, shame, shame! None should utter such words. Many devoted wives keep on living after their husbands' death. Embracing chastity, they devote their lives to the service of the people.'

Khorbur and the frog too argued in a similar vein to dissuade Konkaboti from committing sati.

Nakeshwori spoke, 'Aunt! They are planning to cremate that man. What on earth will we eat then?'

The aunt said, 'Yes, it seems like that!'

Nakeshwori said, 'It is for this slip of a girl that there is all this bother. Now come, let us try to make that girl die too.'

Having said this, Nakeshwori appeared before Khorbur and the others.

Nakeshwori said, 'What are you discussing? Do you intend to take Konkaboti back to her country home? Take her back if you want to, we don't worry about that. But you do not know the customs and rules prevailing in this land of dharma that is India. The people of this country live by and for religion. If someone, whether in profound grief or severe mental agony, pronounces, "I will go with my dead husband," she will have to go, she can never retrace her steps. If she does not keep her word, her husband's clan, along with her father's and mother's, will be irredeemably tainted. All her kith and kin, including her parents, brothers and other relatives, will have to live in abject disgrace. The woman will be cast deep down. One who interacts socially with her will also be consigned to ignominy. Therefore, I say, take this girl back home, and we do not object to that. But listen, you, mosquito mohashoy and Khorbur moharaj, I will reveal all of this to your relatives. Your kith and kin are no atheists like you. They will surely pass adequate shastric judgements. I will see how you manage to marry off your children then!'

Nakeshwori's words struck terror in the mosquito's mind. He would have to settle Roktoboti's marriage with someone very soon. If a good bridegroom now became difficult to come by, there would be hell to pay. The mosquito asked Khorbur, 'Is this really the social order in India?'

Khorbur answered, 'It is true that such was the ancient custom of India. But sati, or the female custom of sacrificing one's life on one's husband's pyre, is no longer in vogue. The sahibs have abolished that.[1]

Nakeshwori said, 'Maybe it has been abolished. But do you know that educated men believe in this custom even to this day? They are striving heart and soul to reintroduce all the erstwhile customs. Educated males are bending over backwards to see their bereaved and grief-maddened mothers and sisters burn in the fire's leaping flames. And we fully hail and patronise such religious fanaticism.'

Khorbur said, 'I don't give a tinker's curse for what is in store for me, and I insist that I will have dealings with Konkaboti. Even if I have to risk excommunication for that, I won't object. I will not bother even if my relatives desert me. But under no circumstances can I bear the sight of this orphaned girl frenzied in unendurable sorrow going up in flames!'

The mosquito said, 'I too am of the same opinion. I am not lily-livered, so I cannot act cravenly. I will take Konkaboti home.'

The frog said, 'I am of the same opinion myself. Let humans be cowards if they want. I won't follow in their footsteps.'

Nakeshwori said, 'You know nothing of what dharma is. You do not know that you will be heinous sinners. If this girl does not perform sati, she will have to go through *projapatya* expiation. But even that will not ensure her going back home. She will be taken away by the undertaker, and she will have to live forever as his wife.'

Konkaboti said, 'You are all engaging in a pointless debate. I have made up my mind to be a sati. I will not listen to anybody's advice. Immolate myself I will. Please do not request me to go on living, for I am in no position to oblige you. Now I implore you to arrange all the articles required for this ritual. And please take me to the riverbank near our village where my mother-in-law's body was cremated. I intend to light my husband's funeral pyre there, and sacrifice my life together with him.'

Seeing Konkaboti's firm resolve, everybody around had to consent to her appeal with a bleeding heart.

The mosquito said, 'Konkaboti, if you have indeed decided to perform this suicidal act, let me go and inform my family. Let my wives and Roktoboti come and meet you.'

Khorbur said, 'Let me go back too to inform my wife. Let her come here with my other relatives. They will arrange everything needed for the ritual of self-sacrifice, and get the barbers, priests and drummers.'[2]

The frog said, 'Let me too inform my relatives.'

The elephant who had stood outside so long, said, 'I will send for my relatives and friends too.'

Nakeshwori said, 'Aunt, why should we then be left behind? You go and get into your basket. And travel far and wide to invite all the ghosts and ghostesses to witness the holy act of sati. This is not a regular phenomenon these days. Ghosts of all ages, ranging from the children to the youths and the old, will surely relish the spectacle.'

In this way, everybody around sent for their relatives. Then they accompanied the elephant which Konkaboti rode and on which the body of Khetu was laid. At the first prohor of the night, they all appeared at the riverbank near Kusumghati.

The pyre was laid out at the spot indicated by Konkaboti.

And at that moment, Roktoboti came to the crematorium with her mothers. Khorbur's seven-arms-tall wife too came with all their relatives and their children. The barber and the priest came along with all the accessories of self-sacrifice, together with the drummers. The relatives of the frog and the elephant turned up. Innumerable ghosts and ghostesses trooped in from all directions. Some other animals, apart from humans and ghosts, came too. The cremation ground of Kusumghati swarmed with all manner of creatures that night.

Roktoboti wound her arms round Konkaboti's neck. Crying inconsolably, Roktoboti said, 'Putrid Water, why are you departing? Where will you go, leaving me behind? I will never let you go.'

Konkaboti said, 'Putrid Water, do not cry. I am going to heaven with my husband, as a devoted wife should. Do not try to dissuade me from that deed. Putrid Water, what else could I do? I came to this earth with such a terrible destiny. I have not been happy on this earth. Let me go to heaven with my husband. I bless you that a princely mosquito be your bridegroom. Live happily with your husband. I do not want even my enemy to be as ill-fated as me.'

Saying this, Konkaboti brought out the bunch of stars and gave it to the mosquito's daughter.

Konkaboti said, 'Dear Putrid Water, please string together three garlands with these stars. You take one garland, and keep the other two for me. I will need them.'

Now people lifted Khetu's corpse and laid it on the pyre. The *pindo*s were prepared ritualistically. The barber cut Konkaboti's nails, and took off all the ornaments that she was wearing. He broke her bangles. And there was a mad scramble to collect the fragments of those bangles because of the superstition that these fragments help in exorcising spirits if those possessed wear them around their necks.

Konkaboti removed the *noa* from her arm, and went down to the river to take a bath. Khorbur's wife then helped her wear a scarlet sari. She tied a string painted with *alta* round her arm. She decked her hair with layers of combs, and smeared her forehead copiously with vermilion.

Being so adorned, Konkaboti rinsed and washed her hands, and holding sesame, water and *kush*, sat facing the east.[3] The priest made her chant mantras, and resolve:

'In this month of *Bhadro,* in this third *tithi* of the dark fortnight, I, Srimati Konkaboti Debi, a member of the Bharadwaj clan, solemnly aspire for the fortune of Boshistho and Arundhoti, and wish to be as happy as them with my husband in heaven for as many years as there are strands of hair on a human body.[4] I wish my parents' and husband's clan to be unsullied and pure. As long as the reign of the fourteenth Indra continues, let the *apsora*s sing hymns and glorify us. Let me be happy with my husband. In case my husband committed sins due to the slaying of Brahmans, and friends, or for treachery, let him be exculpated.[5] With these prayers and longings in mind, I am entering my husband's burning pyre.'

Then Konkaboti offered oblation to the sun, and made the guardian angels of all sides witness her act with these words: 'O eight Lokpals, the sun, the moon, wind, fire, sky, land, water, Lord Yama residing in my heart, the day, the night, the evening, dharma, you all bear witness to the act of my self-sacrifice on my husband's pyre as I follow in his path.'

After the godheads of all directions were made witnesses, Konkaboti tied *khoi*, *batasa* and cowries in the ends of her sari, and circumambulated the pyre seven times, scattering the khoi and cowries about. And the children gathered there scrambled about for them, because people believed that such khoi, if put on beds, chased bugs away.

From among the women present, one approached the sati and obtained from her a speck of her vermilion. This woman's daughter-in-law was a mere child, and so was yet to develop devotion towards her husband; that jot of vermilion put on her forehead would make her a devoted wife.

When the circumambulation was over, the priest made Konkaboti chant the *rrikmantra*.[6] In the end, Konkaboti asked Roktoboti for the two garlands of stars. Konkaboti mounted the pyre, wound one garland round Khetu's neck, and the other around her own. Then, having mounted the pyre, she lay down on the left of her husband.

People bound her to the pyre with the raw bark of a tree. The pyre was then lit from all sides. Bamboo sticks, hay and jute sticks were thrown into the pyre to make the flames leap and spring. Drummers started beating their drums to a deafening pitch. The pyre was now furiously ablaze. The flames licked the sky.

Konkaboti fell into a deep slumber. It really was a happy, an exceedingly peace-giving sleep.

Notes

1. '... The sahibs have abolished that ...': This is a reference to the ban imposed on the practice of sati (immolation of widows) in Bengal Presidency on 4 December 1829 at the behest of the Governor-General Lord William Bentinck. After this ban, abettors in this practice were deemed to be guilty of 'culpable homicide'.
2. '... get the barbers, priests and drummers ...': These three categories feature prominently in a sati act. The barber would cut nails, the priest chanted mantras, and drummers beat drums so thunderously that the sati's screams were drowned.
3. '... holding sesame, water and *kush* ...': These are common elements in a Hindu ritual.
4. 'Srimati Konkaboti Debi': 'Srimati', a synonym for 'Mrs', is used to indicate married women, and 'Debi' is a female honorific title; 'Bharadwaj clan': the clan descended from the ancient sage Bharat; 'Boshistho and Arundhoti': the sage couple respected for their devotion to each other, exemplary between consorts.

5. '... the slaying of Brahmans and friends, or for treachery ...': These three are grievous sins according to Hindu scriptures.
6. rrikmantra: A mantra from the Rig Veda.

Conclusion

It really was a happy, an extremely peace-giving sleep.

The physician said, 'The sleep that has overwhelmed this girl is sound and deep. The spell of delirium has ended. Her pulse beats are regular. Now please take care that there is no noise in the house. Her sleep should not be disturbed.'

The physician departed. The patient was dead to the world in a deep slumber. People in her household started talking in whispers. Silence reigned and even ants could be heard moving, as it were.

The mother sat by the daughter's sickbed. From time to time, she put her hand near her nostrils to see whether she was breathing or not.

The mother had been attending thus on her daughter for twenty-two days running. She had been fighting a valiant battle with Lord Yama, the deity of death, over her daughter's life. Whenever the daughter got up in delirious excitement, the mother laid her down again with great care. When the daughter screamed out, her mother quietly asked her to calm down. The mother's honeyed words put out the fire of delirium, at least for some time.

The daughter lay asleep. Long starvation, a severe ailment and a dreadful delirium had worn her thin, and made her face wan. Even so, one glance at her glorious beauty made one look on the earth as a beautiful place to live in. The mother kept looking with unblinking eyes at that ethereal beauty.

The day broke. It advanced a little. But the daughter slept on. The mother sat by. Another daughter came and sat near the mother.

The patient's lips quivered for a moment. She uttered some indistinct syllables. The sister lowered her head in order to hear the utterance. But she could not make it out.

Once again, the patient's lips moved. Once again some sounds were heard. This time, the mother could decipher the meaning.

The mother said, 'This poor girl of mine has Khetu's name on her lips all the time. For the past few days, that name has never left her lips. Now if only I manage to join their four hands, my agony will be assuaged.'[1]

The mother's dulcet tones entered the daughter's ears. Now, fully awake, she slowly opened her eyes. With a look of wonderment, she started observing her surroundings.

Her mother said, 'Her delirium is not fully cured. The look in her eyes is not yet quite normal. For the last nineteen days, my child could not recognise anybody.'

The sister asked, 'Konkaboti, do you recognise me?'

Konkaboti answered in a very low voice, 'I do; you are my eldest sister.'

The sister asked again, 'And tell me, who is she?'

Konkaboti said, 'Ma.'

Tonu Roy stepped into the room. He asked, 'Konkaboti, how do you feel now?'

Konkaboti answered, 'I am all right, father.'

Tonu Roy sat by her side for a little while. He ran an affectionate hand over his daughter's head and body. Then he went outside.

Konkaboti thought, 'My parents and sisters have accompanied me to heaven, I see! I never got my father's affection on earth. Today, I have got that in heaven. Just as we had our room on earth, I find we have a similar one in heaven. But where is my husband, on whose pyre I sacrificed my life?'

Konkaboti waited for him for quite a while. But he did not show up.

At last, Konkaboti asked her mother, 'Ma, where is he?'

Her mother asked, 'Who do you mean, child?'

Konkaboti said, 'I mean he who turned into a tiger.'

Her mother said, 'The delirium still has its hold! She is still raving!'

Hearing her mother's words, Konkaboti was lost in thought. She came to realise that her body was still very weak. And slowly but surely, her memories came flooding back to her.

Konkaboti asked, 'Ma, have I been seriously ill?'

Her mother replied, 'Yes, child, you are now bedridden for twenty-two days at a stretch. You were completely unconscious. We had lost all hope that you would live.'

Konkaboti said, 'Ma, I have dreamt a strange dream. The dream is etched so deep in my mind that I still believe that it was true. Now, I am remembering so many things. But I cannot determine which was true and which was a dream. So, ma, I will ask you a few questions. Ma, is it a fact that Jonardon Choudhuri's wife has passed away?'

Her mother said, 'Yes, it is true, and that has triggered all the problems that came about.'

Konkaboti said, 'There was a bickering over the eating of ice. Is that true, ma?'

'Yes, child, that too is true. That caused Khetu's ma to be humiliated.'

'Where is she, ma?'

Her mother replied, 'She comes often. And she stays here all day. She loves you more than I do. If I can now place you in her hands, I'll heave a sigh of relief. Your father has consented to this, everybody has. Now it's only left for you to get better.'

Konkaboti now understood that Khetu's mother was not dead, and that her death was a figment of her dream.

Konkaboti asked, 'Just after this wrangling, I had a fever, isn't that true?'

'Yes, indeed, that was the time when you had a severe attack of fever. You turned comatose and delirious. This is the twenty-second day.'

Konkaboti said, 'Then I went to the riverbank to board a boat, didn't I, ma?'

Her mother said, 'What nonsense, why should you have boarded a boat? You have been bedridden ever since.'

Konkaboti said, 'Ma, how shall I describe to you what dreams I had! Looking back, these things alternately amuse me and bemuse me. I dreamt that in order to lessen the burning sensation of my body, I went to the riverbank and sprinkled water on myself. Then I took a dinghy, which took me to midstream. The boat capsized. The fishes made me their queen. Then I stayed in a milkwoman's shanty for some days. From there, I went to the cremation ground. Then I came back home. One year after that, a tiger came to our house. With that tiger, I went to a forest. There I saw ghostesses, frogs, mosquitoes, and so many other creatures. Then I soared up to the sky, did and saw so many things. The dream still lingers in my mind, and strikes me as so very real. Well, ma, tell me what happened after that turmoil over the eating of ice.'

Her mother replied, 'That conflict has been sorted out. Eight or nine days ago, when you were seriously ill, and lay unconscious, one of Jonardon Choudhuri's grandsons died all of a sudden. Jonardon loved him very much. He was maddened with grief. At that time, Gobordhon Shiromoni fell critically ill. And we, as you know, were spending anxious moments over your malady. Jonardon Choudhuri came back to his senses. He sent for Ramhori, who came to his country home from Kolkata, along with his family. Jonardon had a long discussion with Ramhori. Then Ramhori called Nironjon in. Ramhori, Nironjon, your father and Khetu went together to Jonardon Choudhuri's. Jonardon said, "I had taken complete leave of my senses, and so I had that weird idea of remarrying at this age. I forced Nironjon to leave this land, and did grave injustice to Khetu, who is but a stripling. From that time on, I have been beset with perils. Shnareshwor has been put behind bars for embezzling public funds. Gobordhon Shiromoni is stricken with palsy, and is on his last legs. I have had to suffer the loss of my grandson. Konkaboti too may not survive." After saying this, he implored Nironjon to take back his land, which he did. Nironjon now lives in his own house. Jonardon consoled Khetu, and gave him his blessings. The head of our family too is not quite the same man as before. Now he is full of affection, love and pity. Maybe a deep crisis transforms a man in this way. And your elder brother too has changed a lot. He now obeys and respects me just as a good son should. Your ailment worried your brother sick. Once you pull through, you will marry Khetu. There's no chance of this not happening this time. During your illness, Khetu, his mother, Ramhori, Sita—all worked their fingers to the bone. Now you have heard all I had to tell you, do not talk much, please. You are extremely feeble. Overstraining may cause a relapse.'

Konkaboti remained weak for quite a few days. She took a considerably long time to convalesce. Sita always came and sat by her side. Konkaboti narrated the whole tale of her dream to Sita, who reported it to her mother. Khetu's bou-didi, who was Sita's mother, told it to Khetu. Thus Konkaboti's dream narrative became well circulated in her locality. Having heard the entire narrative, Sita nursed an obhiman against Konkaboti.

Sita said, 'Konkaboti, you wore the stars yourself, and gave some to your Putrid Water. You did not keep a single one for me. You do not love me, you love your Putrid Water. I won't talk to you.'

Konkaboti recuperated fully. She became strong as before. Having recovered, she came out in front of Khetu once in a while. One day, Khetu went to Konkaboti's house. A mosquito was flying about there. Khetu got hold of that mosquito, and said, 'Look, Konkaboti, this mosquito seems to be your Putrid Water, isn't that so? Aha, Roktoboti has not seen her Putrid Water for ever so long. She might have been restless for that. Maybe that is why she has come looking for you.'

At this, an embarrassed Konkaboti retired to her room and hid there. After that, she stopped coming out in front of Khetu.

One day, Nironjon said, 'Khetu, I have heard about the strange dream of Konkaboti. How astonishing! Do not curl your lips at it, taking it for delirium or a mere dream. I do not understand if it really was a dream or not. This life of ours, our hopes and despair, joys and sorrows—all appear like dreams, don't they? I never do understand the great illusion of this world. We do not get to know even a single object well enough. For instance, look at this book in my hand; I do not know what it really is. Our sense organs only perceive certain qualities. Our eyes see that it has length, breadth, thickness and colour, our skin perceives that it has hardness, our nose perceives its smell, and our tongue perceives its taste. We cannot get to know the whole of the book, but only the properties. But do these qualities that we perceive belong to the book, or to our senses? Because our eyes, ears, nose, tongue and skin are structured in a specific way, we get to know these specific properties. Had our sense organs been structured in a different way, all the worldly entities would take different shapes. The leaves of the book now look white and black. If my eyes become jaundiced, these very pages would look yellow. So you know, we do not quite get to know the book, but only its properties. And, so to speak, those properties belong to our senses. So now tell me, where does it leave the book, then? Without getting to know the real nature of things, we are simply skimming over this songsar like some imaginary animals that are figments of a dream. So why should we ridicule Konkaboti's dream? Just as the external world is imagined by our wakeful sense organs, so is Konkaboti's dream world made up of her dormant senses. There is very little difference between these two worlds. Konkaboti built a dream world with what she saw, heard and had thought at any time. From the beginning to the end of that dream, Konkaboti is ever present as the subject. The mistakes that Konkaboti is likely to make have also crept into her dream narrative. For instance, mosquitoes' antennae are not akin to elephants' trunks, which are but enlarged snouts, but are elongated strands of hair. Again, in some other places, in the sky, for instance, the goddess of imagination too has played tricks with Konkaboti. However, it must be admitted that it has been an extraordinary dream. But what surprises me is the Sanskrit shloka that the mosquitoes uttered.'

Khetu said with a chuckle, 'Once I made that shloka in jest. That was long ago. I wrote it down on a scrap of paper. But some days later, I threw it away. Konkaboti might have seen that paper.'

After Konkaboti recovered fully, on an auspicious logno and favourable day she tied the knot with Khetu. Since this marriage took place after dreadful trials and tribulations, the people of seven villages around were extremely happy. Jonardon Choudhuri in particular was overjoyed. Despite his old age and chronic cough, he did not stint in any way. On the wedding day, he stayed the whole night at Tonu Roy's.

Clandestinely, he had procured many ice cubes from Kolkata. When the Brahmans were being fed, he told people in jest, 'The bridegroom will not be allowed to cool his body by consuming 'borokh' alone; we too will soothe our bodies a little.'

The people of the countryside, who had never seen ice, were caught flat-footed. Everybody drank soothing ice-cold water in high spirits. And some took a few ice cubes along to show to their people back home.

When the *Shudra*s were being fed,[2] Godadhor Ghosh drank three tumblers of water mixed with ice. And on top of that, he masticated one *ser* of saw-like, sharp-edged ice with his teeth, and gulped that down.

When Konkaboti's mother offered Konkaboti to Khetu's mother as her prospective daughter-in-law, did not the earth seem too small a place to contain their jubilation? Did not Khetu's mother accord *boron* to her son and daughter-in-law with an exultant heart? Did not Khetu, out of shyness, stand with bowed head during the boron? Did not Konkaboti stand like the *kola-bou*, covering her head under a one-arm-long veil? And seeing that, did not a local child even peek into that veil? These questions need not be answered, I believe.

When this ritual of boron was taking place, do you know what Ramhori's wife, alias Khetu's bou-didi, did? She took the opportunity to twist Khetu's ear.

And do you know what Khetu said after this twisting of the ear? He said, 'Enough, bou-didi! Chhi!'

And have you heard what the local women did? *Tthan didi*, who was Komol's wife, said, 'This shaala eats borokh! Hey, Sita's mother, come and pull both his ears off!'

What happened thereafter? Khetu became a moneyed man. Everyone was happy, and went about their domestic tasks. Khetu fathered a number of children. Tonu Roy loved to play with them. If any child perchance beat up the grandson from his daughter's side, he used to bandy words with that urchin's granny, gesticulating wildly.

And after that, what? It won't do to ask 'after that?' repeatedly. The book has already grown oversized. It is not known who will buy this tome. So I am compelled to bring the curtain down on the saga now.

What happened then? Then my story came to an end, and the *noté* tree had to suffer the fate which was exclusively its own.[3] And complaints and grievances poured in about the dismal fate of that creeper.[4]

Notes

1. '... join their four hands ...': A reference to the Hindu marriage ritual in which the bride and the bridegroom have to hold each other's hands.
2. 'When the *Shudras* were being fed ...': Feeding Shudras was part of the marriage ritual in nineteenth-century Bengali Hindu society.
3. '... the *noté* tree had to suffer ... exclusively its own': An allusion to a popular, almost proverbial, Bengali rhyme, which runs thus, '*Amar kothati phurolo / noté gachhti murolo,*' meaning 'My story comes to an end/The *noté* creeper gets mown down.'
4. '... And complaints and grievances poured in ... that creeper': A reference to the next few lines of the verse [see Note 3] in the form of a series of questions put to the creeper, asking to know why it was mown down.

Afterword from the Translator: About the Novel

Konkaboti, Troilokyonath's debut novel, was published on 14 November 1892 in the periodical *Jonmobhumi*. The novel created a flutter among the Bengal literati. Rabindranath Tagore, in an article in the journal *Sadhana*, reviewed the novel with some insightful comments. I quote from Rabindranath's article that I believe will serve as a starting point of my discussion. Rabindranath wrote:

> ... [I] have liked the novel on the whole. The composition is mature and smart. The author has aroused our humour and pity in lucid language with great ease, and has unleashed his power of imagination without flourish. The story is divided into two parts. The first part incorporates real life events, and the second impossible, absurd events suffused with *adbhut ros* (appeal of a sense of wonder). To write such absurd fairy tales with competence is a task of great authorial skill. In the realm of the impossible ... it takes some virtuosity to guide the free-roaming imagination along a path of some arcane rules .... however absurd and bizarre the subject matter is, it must be harnessed to some literary methods ... to create *ros*. That the author has been able to preserve the true nature of the fairy tale, its childlike simplicity, and its sense of unsuspecting loyalty merits high acclaim.
>
> But the author's attempt to pass the second part of his story for a [girl's] sickbed dream has not worked. It is a fairy tale, and not a dream. It is absurd like a dream, but unlike a dream, it is not incoherent. The thread of the story runs all through .... in this dream

> the author narrates events that take place in the background .... Besides, the author projects moods and scenes from time to time that are not exactly within the ambit of the girl's dream. Secondly, in the first part of the story, the real life events have progressed so far that embarking suddenly on the realm of the impossible, the reader feels astonishment tinged with chagrin. It is as if a story has been travelling by a train until suddenly, another train comes along from the opposite direction and rams against it, and everything gets marred ... To treat the reader with such rudeness after having sufficiently aroused his pity and curiosity violates literary decorum. The novel reminds us of *Alice in Wonderland*. That too is an impossible, unreal, crazy dream narrative of a young girl. But in it, there is no such collision between the real and the unreal. And that novel is incoherent, mutable and extremely enjoyable, like a real dream.
>
> But having read the story, we have condoned all these flaws. And we have been stirred by a new optimism that after a long time, an author has emerged in the literary scene of Bengal whose writings are capable of enthralling the children of our country, and also their parents. Very few of this land have the ability to write truly simple books fit for the consumption of our children. We, as a race, are somewhat old by nature, and therefore we regard most worldly activities as puerile, and, as such, childlike acts are contemptible to us. (2005, 617–18, translation by the translator of the novel)

Having extolled Troilokyonath's power of imagination, Tagore raised two valid critical points, the first of which is that the dream narrative in the novel is more of a fairy tale, and second, that the novel 'violates literary decorum' by jolting the readers' expectations through juxtaposition of a realistic narrative with a fantasy in the two parts of the book. I will take up the second point for prior consideration, and then address the first.

Troilokyonath can be called the prime mover of magic realism (an appellation given to him by some Bengali poets of the 1960s and 1970s) in Bengali (and Indian) literature with some justification, but also with some qualification. I consider Troilokyonath a would-be magic realist as in his writings, some features of magic(al) realism preponderated, while some other features were undermined. But Troilokyo as an author had every right to create his own brand of magic realism without any obligation to go by any theoretician's rule book. Besides, 'magic realism' was not known in Troilokyo's time, and he presumably wanted to write non-realist narratives, giving free rein to the imagination. He also wished to accommodate his fantasy in a realist framework. Being somewhat uneasy about acknowledging fantasy in its own right and without reference to reality, Troilokyo sought to *rationalise* his fantasy, and the rationale almost invariably came in the form of a dream narrative; fantasy narratives are always *embedded* in his literature, and the reasons for this, to my mind, are the following.

I think Troilokyonath resorted to dream narratives because he believed dreams are the only points of intersection of reality and fantasy. He presumably failed to distinguish real-life logic from narrative logic. Bengali fictional writing was a burgeoning practice in Troilokyo's time, and he was probably yet to gauge its creative potential. Bankimchandra Chattopadhyay dominated the literary scene then, and his 1866 novel *Kopalkundola* was suffused with supernatural elements, but that was an exception. The latter half of the nineteenth century was a transitional phase in Bengali literature, when narrative literary practice was shifting from poetry to prose. From the early 1850s onwards, 'realist' British novels were starting to gain ground, although the melodramatic novel had not disappeared. As Meenakshi Mukherjee (1985, 17) rued, 'It is really unfortunate that the nineteenth-century Indian novelist had as his model primarily the Victorian novel,' and the Indian reading taste was getting trained on the 'realist' mode of fiction. However, non-realist contents that include supernatural elements or sensational material lurked in the wings, and invaded the realist space whenever the opportunity presented itself. In the period between the publication of *Kopalkundola* and that of *Konkaboti*, which spanned nearly thirty years, the realist mode of writing came to the fore. The fictional convention evolved in such a way that the author needed a pretext (or camouflage) for introducing non-realist contents into his narrative, and dream sequences conveniently supplied that pretext. This, I believe, explains why Troilokyonath did not attempt to write his debut novel entirely in the mould of fantasy, and introduced non-realist material under the guise of a dream narrative. Troilokyo, although deploying the device of dream narratives quite frequently, had recourse to other devices to introduce fantasy. For instance, in his story 'Lullu', fantasy appears garbed in fairly 'realistic' satire and sarcasm, with no reference to any dream sequence. Most of the stories of *Domoruchorit* are replete with fanciful and absurd elements, but without recourse to the strategy of dream sequences. Troilokyo was hesitant to conduct a happy union of the real and the fantastic, which somewhat offsets his appellation as a magic realist author, and the reason for this diffidence was that realism, rather, its Victorian brand, had begun to hold sway in the Bengali (and also, Indian) fictional enterprise. There was little realisation that reality and realism are two different concepts, and that narrative realism is only one of the many methods to delineate reality. Troilokyo subscribed to the prevalent notion of his era.

Now, let me look at Troilokyonath's strategy of juxtaposing the real and the fantastic in the same novelistic space from a different angle. Supriya Chaudhuri, in her essay 'The Bengali Novel' in *The Cambridge Companion to Modern Indian Culture*, points out two different strands of fictional literature in nineteenth-century Bengal. One strand is epitomised by the kind of social realism that informs novels like Pyarichand Mitra/Tekchand Thakur (sobriquet)'s *Alaler Ghorer Dulal* (The Spoilt Son of a Rich Family), serialised in 1855–57 in the periodical *Masik Potrika* and published in 1858, one of the earliest novels in Bengali literature. Another popular genre of fictional literature then was social satire, which went by the name *noksha* (from the Persian word *naqsa*, meaning 'design'). Chaudhuri mentions (102) the nokshas by Bhabanicharan Bandyopadhyay (pseudonym Pramathanath Sharma), like *Nobo Babu Bilas* (The Pleasant Tales of the New Babus, 1825) and *Nobo Bibi Bilas* (The Pleasant Tales of the New Bibis, 1831). But the most remarkable work of this genre is *Hutom Pnyachar Noksha* (Sketches by Hutom the Owl, 1862) by Kaliprasanna Sinha. There was another literary tradition called *bot-tola* literature, meaning 'literature produced under the banyan tree' (for this was sold and purchased in such a place in Kolkata), which catered mainly to the taste of the laity, and was dismissed as obscene by the newly emergent *bhadralok* community. Troilokyonath intended to incorporate the first two strands, namely the realist and the noksha, in his fiction in order to entertain his target readership, the Bengali gentry. In *Konkaboti*, Troilokyonath seems to have been propelled by the desire to deploy both the standard narrative modes to portray the two different aspects of nineteenth-century Bengali society.

I will now dwell briefly on the literary conventions of the dream narrative that Troilokyo drew upon and speculate on what prompted Troilokyo to supplement his realist narration with a dream vision, to which Rabindranath took exception.

In *Konkaboti,* Troilokyonath has used a dream vision as a literary device which has precedents in European canonical literature. One of the earliest known instances is *Somnium Scipionis* or The Dream of Scipio, written by the Roman historian Cicero, the sixth book of his *De Republica.* It describes a fictional dream vision that the Roman general Scipio Aemilianus had two years before he commanded an army that laid waste to the city of Carthage in 146 BC. Boethius's *De Consolatione Philosophie* (The Consolation of Philosophy), published in AD 524, is another example of a dream vision in literature (here, a philosophical discourse). Geoffrey Chaucer was greatly influenced by the technique of a dream vision in the thirteenth-century French poem *Roman de la Rose* (The Romance of the Rose), and deployed it extensively in his own texts like *Legend of Good Women*, *Book of the Duchess* and *Parliament of Fowls*, which are poetically constructed dream visions that serve the purpose of sermonising and/or burlesquing. Shakespeare's *A Midsummer Night's Dream,* written sometime between 1590 and 1596, uses a dream vision as a dramatic technique to depict the darker side of love and present some baffling questions regarding human identity. The romantic poets too used a dream vision to add strangeness to beauty. Coleridge's poem 'Kubla Khan' and John Keats's 'La Belle Dame Sans Merci' are cases in point. In Indian literature, Vasa, the ancient Sanskrit playwright, wrote *Swapnavasabdatta* (The Dream of Vasabdatta), which uses a dream vision as a dramatic device to forge a reunion of two lovers.

A dream vision had thus been an established literary convention in European literature, and to some extent in Indian literature as well. Poets and playwrights used it as a supplement to the real life experiences of the protagonist, either to philosophise so that the misery of life becomes bearable, or to present an alternative and better version of reality. Not long after the publication of *Konkaboti*, Bhudev Mukhopadhyay's *Swapnolobdho Bharotborsher Itihas* (Indian History Derived from Dreams, 1895) and feminist Rokeya Sakhawat Hussain's science fiction story 'Sultana's Dream' (1905) used the literary convention of a dream vision quite successfully.

In *Konkaboti,* Troilokyonath had recourse to this literary tradition of a dream vision as a supplement to his realist narrative but embedded within it, the dream narrative being slightly longer. To my mind, Troilokyonath used his dream vision as a supplement to depict aspects of reality other than those depicted in the realist narrative in Book I of his novel. The dream narrative in Troilokyo's novel does not conjure up an alternative historical or social space as in Bhudev's or Rokeya's works; rather, it creates a somewhat therapeutic space and syncopated time, in that when the dream, which is later revealed to be the addled imaginings of a febrile brain, fades away and Konkaboti regains consciousness, she comes to learn that the troubles that proved life-threatening for her were sorted out in the period of twenty-two days when she lay on her sickbed. Troilokyonath employed his individual talent to re-form or reinvent the device of a dream vision which, in the novel, represents a strategic suspension of a trouble-torn reality in order to enable the author to carry out a narrative surgery, as it were. Troilokyo anesthetises his realist narration with a sickbed dream vision, and once that surgery succeeds, he switches back to the realist mode that makes for a happy ending.

Rabindranath cogently compared *Konkaboti* with Lewis Carroll's *Alice's Adventures in Wonderland* (1865). Rabindranath says that while Carroll's tale is truly a dream vision having a dream-like incoherence of plot, Troilokyo's dream narrative is at best a fairy tale, being 'absurd' but not 'incoherent.' Rabindranath's observation is apt, but I have a few more thoughts about the dream vision in *Konkaboti* that may serve to explain Rabindranath's point. Toilokyonath pits the different conventions of this technique against each other. For example, the anthropomorphic animal characters in Book II of *Konkaboti* have a fable-like quality, reminding one of the animal characters in Carroll's masterpiece; for instance, Frog mohashoy of *Konkaboti* resembles the rabbit in *Alice*. Again, the episode of the capture of the ogre cub in Troilokyo's novel is redolent of similar happenings in the fairy tales of Bengal, as in Dakshinaranjan Mitra Majumder's ever-popular collection of stories, *Thakumar Jhuli* (Grandmother's Sack of Tales). Dakshinaranjan's effort elicited high approbation from Rabindranath. Below, I quote an episode from the story 'Neelkomol and Lalkomol' in *Thakumar Jhuli*, along with the capturing of the ogre cub episode of *Konkaboti* for the readers to compare and judge.

The episode from 'Neelkomol and Lalkomol' goes as follows:

> ... When they heard the name of Neelkomol, the band of ogres retreated three steps in fright. Neelkomol was born in the womb of an ogress in his earlier birth, and so ogre blood coursed through his veins. The ogres knew that. So they said, 'Let us check if he really is Neelkomol himself.'
>
> ... [T]he head ogre said in nasal tones, 'Let us see the tips of your noses.'
>
> Lalkomol pushed Neelkomol's diadem out with his sword for the ogres to see. The ogres took it in their hands, and said to each other, 'Dear O dear, how large is he the tip of whose nose is this large!'
>
> The ogres said again, 'Let us see your spittle.'
>
> Lalkomol sprinkled hot ghee of the burning lamp with his sword. The ogres' fur was scalded ... and they felt it on their toes, groaning in pain.
>
> A little while later, the ogres ... said again, 'We want to see your tongues.'

> Lalkomol ... thrust Neel's sword from behind ... the door which was ajar. The head ogre held that sword tight with both hands, and commanded his comrades, 'Now we will tear this tongue off by pulling it, I will pull, and you pull me hard.'
>
> They pulled the sword hard with all their might, and the naked sword cut deep into the head ogre's hands. Blood spurted out in jets. With loud screams, the head ogre beat a retreat .... (126–27, translation by the translator of this novel)

The episode of the capture of the ogre cub in *Konkaboti* (Book II, Chapter XVII) runs like this:

> The ogress said, 'Don't you know who I am? I am an ogress.'
>
> The mosquito said, '... We are a bunch of *quogresses.*'
>
> The retort gave the ogress the creeps. She said, 'O dear me ...! My name starts with an 'o', and yours with a 'q', which means you are two notches above me in strength. Well, give me proof that you really are 'quogresses' ... [C]ough.'
>
> The mosquito beat the drum a couple of times.
>
> Hearing that 'boom!', the ogress said, 'O my goodness, how terrible is the noise of your cough! .... Yes, I accept that you really are quogresses.'
>
> But the ogress was still a little sceptical .... So she asked, '... throw down a strand of your hair, will you?'
>
> The mosquito now dropped the cord used to tether the elephant. The ogress picked that up, and ... said, wonderstruck 'O dear, ...! When a strand of your hair is so thick and strong, who knows how hefty and brawny you yourselves are! ... it will be a tall order to put up a fight with you.'

And so on. Later, the elephant slides into the ogress's burrow, masquerading as a 'louse'!

> ... The ogress ... was frightened to death on seeing the mountain-size louse with a trunk! She thought, 'Their louse has come here to seize my cub, now what if they themselves barge in and capture me!' In a tizzy, the ogress took flight, leaving her cub behind.

That Troilokyonath adapted the fairy tale mode of narration to suit his purpose should be amply clear from these quotes, especially in the exchanges between the ogres and the humans. The use of rhymes in some other episodes (for instance, in the chapter 'The Boat') is another proof of Troilokyo's adaptation of the story-telling techniques of Bengali fairy tales. No wonder that Rabindranath looked upon the dream vision of *Konkaboti* as a fairy tale. Fairy tale it really is, but here again, Troilokyo effected some improvisations. The most striking of these is his dovetailing of realistic and fantasy modes of narration within the framework of a fairy tale itself. Just as there are fable-like animal characters and fairy-tale-like ghost characters, so there are real-life characters, viz. Khetu, Khetu's mother and Konkaboti's parents and sisters. The realistic narrative of Book I cuts into the fantasy narrative of Book II of the novel. The dream narrative of Troilokyo's novel is not a pure fairy tale, for Troilokyo introduces a dream-like quality by making living characters share the same fictional space with the fantasy characters, and also making them interact. In this sense, Book I and Book II of the novel are not absolutely separate, just as our wakeful and dreamy states are not independent or unrelated, despite being two different realms of existence. The narrative modes of the two books may be different, but the narrative plane is the same.

Coming back to Rabindranath's view that the dream narrative in the novel is 'absurd', but not 'incoherent', we must understand what these terms really mean. In my understanding the word 'absurd', as in the appellation 'absurd drama', means 'occurrences which are illogical and unreal', whereas the word 'incoherent' implies 'logically anomalous'. In my perception, while the absurd refers to events which cannot possibly take place in real life situations, the incoherent implies a disruption of the logical chain of events. To be more precise, in a piece of absurd literature events themselves may be unreal, but the logical chain binding them is realistic, whereas in an incoherent piece of writing, as in surrealistic painting, all elements, whether realistic or 'fantastic', are juxtaposed in free association, with scant respect shown for the common sense logic of association. One way of disrupting the chain of logical association is to dismantle or disorient the spatio-temporal co-ordinates of events. Let me quote from *Alice in Wonderland*: '"I wish

I hadn't cried so much!" said Alice as she swam about, trying to find her way out. "I shall be punished for it now, I suppose, by being drowned in my own tears. That will be a queer thing, to be sure! However, everything is queer today."'(51) Well, this is not simple absurdity, I suppose. Someone drowning in her own tears radically disrupts spatio-temporal co-ordinates of one's existence. It can happen only when someone is not what she was just a while earlier. The event is absurd not only because it is unreal, but because it challenges the logic of possibility itself.

The dream narrative of *Konkaboti* does not thwart or subvert the sense of time and space in the manner in which Carroll's text does. And this explains why Rabindranath chose to call Troilokyonath's dream narrative 'absurd', and yet *not* 'incoherent'. Troilokyo substituted realistic events for the unrealistic ones in the rationalistic chain of logic regarding time and space, but this chain, unlike in Carroll's narratives, remains intact all through.

However, having conceded that, I would like to point out that Troilokyo, too, in a way, subverts the realistic logic of time and space in his dream narrative. This happens when the realistic narrative intersects the fantasy narrative in *Konkaboti*'s dream vision. Real-life characters of Book I of the novel find their way into Konkaboti's dream and interact with fanciful characters. For instance, Khetu and his mother appear in Konkaboti's dream, and Konkaboti helps Khetu perform the funeral rites of his mother. Again, Tonu Roy, Konkaboti's father, negotiates Konka's marriage with a tiger, which actually is Khetu in disguise. This commingling of the real and the fantastic does, to my mind, disrupt the unilinear pattern of time and space, and impart a dream-like quality to the narrative. So we, I believe, cannot fully accept Rabindranath's view that Troilokyo's dream narrative is '*coherent*', nor can we call it an unadulterated fairy tale, even if it incorporates some of its distinguishing features.

Now, I will highlight the different uses the realist and the dream narratives are put to by Troilokyonath in *Konkaboti*. The two kinds of narrative have been used to project two vignettes of nineteenth-century Bengal. The first narrative, which constitutes

Book I, depicts the power structure of colonial Bengal. Lord Cornwallis's Permanent Settlement Act in 1793 made zamindars lethargic vis-à-vis their settlements, and made them greedier and crueller. Jonardon Choudhuri represents this land-owning class. He wields power over people like Nironjon Kobirotno, who once enjoyed some brohmottor land, and lived by teaching students. And alongside this, these people had a band of obsequious flatterers; Gobordhon Shiromoni represents this type. The society had caste and class hierarchies, with patriarchy reigning supreme. Tonu Roy represents this patriarchal set-up, which looked upon nubile girls as mere pawns in the game of marriage. He married his daughters off to old men to earn money in the form of 'dowry' in reverse, so to speak, and supported his deed by doctoring the shastric mandate. His wife and two widowed elder daughters are his helpless victims. And, as is usual with any non-egalitarian social order, the different wings of powers-that-be, viz. patriarchy and social leadership, collude to perpetrate injustice and cruelty. No wonder that in such a social order, Tonu Roy would want to get his minor daughter married to Jonardon Choudhuri, the zamindar, in order to amass wealth, knowing full well that the latter has one foot in the grave. This engenders a crisis in the novel which makes the young girl fall ill in deep anguish, and her mother lament and wail.

Further, the novel portrays the angst and anxiety of a society in transition. This society, having been under colonial rule for more than 150 years, played host to some alien cultural values, but was yet to overthrow its deep-seated orthodoxy. This obviously breeds tension, and also spawns hypocrisy. One classic emblem of this social hypocrisy is the character of Shnareshwor, who lives in Kolkata, organises the singing of hymns of Hori in his backyard like a devout Hindu, and in the upper story of his house, throws grand parties where colonial food and drink like mutton and wine, which were taboo for Hindus, are generously served and consumed. People like Shnareshwor are cultural chimeras who parade their cultural moorings in the orthodox social order to enjoy social prestige, and simultaneously (and surreptitiously) relish what luxury and pomp the exotic culture has to offer. Shnareshwor's hypocritical hedonism, symptomatic of a society in the throes of social transformation, has been vividly laid bare in the novelistic space of *Konkaboti*.

The character of Khetu comes through as the unsullied soul of pristine rural Bengal. He is an embodiment of courage, physical prowess and moral rectitude. He has profound love for his widowed mother who brought him up against heavy odds, and feels respect and gratitude for people like Ramhori and Nironjon, who stood by his side in times of crisis. Khetu's struggling childhood, his strength, his scholastic temperament, and his love for his mother suggest that his character has been modelled on the persona of Ishwarchandra Vidyasagar. His attitude to people associated with him represents a silver lining in a decayed, degenerate social order driven by and besotted with power, obsessed with effete customs and reeking of avarice.

The Bengali society presented in the novel had already witnessed some historic changes in the colonial legislation. Social reform was in the air, and some of the reforms had taken place. A story narrated by Godadhor, a one-time dacoit, gives chilling details of how a group of silk-selling Brahmans was killed by brigands called *thangares* (see Glossary) in late eighteenth- and early nineteenth-century rural Bengal. These gangs of highwaymen, who killed stray, helpless pedestrians on their travels by night, were a menace, which was extirpated by Lord William Bentinck and his administrative chief William Henry Sleeman in 1830. There are also other historical references that include the Age of Consent Act (vide note 4, Chapter III, Book I), which a person like Tonu Roy often cited in support of his practice of marrying off grown-up daughters to elderly men for monetary gains, and the Sati Act of 1829 (vide note 1, Chapter XIX, Book II). These allusions place the novel in a specific historical perspective, and contribute significantly to the reconstruction of the discursive domain from which the novel emerged.

Another point worth noting is the incident concerning the eating of '*borokh*' or ice by Khetu, which scandalises the orthodox section of rural society, leading to his excommunication. Ice was a source of both wonder and worry in a transitional Bengal society, and rumours bandied about regarding it spawned superstitious beliefs. For example, it was believed that ice was manufactured with cow's blood, and hence was taboo for Hindus. In this context, one recalls the memorable opening sentence of Garcia Marquez's 1967 magnum opus *One Hundred Years of Solitude*: 'Many years later, as he faced the firing squad, Colonel Aureliano Buendía was to remember that distant afternoon when his father took him to discover ice.' Indeed, the village Kusumghati in *Konkaboti* is in some ways like Macondo in Marquez's novel, in that both are strangers to technology. The intervention of technology, which is a gift of Western/colonial culture in an otherwise predictable, prosaic order of life, introduces an element of magic to the rural folk. In Macondo, the gypsies visiting the village from time to time provided the rustics the gateway to the magic world of technology. In a passage in Marquez's novel, José Arcadio Buendía takes his son Colonel Aureliano to the tent of the gypsies to show him ice for the first time—and the latter was astounded to see '... an enormous, transparent block with infinite internal needles in which the light of the sunset was broken up into colored stars,' which, he was convinced, was '... the great invention of our time.'

'Fear and jubilation at the contact with mystery' is the colonised's standard response towards technological innovations and interventions of the colonisers. In Marquez's novel, the village Macondo in the pre-colonial phase of its history was introduced to the magic of technology through the gypsies, whereas in Troilokyonath's novel, it was Khetu who exposed the rural folk of Kusumghati to the delicious scandal of '*borokh*' eating. In Macondo, there never were orthodox precepts governing the life of its people, and so the amazement at 'the great invention' of their time was uninhibited and spontaneous. But Kusumghati in *Konkaboti* is a village in which the precepts of dharma, deriving from shastric scriptures, are the motive force of life in the caste-ridden society, and as such, the wonder is overtaken by a sense of insecurity and outrage at the prospect of a breakdown of an established social order, as the following extract (Book I, Chapter XIII) from my translation of *Konkaboti* will show.

> ... Gobordhon Shiromoni said, '... [Ksetrochondro] drinks water from *jobons*. He eats what you people call *"borokh"*—the thing that the sahibs manufacture in their factories ....'
>
> Jonardon Choudhuri asked, 'What? What did you say?'
>
> Shnareshwor said, '*Sorbonas*! Calamity! He eats "borokh"? The thing that the sahibs produce with the blood of cows? ... our dharma is heading for perdition. *Hai, hai,* the end of the Hindu dharma is nigh!'

The fantasy part of Troilokyonath's narrative, that constitutes Book II, portrays the sycophancy and mimicry in the colonised culture, as well as the colonial claim to the superiority of the European race. Troilokyo's fantasy is steeped in satire in Book II, as demonstrated in Konkaboti's conversation with the frog (Chapter XII) attired as a sahib, aspiring to attain social respectability.

> ... Seeing the appealing grace of the frog, Konkaboti allowed herself a faint smile ....
>
> Konkaboti asked, 'Frog mohashoy, which way leads to the village? ...'
>
> The frog answered, 'Hit mit fat.'
>
> Konkaboti said, 'Frog mohashoy, I could not quite make out what you said ....'
>
> The frog said, 'Hish fish dam.'
>
> Konkaboti said, 'Frog mohashoy, you are speaking English, I see. But I have not studied English .... If you do me the favour of speaking in Bengali, I will be able to understand.'
>
> The frog ... feared that if he was heard speaking in Bengali, he would lose his caste... When he found that no one was around, he mustered the courage to speak in Bengali.
>
> '... What an obnoxious slip of a girl you are! ... You see that I am a sahib, but still address me as "Frog mohashoy"! What prevents you from calling me a sahib?'

This obviously is the outcome of the project of Thomas Babington Macaulay, who in paragraph number 34 of his 1835

Minute on Indian Education, articulated his desire to form a class from the native population '... who may be interpreters between us [that is, the English colonisers] and the millions whom we govern—a class of persons Indian in blood and colour, but English in tastes, in opinions, in morals and in intellect. ...'

Frog sahib in Konkaboti's dream vision is a brilliant caricature of the class conceived by Macaulay. Charles Wood, a British liberal politician, member of the British Parliament in the mid-nineteenth century, and President of the Board of Control of the East India Company, sent a despatch to Lord Dalhousie the Viceroy, in 1854, charting out his plan for refurbishing the system of education in India; known as 'Wood's Despatch,' it contained the proposal, among others, that universities should be set up in various provinces of the country, modelled on the London University. Although the Despatch had clauses related to the teaching of vernacular languages and women's education, its main area of thrust was the creation of civil servants for the smooth functioning of the administrative machinery. Frog sahib in Book II of *Konkaboti* is emblematic of that class.

The master–servant relationship has been the mould in which the relationship of the colonial and the colonised was mostly cast. This fact is underscored in Chapter XIV ('The Master Mosquito') of Book II, where the master mosquito asks Konkaboti about her proprietor.

> The master mosquito asked, 'I must know to whom you belong.'
>
> Konkaboti replied, 'Mohashoy, I was my father's property before. Human girls are their father's property in childhood. The father enjoys the right to sell or give them away to any blind, crippled, old or diseased fellow he wishes .... My father sold me to my husband for three thousand gold coins. Now I am my husband's property ...'
>
> The master mosquito said, '... My question is—which mosquito's property are you?'
>
> Konkaboti answered, 'Which mosquito's property! ... I don't think I am any mosquito's property.'
>
> ...

> ... The master mosquito said, 'Listen, human child, all men and women in India are the mosquitoes' property .... I ask you ... Which mosquito sits on your body to drink your blood? ...'

The mosquito in the passage represents the master class that can be identified with the colonisers, for whom exploitation of the colonised mass was the natural order of things (apart from suggesting the large-scale blood-sucking ubiquity of mosquitoes in a tropical country like India, and frequent outbreaks of malaria in colonial times). The colonised were the colonisers' property, and hence would have to accede to the system of exploitation *for their own benefit*—this was the maxim or motto of colonisation. But it would be unfair to apportion blame squarely on colonialism. British colonialism and Indian feudalism joined hands to manufacture this 'neo-liberal' policy. As Ranajit Guha writes in *Dominance and Hegemony* (1997), '... This mediocre liberalism, a caricature of the vigorous democratic culture of the epoch of the rise of the bourgeoisie in the West, operated throughout the colonial period in a symbiotic relationship with the still active and vigorous forces of the semi-feudal culture of India.'

Guha shows that although colonialists were averse to feudal systems and were champions of human rights in their own country, their functional modalities in this country only show their complicity with the feudal system and a disregard for humanitarian values. The master mosquito in *Konkaboti*'s dream narrative is a liberal overlord who wants to be benevolent towards the human child, but to do so, he decides to purchase her from her owners. The colonial masters too sought to 'legally purchase' their subjects from their feudal proprietors before they could offer them their 'liberal' measures, in terms of education or democratic rights.

The master mosquito in the dream narrative does, to my mind, also come through as a representative figure of the concept of 'governmentality.' In his essay of that name, Michel Foucault has demonstrated how the notion of sovereignty with respect to governing people has traversed centuries until, from the late eighteenth century onward, with the rise of population, it came to depend heavily on the concept of the economy as an independent and separate sector of reality. 'Political economy' came to signify a combination of techniques for governmental intervention in this specific sector, with a view to managing the swelling population.

The political economy of the Foucauldian thesis is burlesqued in the dream vision of *Konkaboti* when the master mosquito, Long Antenna, makes his stirring speech (Book II, Chapter XIV), demanding an immediate end to the Indian habit of travelling.

> Long Antenna then addressed ... other mosquitoes, and said, 'O great souls, I find that we are faced with a grave danger! ... All the mosquitoes of the world have so long been drinking the Indians' blood, and living in clover .... Humans keep their livestock within an enclosure, and we did the same with the Indians. And the Indians too ... have been humbly serving us, and nourishing us with their blood. But regrettably, some Indians have become adventurous enough these days to set sail on oceans and cross mountains .... those who do such things and deprive us of our right to drink their blood commit the most heinous of sins. Now we must dissuade Indians from committing such reprehensible acts .... Besides this, Indians are showing a disturbing ... inclination for travelling from this village to that .... we need to find ways to stop Indians from ... travelling ....

This is a classic example of political intervention in the sphere of the economy to tackle the issue of a migratory population. Unrestricted travel was considered a scourge for the British government in their homeland too as early as in the sixteenth century, when Sir Thomas More wrote *Utopia* (in 1516 in Latin, translated into English in 1551). The sixth chapter, titled 'Of the Travelling of the Utopians' in More's book, describes how a Utopian who travels without leave or permission is

> ... punished as a fugitive, and sent home disgracefully; and, if he falls again into the like fault, is condemned to slavery. If any man has a mind to travel only over the precinct of his own city, he may freely do it ...; but when he comes into any of the country houses, if he expects to be entertained by them, he must labour with them and conform to their rules ... (92)

We see how travelling was integrated into the system of labour, which is a clear indication of governmental intervention in a field of activity such as travelling, which impinges on the territorial identity of a populace. In *Konkaboti*'s dream narrative, Long Antenna imposes severe restrictions on travelling by summoning a shastric mandate from the pundits. The law prohibiting travel in this context, according to Foucault, supplements other government apparatuses.

Delivering an address derived from fables is a standard literary device of purveying social satire. The fable is a literary mode adopted by satirists who want to present their satire as a political allegory. George Orwell's 1945 anti-communist classic *Animal Farm* is a case in point, with its famous dictum, 'All animals are equal, but some animals are more equal than others.' In Bengali literature, too, speeches in fables have been put to good use by Bankimchandra Chattopadhyay in his satirical essays in *Lokrohosyo* (Mystery about Mankind), published in 1874. The first essay of this book is titled *Byaghracharyo Brihollagul* (Long Tail, the Tiger Savant), in which tigers make declamatory speeches on the attributes of the human race so dear to them as food. I quote from a representative speech in this essay, strikingly similar to Long Antenna's speech in form, content and tenor. The following is the address of a tiger called Omitodor ('Huge Belly'), who presided over a two-day seminar of the tiger community:

> ... the humans are uncivilised animals. We are, however, civilised. So it is our duty to make the humans civilised like ourselves. Maybe God has sent us to this beautiful wilderness to make men civilised .... if men become civilised, their flesh will be more savoury, and they can be captured with more ease .... humans will then realise that it is their sacred duty to offer their bodies to satiate the tigers' appetites .... (25, translation by the translator of the present book).

This skilfully caricatures the (in)famous 'civilising mission' of the colonisers, as does Long Antenna's speech. Long Antenna uses speech as a literary device, as does Huge Belly. In fact, Huge Belly's speech makes its comparison with a conversation between the master mosquito and Konkaboti (Book II, Chapter XIV) irresistible.

> ...The master mosquito said, 'Tell me why ... these crores of people .... in India exist at all. Why were they created? ...'
>
> Konkaboti said, '... I do not know ...'
>
> The master mosquito said, 'O this girl is a dolt ...! ... She knows nothing! ... Roktoboti is just a child, but ... she is a thousand times better ... in terms of common sense. Now Roktoboti, dear child, will you tell me why Indian people have been created?'
>
> Roktoboti said, 'Why, father ... so that we can drink their blood.'
>
> The master mosquito said, '... Now, have you understood ...?'
>
> Konkaboti replied, 'Yes, ... Human beings were created so that mosquitoes can feed on them.'

The mosquito of *Konkaboti* is clearly a close kin of the tiger in Bankimchandra's essay. Civilising is a pompous-cum-self-aggrandising colonial agenda, which functions as part of an efficient exploitative machinery.

The realistic and fantasy parts of *Konkaboti* do not treat reality from two radically different angles, and there are areas of overlap. For instance, delineations of patriarchy interlard both the narratives. In the dream vision, the mosquito household where the three wives of the master mosquito live indoors and the life of the stars' wife, who too lives an interned life, are cases in point. Again, the reverse kind of social reality is also depicted in the dream narrative. This consists in the phenomenon of wives beating their husbands, which was occasionally a subject of social satire in Kalighat *pot* paintings.[1] In Chapter XV, Book 2 ('Khorbur'), the incident of Khorbur's getting even with his formidable physically abusive wife with the assistance of elephant-the-brother-in-law is a throwback to that social reality.

I hope the above discussion will encourage an introspective reading of the Troilokyo literature. Such an effort, I believe, will be rewarding.

Note

1. Kalighat painting or Kalighat *pot* originated in nineteenth-century Bengal, in the vicinity of the Kali Temple, Kalighat, Kolkata. These

'pots' were pieces of coarse cloth or paper (later, wood), on which *potua*s or painters hailing from districts like Birbhum and Bankura painted with thick brush strokes. A popular form of folk art, they were bought as souvenirs by visitors to the Kali temple. From the depiction of Hindu gods, goddesses, and other mythological characters, the Kalighat paintings developed to reflect a variety of themes, including those related to social justice and social evils, and in some cases, were noted for their wry humour.

Bibliography

Carroll, Lewis. *Alice in Wonderland* and *Through the Looking-Glass*. London: Wordsworth, 1993.

Chattopadhyaya, Bankimchandra. 'Byaghracharyo Brihollangul.' In *Bankim Rochanaboli* (*Probondho*). [Works of Bankim: Essays]. Kolkata: Dey's Publishing, 2009.

Chaudhuri, Supriya. 'The Bengali Novel.' In *The Cambridge Companion to Modern Indian Culture*, edited by Vasudha Dalmia. Cambridge: Cambridge University Press, 2012.

Foucault, Michel. 'Governmentality.' In *Power,* edited by James D. Faubion, trans. Robert Hurley and others, 201–22. Web, accessed 22 April 2014.

Guha, Ranajit. *Dominance without Hegemony: History and Power in Colonial India*. London: Harvard University Press, 1997.

Macaulay, T. B. *Minute of 1935*. http://www.mssu.edu. Accessed 24 April 2014.

Marquez, G. G. *One Hundred Years of Solitude*, 1967. Trans. Gregory Rabassa. http://www.intexblogger.com. Accessed 24 April 2014.

Mitra Majumder, Dakshinaranjan. *Thakumar Jhuli*. Kolkata: Mitra and Ghosh, 1969. Reprint.

More, Thomas. *Utopia*. http://www.planetpdf.com. Accessed 24 April 2014.

Mukherjee, Meenakshi. *Realism and Reality: The Novel and Society in India*. New Delhi: Oxford University Press, 1985.

Tagore, Rabindranath. 'Kankabati.' In *Troilokyonath Rachanabali*. Kolkata: Sahityam, 2005, 619–21. (This is a reprint of the article published in *Sadhana,* 1892).